I

The Liar

A Death at the Hotel Mondrian

Anja de Jager

CONSTABLE

CONSTABLE

First published in Great Britain in 2019 by Constable

1 3 5 7 9 10 8 6 4 2

Copyright © Anja de Jager, 2019

The moral right of the author has been asserted.

A CIP catalogue record for this book
is available from the British Library.

ISBN: 978-1-47213-043-3

Typeset in Bembo by Photoprint, Torquay
Printed and bound in Great Britain by Clays Ltd, Elcograf S.p.A.

Papers used by Constable are from well-managed forests and other
responsible sources.

MIX
Paper from
responsible sources
FSC® C104740

Constable
An imprint of
Little, Brown Book Group
Carmelite House
50 Victoria Embankment
London EC4Y 0DZ

An Hachette UK Company
www.hachette.co.uk

www.littlebrown.co.uk

Chapter 1

The only reason that I was in the Lange Niezel on the edge of Amsterdam's red-light district at 5.52 a.m. was because I was doing Detective Ingrid Ries a favour. She'd sounded in a panic when she called. You had to love a job where helping out a friend led to standing at a crime scene at this ungodly hour of the morning. It was neither raining nor below zero, but I was glad I'd grabbed my woollen hat on the way out. It was late November, and winter didn't feel that far away. The lingering darkness made it seem as if the night had hit snooze on the alarm clock and had settled in for at least the next hour and a half, wrapped in a duvet of thick grey clouds.

Two seagulls were strolling down the silent alley as if they owned it, picking up thrown-away fries on their morning patrol. Twenty minutes ago, when I'd first got here, there had been the noise and bustle of an ambulance crew and some of my uniformed colleagues. Now the assault victim had been taken to hospital and the others had gone. I shivered in my thick coat and hopped from one foot to the other to reduce the time that my boots made contact with the ground. The flapping of a shop awning dominated the

3

otherwise silent street. A street cleaner and I were the only people here. I checked my watch: what was keeping Ingrid? Sure, I lived closer to the crime scene than she did, but if she'd called me out of bed to fill in for her boyfriend, the least she could do was not leave me here by myself.

The street cleaner was still waiting patiently, because nobody had told him to leave. He was one of those anonymous people who kept the city tidy. He was African; I would guess Somalian. His head was too small compared to his body, which was bulked out by an enormous thick coat. He glanced around him. I showed him my badge, but that did nothing to reassure him. A gust of wind pushed a McDonald's wrapper down the road and lifted it in the air as if to taunt the man. His eyes followed it regretfully. His back was bent over the bin on wheels that he pushed all day. Clearly he would much prefer to chase the wrapper than talk to me. I didn't take it personally.

'When did you first see him?' I asked. I shivered and wrapped my coat around me. The autumn air was thick with moisture.

'First? Maybe four thirty?' The man's Dutch was basic and heavily accented.

'Four thirty? You called us at . . .' I looked at my phone, 'five minutes past five.' I thought about switching to English, but he seemed to understand me as long as I spoke slowly and articulated carefully. The victim, still unconscious and unidentified but at least now in the hospital, had been found slumped in the doorway of a coffee shop with his face turned towards the wall and half hidden by the facade. I had seen him as he was being loaded into the back of the

4

ambulance. People must have noticed him but assumed he was drunk or drugged up, and sleeping it off, and would have hurried past.

'He hadn't moved.' The African's voice was halting and soft and I had to concentrate to hear him over the sound of the wind.

'How many times did you come past?'

'Four times. Four circles.'

Circuits, I corrected automatically in my head, but I knew what he meant. 'He was already here when you started work?'

The cleaner nodded.

'Did you see anything? Did you see someone punch him?' The victim's face had been severely battered. I'd had a chance to swap a few words with the paramedics before they carted him off. They suspected a broken cheekbone and nose, in addition to a number of broken ribs, judging by the severe bruising around his torso. 'Did anybody kick him?'

The man shook his head. 'No, no fights tonight. Just the man.'

The fight must have taken place before the cleaner got here.

'Can I take your name, please?'

'I have a passport. I have a job.'

I smiled to allay his fears. 'I know. But just in case we have any further questions.' Depending on where this man originated from, it was quite possible that he'd had a bad experience with police en route to the Netherlands. To be honest, he could have had a bad experience with the police here. 'And I'm sure the victim will be grateful to you for calling an ambulance.' I spoke very clearly. 'Thank you for that.' Especially since you're scared of the police and just want to keep your head down and the street clean. He'd been the Good Samaritan who'd done what plenty of tourists and people out drinking in the early hours of the morning hadn't.

The man shivered. He had two scarves tied around his neck. One looked like a football scarf, but I couldn't identify the team. The other was dark blue, the same colour as his coat. Maybe it had been provided by the council.

'Can I buy you a coffee?' I said.

'Can I go? Please?'

I asked for his name and telephone number again. This time he gave me the details without arguing. After I'd written them down, I wished him a pleasant rest of the day and let him go. He seemed more grateful for being allowed to leave than for my thanks or my offer of a coffee.

The glow from a streetlight exposed the early-morning aftermath of a night filled with too much fun, empties and cigarette butts littering the places the cleaner hadn't yet got to. A deadly silence hung around the area. In the evening it would be swarming with punters, tourists and people out drinking, but now there were just the two of us: a police detective and a street cleaner. He reached the McDonald's wrapper and speared it with a pointed stick, then shivered again. It wasn't even real winter yet. On an impulse, I pulled the hat from my head, rushed after him and gave it to him. He pulled it on, stretching it far enough to fit him, and thanked me four times before moving on. I watched him as he made his way carefully down the street, sweeping up cigarette butts and crisp packets.

When he turned the corner, I started to focus on the walls of the buildings along the street, looking for CCTV cameras.

I hadn't found any by the time Ingrid finally joined me. As she walked over to me, she was stuffing the last of a croissant into her mouth. Flakes of pastry fell on the front of her coat. I was always surprised how she managed to stay so skinny. The bumps of her wrists were visible where the sleeves of her jacket didn't cover them perfectly. She'd once told me that it was hard to find clothes that fitted because her arms and legs were so long. Her short blonde hair was brushed up into spikes.

'Thanks for helping me out, Lotte,' she said. 'I should have called Bauer or someone else from the team, but I wasn't thinking straight.'

Bauer was her boss. I understood why she hadn't called him. 'It's not a problem,' I said. 'How's Tim now?' Tim was her boyfriend. They worked together in the serious crime squad. Ingrid had been on my team before moving to join him a month ago.

'He's better now that we know what it is. He has to have his appendix out.' She rubbed her eyes. 'We were at the hospital for most of the night. They're keeping him in until the surgery.' She walked towards the coffee shop where the victim had been found. 'Was there any ID on the guy?'

'No, nothing. His pockets had been cleared out. No wallet, no phone, no car keys, not even a public transport card.'

'It's the fifth violent mugging around here in two weeks,' she said.

'Weren't the others a bit closer to Centraal station?'

'True, but I wouldn't rule out the possibility that they were all done by the same lot. They probably just spread their net a bit wider.' She bent down to examine a scuff mark on the door that could have been there for weeks. There would be little forensic evidence available to us. If he'd been punched and kicked, there wouldn't even be a weapon.

'Our only hope is CCTV footage,' I said. 'There's got to be a security camera around here somewhere.'

But most of the shops along the Lange Niezel still had their shutters down. Early morning was the red-light district's equivalent of the middle of the night. It would be worth coming back once they'd opened again. One of them might have caught something on their internal security cameras.

'Did you talk to the guy who called it in?'

'Yeah, the street cleaner. He didn't see anything; just the guy slumped in the doorway.'

As Ingrid continued to examine the coffee shop doorway, a man approached me.

'Are you the police?' He wore a woollen trench coat, a green and white checked scarf wrapped around his neck. He was smartly dressed for this time of the morning. Probably on his way to work.

'Yes, I'm Detective Lotte Meerman.'

'Great,' the man said. He was wearing glasses, and his dark hair and beard were shot through with grey.

I could feel a smile growing on my face. It was possible that he'd witnessed the assault. He looked like the kind of person who would come forward if he had. The kind of person who thought it was his duty to society to report what he'd seen.

'I thought it was important,' he said, 'to let you know that I'm not dead.'

Ingrid grinned at me. Her mobile rang and she quickly walked away.

I pushed my hair off my face. 'Of course you're not.' I tried to keep the disappointment out of my voice. There was no reason not to be polite. After twenty years in the police force, I'd seen my share of delusional people. Early on in my career, an elderly woman came to the station every week to tell us that her neighbour had killed her cat. When I went to her house after her second or third visit, I found the cat very much alive, but also very overweight. The surprisingly understanding neighbour told me the row had started because he'd told the cat's owner that she was feeding the animal too often. Since then, she'd got it into her mind that he was trying to kill it.

The man standing opposite me this morning was at least two decades younger than that elderly lady – probably in his late forties. At first glance there was nothing to indicate that he was mentally disturbed. His eyes were focused as he looked at me. But his hands were so tightly folded together in front of him that it looked as if his fingers were strangling each other. There was a bruise on his left cheekbone. It appeared to be recent.

'When I saw you,' he said, 'I felt I should at least tell you that I hadn't died.'

There was something odd about his speech. His Dutch wasn't the basic and accented version that the street cleaner had used earlier on, but it was halting. Almost as if he hadn't spoken for years.

He swallowed. 'I . . .' he started, then fell silent again.

'Take your time,' I said, glancing at my watch. 'Have you been ill?' Maybe he'd had a stroke. I scrutinised his face, but there were no signs of it.

He shook his head.

'Is someone saying you're dead?' A celebrity's obituary had been mistakenly released the other month. Maybe something like that had happened to this man too.

I shot Ingrid a glance that would hopefully tell her I wouldn't mind being interrupted, but she was still on the phone. 'What happened to you?' I pointed to his bruise.

'Nothing. That's nothing.' He seemed to come to a conclusion. 'I'm Andre Nieuwkerk,' he said. 'Andre Martin Nieuwkerk.'

The name took my breath away, and it was a second before I could answer. He was the right age.

Or at least the age Andre Martin Nieuwkerk would have been if he hadn't been murdered as a teenager thirty years ago.

'You can't be,' I said.

Colour flared up on the man's face. 'I'm at the Hotel Mondrian for another day.' He rearranged his scarf with deliberate care. 'People should know,' he said, 'that I'm not dead.'

10

Ingrid ended her call and came over. 'That was the hospital,' she said. 'Our victim has woken up and named his attacker.'

The man in the long coat turned and walked away. I thought about calling him back.

'We can speak to him now,' Ingrid said, more urgently this time.

Even though I could see the excitement in her eyes, because this was the first solid lead in this series of assaults, she sounded exhausted and looked frazzled. She hadn't slept all night because she'd been at the hospital with her boyfriend. Tired people didn't always ask the right questions.

'Okay, let's go,' I said as I watched the man cross the bridge.

Chapter 2

At the hospital, we followed the yellow line on the floor that would lead us to our victim's room. We now knew he was called Peter de Waal. I knocked on the door and we went in.

De Waal's face was bruised and swollen and it was hard to guess his age – mid to late thirties probably. His left eye was closed, the socket black and blue. He had an oxygen mask over his mouth. A doctor was by his side, hooking him up to some machines.

'I'm Detective Lotte Meerman,' I said. 'Can you answer a few questions?'

'Keep it short,' the doctor said. 'Five minutes at most.'

A woman was sitting at the bedside, but she stood up as we came in. She had dark shoulder-length hair, and was wearing a tight skirt and knee-high leather boots.

Peter de Waal raised his hand, slowly, as if the movement was a huge effort, and pulled the oxygen mask away from his face. 'Erol Yilmaz,' he said. Talking opened up a cut in his lip, and he grimaced against the pain. 'It was Erol Yilmaz.' He put the mask back.

'We told you he was dangerous,' the woman said.

'And you are?'

'Caroline de Waal. Peter's wife.' She was still standing. 'We told you and you didn't do anything.' Her voice got louder. 'A restraining order. As if that made any difference.'

'So you saw him clearly?' Ingrid asked.

Peter removed the mask again. 'I came out of the bar and heard a voice behind me. I turned round and saw Erol. He punched me in the face and that's all I remember.'

'And Erol Yilmaz is . . .'

'My ex-husband,' Caroline said.

I nodded. I could see where this was going. Ingrid left the hospital room to make some phone calls. She'd get us Erol's address so we could go round and ask him some questions. Maybe he was linked to the other assaults, or maybe this was a one-off. If we could close even one GBH case, the boss would be happy. Sometimes police work really was this easy.

'He's been harassing us for the last year,' Caroline continued. 'There've been constant threats. Phone calls, emails.'

'So you got a restraining order?'

'Because you refused to do anything else. You didn't protect us.'

'What time was the assault?' I felt bad asking questions, as Peter had to move the mask away from his mouth every time to answer them, but we had to know these things.

'Around three a.m.'

The cleaner had first seen him at 4.30. If he'd got the time right, Peter had been unconscious in that doorway for an hour and a half without anybody calling it in. He was lucky he hadn't got pneumonia lying on the pavement in the November cold. 'Were you by yourself?'

'With a group of colleagues. They all headed in a different direction.'

'Can you give me their names?'

Peter lay back against the pillow with his eyes closed. He seemed to find it hard to breathe even with the mask. I looked around for the doctor.

'What's the point?' Caroline said. 'He told you who did this.'

'We'll still have to check the details. If one of your colleagues can confirm the time you left and the bar you were in, that would be a big help.'

'Just arrest Erol. Before he leaves the country.'

The doctor came back into the room. 'Please leave for now. The patient needs to rest.'

'Sure.' I left and waited in the hallway until the doctor came out. 'What's his prognosis?'

'He's got a shattered cheekbone and a broken nose. Probably concussion from the fall. Also a couple of broken ribs.'

'He's on oxygen?'

'Yes, bruised lungs.'

'He says he only remembers a single punch. This wasn't a single punch, was it?'

'No, definitely not. From the bruising around his torso, I would guess he was kicked when he was on the ground.'

That was what it had looked like to me as well. Maybe the first blow had knocked him out and he hadn't been aware of the rest of the assault. The punches and kicks could indicate that there'd been more than one person. Had Erol Yilmaz brought some cousins to rough Peter de Waal up? It wouldn't be the first time that a group of Turkish men with a grudge had attacked someone.

'If you have more questions, come back this afternoon,' the doctor said. Without waiting for an answer, he strode off.

Ingrid joined me. 'I've got the address,' she said. 'Let's have a chat with Erol Yilmaz.'

We were going through the revolving doors of the hospital when the sound of engines destroyed what had been a peaceful lull. I expected ambulances, but over Ingrid's shoulder I saw a large car pull up, followed by a van, stopping on the edge of the hospital car park. The emblem of the main Dutch TV channel was printed on the side of the van.

'Ah shit,' I said. 'What are they doing here?'

The car doors opened and Commissaris Smits got out. Our new chief of police was the youngest we'd had in a long time. Modern, we'd been told in the initial introduction. He didn't look our way, but turned towards a woman, who handed him a hat to complete his uniform. She positioned it carefully and straightened it out.

'You've got to be kidding me,' I said. 'Why's he here?' 'Modern' clearly meant talking to the press a lot.

'Isn't that obvious?' Ingrid said. 'He looks good on the screen. It's that strong jawline.'

I shot her a glance. 'Please tell me you're joking.'

She winked. 'It's what my mum said when she saw him on TV when he first got the job.'

We could have walked to the car and driven off. Instead we watched the preparations for the interview. The van spat out the camera crew. I recognised the interviewer: Monique Blom had been on the *NOS Journaal* last night, asking the

Minister for Economic Affairs about rising unemployment numbers. This whole media circus seemed over the top and inconsiderate.

They set up about thirty metres away from where we stood, ignoring us completely. They probably didn't know we were police detectives; they must have assumed we were visiting sick relatives. The crew finally seemed happy with how the interviewer and the commissaris were positioned and gave them a nod.

'We're outside the hospital where the victim is recovering,' Monique Blom said. 'I'm here with Commissaris Smits to ask him for his comments. Thanks for your time, Commissaris.' The wind messed with her perfect hair, but it also blew her words in our direction.

'My pleasure.' The commissaris's dark hair was better protected by the cap that was part of his uniform.

I suddenly realised why they were here. A TV crew was the last thing we needed.

'This is a disaster,' I muttered.

'It'll help us get witnesses,' Ingrid said.

I threw her a glance. The publicity would only get her extra headaches, because it would increase the pressure on the team to get results. It wasn't worth it for the small chance that seeing the coverage on TV would shame someone into coming forward. None of the tourists who had been here last night would watch the Dutch news anyway.

'But still, doing an interview here? Now?' I shook my head. 'That's quick. Peter de Waal has only just regained consciousness.' Maybe 'modern' meant enjoying the attention. To my eyes, Smits looked more like a youthful politician than a chief of police.

'He likes doing all these interviews,' Ingrid said.

The scarf around the commissaris's neck was the same blue as the band around his cap. The flame, the symbol of the Dutch police force, was clearly visible on the front of the hat. I thought he was brave to wear it, as the wind could easily grab the peak of it and blow it from his head, and the resultant clip would be on the internet in seconds.

'We've increased the number of police officers dealing with this current series of assaults,' he was telling the interviewer.

I exchanged a look with Ingrid. If only he had increased the size of the team, she wouldn't have had to call me this morning in a panic to help her out.

'We're doing everything we can to stop these gangs from terrorising people in the area,' he continued. 'That's our number one priority at the moment.'

'Seriously,' Ingrid muttered, and shook her head.

I didn't like the emotive language he was using. Words like 'gangs' and 'terrorising' should be kept for when we actually knew what was going on with these violent muggings. The attack on Peter de Waal sounded as if it had been entirely personal.

'These are deeply worrying incidents,' Monique Blom said, seemingly revelling in the sensationalism. 'What's your advice for people?'

'We're asking everyone to be extremely vigilant and contact us if they witness anything. As I said, we've got additional manpower on this case, including one of our most decorated detectives.' Suddenly the commissaris's eyes swung my way. I'd had no idea he actually knew who I was. The cameras followed his line of vision. I quickly turned my back on them to stop my face from plastering the screens again. My previous cases had brought me more recognition than I'd ever wanted, and I hated being singled out.

'Additional manpower', he'd said, only to make himself look good. I wondered if he even knew who was actually working on the cases. Ingrid must be pissed off about this.

I stood in silence with my back turned until the interview had finished. Then I had a look to see what was going on. Once the cameras had stopped rolling, Commissaris Smits had a pleasant chat with Monique Blom. They seemed to know each other well enough. He shook her hand and went back to his car. As he opened the door, he looked over his shoulder in my direction and gave me a nod.

I was still puzzling over that as Ingrid drove us to Erol Yilmaz's house.

The man who opened the door was smiling, but as soon as he saw us, the smile disappeared and was replaced by a frown so deep that it made his eyebrows meet in the middle. He had been expecting someone, but it wasn't us. He started to push the door shut again, but I put out my hand and stopped it. I normally only got that kind of reaction after I'd identified myself. It seemed that for this man, most strangers who came to his front door were bad news.

Or maybe he'd been expecting the police.

'Are you Erol Yilmaz?' I asked.

The sides of his head were shaved and the rest of his dark hair was brushed up and gelled in the centre. His skin was darkened by the emergence of a beard. He was tall and muscular. His biceps bulged from under the sleeves of a black T-shirt.

'What do you want?' His voice was aggressive and confrontational. I could imagine him taking out Peter de Waal with a single punch.

'Detective Lotte Meerman,' I said, showing my badge to identify myself.

He rubbed the back of his neck. 'What is it this time?' He didn't look like an innocent man.

'Can we come in? We want to ask you a few questions,' Ingrid said.

'Do I have a choice?' Anybody who looked at him would say: yup, I can imagine that this guy has beaten someone up. I could feel the anger radiating from him.

'Not really,' I said.

He sighed and pulled the door open. Ingrid and I followed him down the small hallway, past a rack full of coats. I wondered how many people lived here. The weight of my gun sat comfortably under my jacket. He paused at the end of the hallway as if he was considering where to take us, then led us into a living room.

It was chaos. The floor was covered with an explosion of colourful children's toys. A blue mouse, a doll, an elephant and three balls sat in a line behind a teddy bear, as if it was a train, with the bear the engine pulling the other toys. In one corner someone had started a building project with

Lego. It looked like a small castle, but the roof and one wall were still missing.

Erol stopped in the middle of the room. His fists were balled at his sides, so I couldn't get a good look at his hands. His body language was so incongruous among the toys that he was like a raven in a meadow full of flowers and butterflies.

The smell of cinnamon and cumin drifted in from the kitchen.

'Where were you between two and four o'clock this morning?' I asked.

'I was at home.' There is a particular look on a suspect's face that makes them seem guilty, and Erol's was a textbook example of it: a mixture of aggression and defensiveness. It implied that whatever he was going to say, we weren't going to believe it anyway and therefore answering was a complete waste of everybody's time. 'I was asleep.'

I looked at the toys. 'Any witnesses to that?'

'No, I live by myself.'

The door slowly opened and a small girl waddled into the room, dressed in a miniature pink princess dress. She was a toddler, too young to be the builder of the castle. Dark curls circled her round face. As she wobbled up to Erol, she stared at me with her thumb in her mouth. She collided with his jeans-clad leg and wrapped one arm around him for stability. He stroked the top of her head and finally his hands relaxed. There were no marks on them. No cuts, no bruises.

'She's cute, your daughter.' I smiled at the child and made a little waving gesture at her.

The girl didn't respond but only sucked her thumb with more concentration.

'She's not my daughter.' His abrupt tone of voice made it clear he didn't want to talk about the child.

'Okay.' Whoever she was, she was clearly comfortable with him. My attempt at casual conversation had fallen flat, so I decided to come straight to the point. 'Peter de Waal was beaten up last night. He said it was you.'

Erol shook his head. 'It wasn't me. I was here all night.'

'Any witnesses?'

'No, as I said, I was alone.'

'You divorced two years ago,' Ingrid said. 'You've been harassing Peter and Caroline de Waal for almost a year now.'

Erol slowly shook his head again but didn't respond. It seemed more a gesture of exasperation than a denial of what he was hearing.

'But Caroline de Waal *is* your ex-wife?' I said.

'That's right.'

'Did you beat up her husband?'

'No, of course not.'

'You've made trouble for him and his wife before.' I kept my tone light, so as not to scare the kid.

'I stopped that.'

If only this didn't look so much like the sad aftermath of a mixed-culture marriage gone horribly wrong.

Ingrid made a show of scrolling through a report on her phone. 'You broke their windows,' she said. 'You sent them threatening emails.'

'I haven't been near them in over a year,' Erol said.

'They took out a restraining order against you.'

Erol shook his head once more. He took hold of the child as she tried to duck further behind his legs and lifted her up to his chest. The little girl squirmed and fought to get her freedom, and he eased her back to the floor. She toddled to the train of animals, grabbed the elephant and sat down in a corner, hugging the toy to her chest.

'Were you violent towards Caroline?'

'No. Never.'

'So what happened?'

'We got divorced. What does it matter? Stop coming here!' His voice was suddenly loud.

'That doesn't give you the right to threaten her.'

He balled his fists again, then looked over at the child with the elephant and uncurled his fingers with a definite effort. 'I know that.' His voice was softer now.

'So tell us what happened, Erol.' Ingrid leaned forward. 'You saw him? You were in the red-light district and you saw Peter and hit him?'

The door opened again and a second child – a boy – walked into the room. He had to be eight or nine years old. The Lego castle's architect.

Erol turned to face him. 'Didn't I tell you to stay in your room when there are visitors?'

'I need to go to the toilet.'

'Okay, but be quick about it.'

The boy rushed down the corridor. As soon as he was out of sight, Erol took a couple of deep breaths and pulled a hand through his hair. He looked down at the floor in front of him. The boy's interruption must have made him realise that being aggressive was counterproductive when trying to prove you hadn't beaten someone up in a flare of red mist.

Ingrid continued with her questions. 'Are you involved in any gang-related activities?'

'No. I work in IT for an insurance company.' The answer was soft, as if he had to say the words but didn't expect us to believe them.

And he would be right. What he said didn't make me think he hadn't done it, but I could see that his hands didn't have any cuts on them. Peter de Waal had said he'd been punched, and I would have expected some marks on the knuckles of the guy who'd done it. When your hands connect with someone's bones, they normally don't come away unscathed. I couldn't see a single scrape or bruise on Erol's hands.

'Is there somebody who can vouch for where you were last night?' I looked at the girl in the corner. 'Like the children's mother?'

'As I said, they're not my kids. They're my sister's. She'll come and pick them up soon.'

He'd probably been expecting his sister when he'd opened the door and was faced with us instead.

We could have done with some witnesses. Not everybody would be willing to admit they'd been in the red-light district and had seen an assault, even though the place where it had happened featured more bars than brothels. Even under normal circumstances it was hard, because people liked to keep their heads down.

'You can check my car, my mobile phone. I was at home

from about seven last night. I took a day off to help my sister out.'

He could have walked or cycled, and he could have left his phone at home. Neither of those things proved anything. Still, there was nothing that proved he'd done it either. Until there was a witness, it was one man's word against another's, and Erol's unscathed hands made me inclined to believe him. For now at least.

'Thanks for your time,' I said. 'We might come back with some more questions.'

'I'm sure you will.'

As we left, the boy came out of the bathroom as if he had been waiting there until we were gone. 'Who were they?' I heard the high-pitched young voice say.

'It's okay,' his uncle answered. 'They just had some things they needed to ask.' For the first time since we'd arrived, he sounded calm and natural.

Ingrid and I walked back to her car.

'What do you think?' she said. 'Did you notice his hands? He must have worn gloves.'

'Or maybe he didn't do it.' I was glad I'd gone with Ingrid this morning, instead of talking to the crazy man.

Chapter 3

I missed Ingrid in our team, but there was one good thing about her having left: I finally had my long-wished-for seat by the window. It meant that I could observe the seasonal thick clouds outside with renewed clarity. Our office had four L-shaped desks in it, pushed together to form a plus sign. When you only have two people in a space that was originally meant for four, those two people automatically get to sit by the window.

'You know this is entirely your fault, don't you?' my colleague Thomas Jansen said, pulling me out of my thoughts. He had the desk opposite mine. He always wore a blue shirt because he thought it brought out the colour of his eyes. He also had a year-round tan. He was vain like that.

'I don't know what you're talking about.' I looked studiously at the clouds, then turned to throw him my best innocent look. We'd worked together for long enough that we knew each other very well, and I knew he wasn't buying it. But I hadn't put in a good word with the chief inspector, whatever Thomas might believe. I was going to see how it worked out, and deny any responsibility if it all went horribly wrong.

'I'm going to watch him closely, and as soon as he messes up, he can go straight back to traffic police.'

'It will be fine. He'll be fine.'

'I was talking to one of his colleagues, and the guy really isn't very smart.'

I was going to defend him, but then I caught movement out of the corner of my eye. Charlie Schippers was standing in the doorway with his box of stuff.

'Where do you guys want me?' he said.

When I'd worked with him before, he had reminded me of an overexcited spaniel who could never stay still. Now he stood there with a fixed smile on his face that told me he had heard at least part of what we'd been talking about. However smart he might or might not be, there was no way he didn't know he'd been the topic of our conversation. He was about ten years younger than Thomas, and I wondered if part of the other man's animosity came from nothing more than jealousy.

'Sit there.' I pointed to the desk diagonally opposite mine. 'Next to Thomas.' The one next to me was my old desk. I'd always hated sitting there, with my back towards the door, and I didn't want Charlie to have to deal with that.

'Sure.' He put his things down with some reluctance. It was odd to see him with anything other than the boundless energy he had previously displayed and that had made me think that having him join our team would not be a bad thing. That was what I'd told the chief inspector. It was hardly the glowing review that Thomas thought I'd given the guy.

Only then did I think about how telling Charlie to sit

next to Thomas would look to him. As if even his one friend didn't want him next to her. But to say now that I had changed my mind and that he should sit next to me instead would only draw more attention to it.

It was just like being back at school.

'That was my old desk, but I never liked sitting there,' I said instead. It was too obvious. I was trying too hard. He was a grown-up. He could deal with it. 'Do you want a coffee?'

'No,' he said. 'I'm okay.' And he started to unpack his stuff. I popped down to the canteen to get myself one, just to get out for a bit.

There was something about that first coffee of the morning, the caffeine rushing through my veins, driving every last bit of sleepiness from my brain. Just one cup could make all the tiredness go away. I loved sipping it in the quiet canteen with just a few people sitting there, other cops taking ten minutes away from their desks and their cases, gathering their thoughts before getting back to whatever they were dealing with. I knew I was lucky that all I had to worry about right now was tricky colleagues.

When I got back to our office half an hour later, Thomas looked up from his screen. 'Ingrid popped in just now and showed me this.'

'What is it?'

'Some news footage. He did another interview just now.'

I didn't even have to ask who he was talking about. *He likes doing all these interviews*, Ingrid had said. She wasn't wrong. 'Is this about the assaults again?' I said.

'Yes. For a different channel.' Thomas beckoned me over.

I looked at the screen over his shoulder. The news segment was just ending, the interviewer thanking the commissaris for his time.

'If anybody saw anything last night,' the commissaris said, 'please contact us immediately.' He stared directly into the camera, his eyes narrowed. 'We're going to get the people who are doing this.'

I could see what the police force had been going for when they chose him for the job. Unlike our previous commissaris, who retired a month ago, Commissaris Smits came across as an energetic man who looked as if he was personally going to chase the criminals who attacked and robbed people after they'd happily got drunk in the town centre.

I didn't envy Ingrid her new job. The pressure to make an arrest was increasing with every interview the commissaris did. They should add the manpower to the investigation that he'd talked about this morning.

Or maybe they had, but nobody had come to talk to us. We probably didn't have enough experience with what the commissaris kept saying was gang-related violence to be considered.

'Did she fill you in?' I asked Thomas.

'She told me about your Erol Yilmaz guy,' Thomas said. 'I can't see him for those other assaults. Beating up Peter de Waal, sure, but not the rest of them.'

I nodded.

'From his history, he just isn't the type,' Thomas continued. 'The others all seem to be aggravated robberies. The attacks happened around the station and the victims had their wallets and cameras stolen. Passports, smartphones, that kind of stuff. This one, from what Ingrid told me, was personal, and there was lots of stuff leading up to it: threats, harassment. Very different.'

'And he had a restraining order.'

'Yes, after he'd pelted the couple's windows with dog excrement. That's the official term used in the file.'

'That's nasty.'

'Stuffed it through the letterbox too.'

'But I'm wondering if this one really was different. Peter de Waal was robbed too,' I said. 'He had no wallet on him, and no phone either. That's why we couldn't identify him at first.'

'Maybe Yilmaz tried to make it look like a robbery,' Thomas said. 'Or he punched the guy, knocked him unconscious and left him in the doorway, then someone else thought it was a great opportunity to take his stuff.'

'I don't think he did it,' I said. 'Didn't Ingrid tell you that?'

Thomas continued as if I hadn't spoken. 'Who was the guy who called it in?'

'A street cleaner,' I said.

'It could have been him.'

I thought back to my talk with the African man this morning. 'He was nervous,' I said, 'but I think that was just because of me. Because he had to talk to the police, I mean. If he'd taken the wallet, he probably wouldn't have called us.'

'Maybe so,' Thomas said. 'Erol Yilmaz works in an office somewhere. He's got a proper job. I just can't see him for the other assaults. Apart from the hate campaign against the de Waals, he doesn't have a criminal record.'

'He said he worked for an insurance company,' I said. 'Anyway, I'm pretty sure he didn't do it. Ingrid must see that too, surely?'

'Is that what we're working on?' Charlie asked.

'No, Lotte is just helping Ingrid,' Thomas said.

'I'm not really.' I was only following it because I was interested to see what was going to happen with it. 'Just this morning.'

But talking about this morning made me think of the other man I'd talked to. The man who'd said he wanted people to know that he wasn't dead.

Even though he couldn't possibly be the person he'd said he was, I woke up my PC and googled the name the man had used: Andre Martin Nieuwkerk. This huge success story for the police had happened so long ago that there wasn't anything about it in our internal database, and I would have to check what was in the public domain.

I wasn't really cyber-skiving as I read old newspaper articles about the Body in the Dunes. That was what the press had called the case, which had been widely reported twenty-five years ago, after the bones had been found by a man walking his dog. I'd seen all the articles before.

I remembered old cases as clearly as other people remembered football teams. I'd read somewhere that the music you liked when you were a teenager influenced your music taste for ever. I hadn't really been into music. I hadn't really been into football, even though I'd worn orange the whole week after the Netherlands won the European Championship in '88. What I had been into was looking at crime cases. It had started when I was a kid. My parents had divorced and I didn't see my father; my mother told me that he was too busy with his job as a policeman to meet with me.

It had led to me scanning every photo of every crime in the papers, hoping to catch a glimpse of my father. If he was so busy, then he would be working on some of these high-profile cases, I'd thought. I'd been the strange kid, not into anything other than reading about crime and trying to follow every clue available to the general public in all the cases that were reported.

I never saw my father in any of the photos. He hadn't been too busy; my mother was just too angry with him to allow him access. Even when people loved you, they still lied to you.

Everything changed when I went to university, around the time the Body in the Dunes case was closed. All of a sudden I was no longer the strange kid because everybody else around me was just as fascinated with this case as I was. Together with my fellow students, I tried to puzzle out what had happened. There had been no clothes or any other items that would help identification. The bones had been those of a male between fifteen and twenty-five years old, and the victim had been dead for at least four years because the body had decomposed entirely to a skeleton. The cause of death had been strangulation. We decided that there must have been fractures in the small bones of his throat, otherwise they would not have been able to establish that.

I remembered so many things about this case because it was the first one I looked at after I'd found my tribe. After I'd met all the other people who understood, who were as fascinated with it as I was, who also tried to make sense of the world around them by making sense of crime. Suddenly my weird obsession was normal. In fact, it was useful. I never felt as if I was studying; I was just continuing to do what I had always done, only in a more structured way, with other people who did the same thing. This wasn't hard work; this was heaven.

I found a photo of Nieuwkerk's parents and his younger sister Julia. It had been taken at a press conference, not after he'd initially gone missing, when you'd normally see the crying parents, but four years later, when his body had been found.

After he'd been identified.

The press had given the family a hard time because they'd waited for days after they'd last seen him before they'd gone to the police. In class, we'd been taught that the first twenty-four hours were vital. We had made judgements on what this family must have been like to have missed that crucial slot. Had not going to the police immediately made them suspicious?

The suspicion had only lasted until the real murderer had been caught.

One of the papers had carried a picture of Andre's geography teacher. The press had had a field day with this. The investigation into Andre's death had quickly honed in on the teacher, a man Andre had seemed very close to, and when police detectives had started asking questions in the school, more students had come forward to say that he'd abused them. Rumours had started to fly around. Those rumours had reached a number of journalists, leaked by either the police or parents. The article had called for the man's arrest. Screamed for it was probably a more accurate description.

I looked at the photo on the front page of that old paper. Even though there were some privacy laws that the press had to stick to, his identity hadn't been protected at all by the small black bar that covered his eyes, or by calling him Paul V. rather than using his full surname. It wasn't that hard to track down a geography teacher called Paul V. Paul Verbaan. A married man with a child. An entire article had been written about how he and his family had been refused access to their local church.

The remains had been found near Haarlem, by the coast, in the west of the country, close enough to my home town Alkmaar that my father could have worked on the case. Only he hadn't. I'd looked for that like a reflex, checking for his face in the photos, even though we'd been in touch by this point.

But the victim and the murderer hadn't come from Haarlem. They had lived in Elspeet. Right in the heart of the Dutch Bible Belt. The place where there'd been an outbreak of polio in the seventies because the orthodox Calvinist community had refused to vaccinate their children. The place where, even today, eighty per cent of people voted for one of the ultra-religious political parties.

It had of course given the whole story a new twist, or made it even sadder, depending on what your views were.

In my eyes, with my background, it had made it even more interesting.

I still remembered that I had been surprised to be surrounded by people who had totally agreed with me.

Chapter 4

After work, I went home, got changed and cycled to Mark's place in Amsterdam Zuid. Tomorrow morning, I would cycle back to my flat on the canal to feed my cat, get changed again and go to work. We'd got into this routine of being at his place on Tuesday nights, at mine on Thursday nights, and at either place, open to negotiation, at the weekend. It was very good, but not ideal. But then could you expect any relationship to be perfect? Everything took compromise.

The trick was to find a relationship in which you could live with the compromises you had to make.

I unlocked the door to Mark's house with my own key. However much I liked being greeted by him at the door, I liked the sense of belonging that the key gave me even more. It was the same when he came to my flat. I liked the antici-pation of the sound of the bell, but I loved the sense of permanence when I heard his key in the door. I hoped he felt the same when he heard me come in.

'Hi, Mark, I'm home,' I said loudly, in case he'd missed the sound of the door. What the hell was I saying? When had his house become home? This wasn't home. My flat by the canal was home. I shook my head. It was just something you said. I was clearly over-thinking things.

'How was your day?' he called from the kitchen. He liked cooking and had once said that making dinner for me was his way of taking care of me.

'It was fine.' My way of taking care of him was to not dump what had happened to me during the day on him the moment I walked through the door. I walked a careful balance between letting him into my experiences without talking about death and crime every time I saw him. It wasn't always an easy tightrope to negotiate.

I gave him a hug from behind and sneakily looked over his shoulder to see what was for dinner. The chicken breasts were easy to recognise, but I struggled to identify the small things floating in the mustard-yellow sauce. 'What are those green bits?'

'The *green bits* are capers.' I couldn't see his face, but I could hear that he was laughing at me.

'Okay.' I didn't think I'd ever knowingly eaten anything with capers in. Maybe they tasted like raisins. They were the same size. I didn't dare ask, because that would give away, once again, that I really didn't know anything about food or cooking, even if Mark did his best to educate me. 'And how was your day?'

As he stirred the sauce, he told me about his latest project. With my arms around his waist and my chin resting on his shoulder, I made encouraging noises to keep him talking and to show I was listening. I liked hearing about his job. I didn't want him to think that dealing with death and crime was by definition more important than redeveloping office blocks and houses. There was something creative and constructive in what he did: he was building things up, whereas I too often dealt with the aftermath of when things had irrevocably fallen down. If I talked about my work, I would always be discussing crime. It was a subject that was easy to talk to colleagues about, but I had to be careful at home.

'What do you want to do for Sinterklaas?' Mark said.

I wondered for how many years we'd continue the Dutch tradition of swapping gifts on 5 December. More and more people were moving to presents at Christmas instead. A number of the large department stores didn't have Sinterklaas decorations any more but already had Christmas trees. It was too early for that – only late November.

The controversy around Sinterklaas and Black Peter had flared up in earnest this year. I remembered being glued to the screen when I was small for the annual live TV broadcast of Sinterklaas coming to the country. I still believed he was a real bishop, based in Madrid, and of course he had to travel to the Netherlands on a special steamboat to deliver our presents. That Madrid was nowhere near the coast and that a bishop would have more important things to do than hand out gifts never entered my mind. At age six or seven, it hadn't seemed weird at all that a different town was chosen every year to host this big event. Once Sinterklaas had arrived, the period of about two weeks leading up to the 5 December celebrations would start. There would be more candy, especially chocolate, and then there would be presents. The shops would begin their seasonal advertising. It was the start of something good happening. That was the point.

This year there had been police presence at Sinterklaas's festive entry by boat to keep apart the protesters against Black Peter and those who hated what they saw as an attack on a children's festivity. However much I loved our childhood tradition, you had to accept that when part of the population saw the blacked-up face of Sinterklaas's helper as inherently racist, there was a problem. And when the people who wanted to protect what they saw as our national heritage used violence at what should have been a happy occasion, there was also a problem.

I could imagine that a decade from now, nobody would celebrate Sinterklaas any more. When the Dutch had first settled in New York, then New Amsterdam, they had taken the Sinterklaas with them, where over time he'd morphed into Santa Claus. It was ironic to think that maybe Santa was going to be the present-giver of choice here in years to come. Elves were far less controversial than Black Peter. But the traditional Sinterklaas celebration was a lower-key affair than the Christmas that American and UK television and movies showed. I liked low-key. I'd always spent the evening with my mum; we would swap a few presents and have almond pastries and *pepernoten*. What was I going to do this year?

'I need to check,' I said. 'I'm seeing my mother tomorrow anyway.'

'Sure. Just let me know.'

When we were together, the rule was no TV during dinner. So there was no escape when I felt Mark's eyes on me before I'd even cut the first bit of chicken breast. 'Something's happened,' he said. 'I can tell.'

'It was bizarre.' I sighed. 'A man came up to me this morning and made a point of telling me he wasn't dead.' I speared one of the green capers with my fork and tried it.

'That's . . .' he seemed to be searching for the right reaction, 'odd.'

Capers very much did not taste like raisins, but I managed not to pull a face. It wasn't that they tasted bad; I'd just expected something else. Sweet, not salty. I should have guessed that they wouldn't taste like raisins, because raisins with mustard would be revolting, and Mark never cooked anything that was revolting. Well, I'd learned something new, again.

'Odd. Yes. It was a very strange situation. He said he should let people know that he wasn't dead. Or at least I think that's how he phrased it.'

'Did he say who he was?'

'Yes. He said he was Andre Martin Nieuwkerk.'

Mark nodded, lifted a piece of chicken on his fork and examined it. 'Maybe I've overcooked it a little bit.'

The name clearly meant nothing to him. There was no reason why it should.

'It tastes good to me,' I said. 'Thanks for cooking.' He was less obsessed with murders and death than I was. That was probably a good thing. 'You haven't heard of Andre Martin Nieuwkerk?'

He looked up from his food. 'No,' he said. 'Should I have?'

'It was quite a famous murder case twenty-five years ago. The Body in the Dunes?'

He shook his head. 'Doesn't ring any bells.'

It was as if someone didn't know your favourite band.

'Tell me about the Body in the Dunes,' he said, as if he was asking me to tell him the plot of a movie.

'Okay. In the early nineties, a man walking his dog found a skeleton in the dunes near Haarlem: a young man between fifteen and twenty-five who'd been dead for a while.' I looked at Mark eating his dinner. 'Stop me if it's too gruesome,' I said. I knew my tolerance for these stories was higher than most people's.

'No, I'm fine,' he grinned. 'There are no bones in the chicken. That helps.'

It made me laugh. 'Okay. So there were just the bones, no clothes, no bag, nothing. So the police had a hard time identifying him.'

'What about DNA?'

'This was before they used DNA. That's why they dug up all those unnamed bodies from cemeteries a couple of years ago, to try to identify them with new technology.' I shook my head. 'Never mind, that's a complete tangent. Anyway, the investigating team were smart: they looked at the skull, and at photos of men and boys of the right age who'd been missing for at least four years.'

'That must have been a lot of people.'

'True. I don't know how many they checked, but they realised quite quickly from the photos that the remains were those of Andre Martin Nieuwkerk. He'd gone missing four years before, which fitted perfectly.'

'And that's the man who told you this morning he was still alive.'

'Well, that's who he claimed to be, yes. Because the case

was closed. They found the murderer. It was his school teacher. It was a real mess.'

'His teacher? How old was the kid?'

'Fifteen.'

Mark pulled a face that was not dissimilar to the one I'd wanted to pull when I'd bitten on that caper. 'So now this guy says he's him?'

I nodded.

'Could that be right? Could they have made a mistake?'

'I don't think so.' I put my knife and fork down. 'That would have meant they'd misidentified the skeleton, and the kid, the man now, had stayed hidden for over thirty years, officially declared dead.'

'Didn't you say this happened twenty-five years ago?'

'The remains were found twenty-five years ago, but he'd been missing for four years before that. So roughly thirty years in total.'

'Is it possible to have a normal life,' Mark asked, 'after you've been declared dead?'

'Depends on what you mean by normal. If you've been declared dead, you can't get a passport or a driving licence. You can't even get a bank account. You'd have to live off-grid. Only do cash-in-hand jobs.' I thought of the man I'd met this morning. He'd been smartly dressed. He hadn't looked like someone who lived without a bank account. 'I probably talked to a crazy person this morning.' I started eating again.

'Did he say anything else – apart from that he wasn't dead?'

'Not really. I had to go and help Ingrid with something.'

'Is she back in your team? I didn't know that.' Mark had come to the drinks we'd had when Ingrid left our department.

'No, I was just filling in for Tim.'

He winked. 'Trying to prove that you're more reliable than him?'

'Tim's in hospital. It's got nothing to do with being reliable.' Even to myself my voice sounded defensive.

'It's okay, I'm not jealous of your colleagues.'

I ate some more of my chicken. 'She'd been up all night with him, so I thought it was best to give her a hand. In any case, this man's story was so outlandish that I couldn't really take him seriously.'

'So what was Ingrid's case about?'

'It's to do with those violent muggings.'

'Ah yes, I saw about those on TV.' He reached out and rubbed my arm. 'That was probably more important.' He grinned. 'And you escaped a crazy person.'

Even though I'd used the phrase myself, it was when I heard Mark say it that I realised the man hadn't seemed crazy.

He'd been more like someone who had been trying to make a point. I just didn't know what that point was.

Chapter 5

The next morning, it was still dark as I cycled back to my flat to feed Pippi. It had been hard to get out of the warmth of the bed and Mark's embrace and I felt that the cat wasn't suitably appreciative of my efforts. She looked at me with that mixture of gratitude and blame – a mixture that cats seem to specialise in. She ate greedily whilst keeping an eye on my every movement as I cleaned her litter tray, making sure I was doing it properly. I knew that cats slept sixteen hours a day, but I could only imagine that she must be bored when there was nobody home. It wasn't that I'd never left her by herself for a night before, but it was now becoming a regular thing, and that made me feel guilty.

The look of blame Pippi was giving me clearly worked, because as I got changed, I told her I would be home early tonight and would spend all evening playing with her. The ball of string would get a proper workout. All other cat toys were studiously ignored. Even the wind-up mouse that I thought was quite amusing wasn't as interesting as string.

I sat down at the table by the window and got my laptop out. I would keep Pippi company for another half an hour or so. I googled Andre Martin Nieuwkerk again, as I'd done in the office yesterday. Not because I believed the man I'd met yesterday morning had actually been the Body in the Dunes, but because there was a possibility that he'd used that name to make a point. Maybe he wanted to flag something else up. All night I'd been turning his words over in my head. When he said that he wanted people to know that he was still alive, it could be taken in another way. Maybe I was over-thinking this, but I'd heard words like those used by other people.

Like cancer survivors.

Like people who survived other kinds of severe trauma.

What if this guy had survived something too? What if it had been the kind of thing that Andre Nieuwkerk had suffered?

What if this guy was another child abuse victim?

I clicked on the first image search result and the murdered boy's face filled my screen.

Pippi put her claws into my leg for attention and I reached down and scratched her head, but I couldn't tear my gaze away from the screen.

He looked so young.

It was obviously a school photo. I remembered when I'd been that age and the photographer had turned up to take individual photos, as well as a class portrait. Photos like the one that was on my screen now, which we'd taken home to hand out to loving parents and grandparents.

You couldn't always tell much about a kid from those school photos. If the photographer was good, he could make even the most rebellious children look like well-behaved angels. Still, the impression I got from the boy who looked out at me from the screen was that he had been a quiet kid. A shy smile hung around his lips, and his dark hair was cut with a thick, blunt fringe that didn't do him any favours. He wore a buttoned checked shirt that was more suitable for an old man than a teenager but had the effect of making him look even younger than the fourteen or fifteen he must have been.

I hadn't worked in the Kinderpolitie myself, the department of the police force that dealt with crimes against and perpetrated by children, but I still recognised the kind of kid who would keep quiet if anything happened to him. It made me wonder if the man who had talked to me yesterday morning had been a kid like that as well.

Even though my decision to go with Ingrid to interview Peter de Waal still felt like the right one, especially in light of Erol Yilmaz's reaction, I now felt bad about not talking to the man for longer. It could have taken all his courage to come up to me, and I'd just brushed him off.

I checked my watch. It wasn't even eight o'clock yet. The man had mentioned the hotel he was staying at. I looked the place up. It was only a fifteen-minute cycle ride away. I shut down my laptop and put my coat on.

I could still hear my cat meowing after I'd pulled the door closed behind me.

There was a chill in the air this morning that reminded me that winter wasn't far away, but the stars that showed faintly in the sky told me it was going to be a nice day. The sun would come up in an hour or so. At least the stars gave me hope that I would see it today.

The trees along the canal had been stripped of their leaves weeks ago and, lit by the street lights, they threw eerie shadows on the road. Two more turnings and I was at the Hotel Mondrian. I locked my bike up and went inside.

The clientele inside the hotel seemed to be a mixture of business people and tourists. One of the long tables by the entrance was occupied by a group of ten women who were at least a decade older than the rest of the people milling around. They spoke English and were surrounded by a collection of small backpacks and cameras. They seemed ready for a busy day of sightseeing. One of them looked at her watch and sighed.

I didn't pay them close attention, but instead turned to the receptionist. He was a tall young man with close-cropped dark hair. His desk was enclosed at either side by large bunches of tulips in glass vases. Behind him hung a print of a Mondrian painting, blocks of primary colours edged with thick black lines. He was clearly keeping one eye on what was going on around him at the same time as talking to a man who was checking out, because as soon as I took a step towards the desk, he caught my eye and asked if he could help me.

I showed my badge. 'I'm Detective Lotte Meerman,' I said. 'I'm here to talk to one of your guests.'

'Of course,' the receptionist said. 'What's his name?'

Now that was a good question. 'Andre Nieuwkerk.' I didn't think he would have used the middle name at check-in.

The receptionist checked his computer. 'We don't have anybody here under that name,' he said.

I wasn't entirely surprised. 'Maybe it's under Martin. Martin Nieuwkerk.'

The man behind the desk shook his head. 'There isn't anybody here with that surname at all.' He seemed relieved that he couldn't help me, so that we wouldn't cause problems in his hotel.

'He's Dutch,' I said. 'Probably in his early forties?'

'Dutch? I don't think we have many Dutch people staying here at the moment. An elderly couple in their seventies . . .'

'No, not them.'

'Two men in their twenties . . .'

'Not them either.'

'And that's it. No other Dutch people.'

'Did anybody leave a note under that name?' The man had specifically said I should come to this hotel. Had he changed his mind? Decided not to talk to the police after all? Maybe there was more than one Hotel Mondrian. I might just be at the wrong place.

The receptionist did me the courtesy of looking through a pile of papers and checking the pigeonholes for the various rooms. 'Ah, here's something,' he said. '"If anybody asks for Andre Nieuwkerk, it's Room 14."'

'I thought you said he wasn't here,' I said.

'Well, he's not registered under that name.'

'Can you call him for me?'

I waited as he dialled the room. After a minute or so, he shook his head. 'No response.'

He must have gone out already. Yesterday he'd been up

early too. It had been well before eight o'clock when he'd spoken to me. I gave the receptionist my card. 'Please call me when he gets back.'

The manager of the Hotel Mondrian contacted me four hours later. 'I'm sorry to call,' he said, 'but you left your card with us this morning.'

'Is Andre Nieuwkerk back?'

'Well, the guest in Room 14 had his Do Not Disturb sign on his door and he should have checked out by ten a.m. It's midday now. We've knocked and there's no response . . .' His voice petered out.

I understood what he was saying. It wouldn't be the first time this had happened in a hotel. They probably preferred to have a police officer discover what was on the other side of the door than the cleaner.

'Is the guest Dutch?'

'No, he's British. He's got a British passport.'

'What's his name?' I didn't have to go myself. I could just send some cops in uniform. I could even insist that the manager open the door himself.

'His name is Brand. Theo Brand.'

I was about to say that I would get someone over there, but something about that name pulled me up.

Brand. Nieuwkerk.

Brand Nieuw. Brand New.

Someone who wanted people to know that he was still alive.

'I'll be right there.' I ended the call and grabbed my handbag. 'You're coming with me,' I said to Charlie.

Charlie drove us to the Hotel Mondrian through the midday sunshine that the stars had promised this morning. A girl waiting for a traffic light had her eyes closed and her face turned towards the rays of the low-hanging sun as if this was the last fix she was going to get before winter hit.

I had to narrow my eyes to slits in order to see anything where the beams crept over the top of the houses. I should have worn my sunglasses. Even the street cleaner probably didn't need his woollen hat and two scarves today.

The hotel manager was waiting for us on the other side of the revolving door with a calm expression on his face, as if this was an everyday occurrence. 'Police? Please come in.' His voice was soothing in the midst of the chaos. Dark suit over a grey waistcoat, short blond hair. Nothing would faze him. Deaths were not uncommon in hotels but had to be kept quiet at all costs. Nobody wanted to sleep in a room where someone had died the night before.

I followed him up the stairs and into a smart corridor with Charlie close behind me. A woman rattled down the hallway dragging a wheelie bag. The manager said a friendly good morning as if nothing unusual was happening at all. It was clear which room we were after: the red Do Not Disturb sign dangled from the door handle. The manager waited, swipe card in hand, until the woman with the bag had stepped into the lift. Then he opened the door and let me go through first.

A man was lying on the bed, fully clothed. It amazed me that his shoes were still on his feet. He hadn't even undone them to get into bed. His tie was perfectly done up too. He'd just fallen backwards. Had he died as he was sitting on his bed? There was no sign that he had struggled for air; the bed covers were undisturbed. A bottle with a white label that screamed prescription medicine stood on the bedside table.

I was looking at those things because I wanted to delay looking at the dead man's face.

'We should secure the scene,' Charlie said. 'I'll call Forensics.'

I didn't stop him.

There was no doubt that the body on the bed was that of the man I'd refused to speak to yesterday. The man I'd come to see this morning. I felt a pressure behind my eyes that wasn't caused by being confronted with a dead person. It was the feeling I got when I was driving along the motorway and someone suddenly cut in front of me. The feeling that said: you couldn't have waited? It was so urgent that you couldn't have waited for a few seconds?

You couldn't have waited until the next day?

Suddenly I was that school outcast again. I was the kid whose feelings were out of sync with everybody else's. A better person, a normal person, would feel sorry for the guy, that his life had got so bad that he'd killed himself. They would feel sad that they hadn't been able to help him.

I didn't feel any of that.

I felt anger. Anger that he hadn't waited for me, anger that he had put me in this position, that he had made my choice a mistake.

I stepped out of the room and scanned the ceiling of the hallway for the cat-eye that would have recorded all the comings and goings on this floor. It was located in the middle, only a few doors away from Theo Brand's room. I turned to the manager. 'Can you get me the footage from that camera?'

'I'm sorry, we're having some problems with our CCTV at the moment.' He could just as easily have been telling a guest that the hot water wasn't working. 'We contacted the company, but just having them there is a deterrent, don't you think?'

I wanted to swear, but I kept a professional face on. It might be a deterrent, but it was also a hindrance to this investigation. We relied too heavily on the surveillance that individual firms were providing us with.

I heard a noise behind me. It was a chambermaid, trolley stacked high with towels and replacement shampoo. 'Sorry,' she said. She was African too, her hair tidied away under a pale green scarf, her eyes cast down to the floor just in front of the trolley. It was hard to get a job that didn't involve cleaning if you didn't speak the language.

I realised I was hindering her progress along the corridor. I took a step sideways to let her pass. These hallways were really narrow. She went past without looking into the room.

Edgar Ling was one of the first members of the forensics team to turn up. He was short and bulky and the plastic coveralls weren't particularly flattering. His eyebrows and eyelashes were so fair they were barely visible, and his eyes were glossy, as if marbles the colour of wet soil had been inserted into his skull.

I pointed out the key that was lying on top of the desk in the room. 'Check what time that was used,' I said to the hotel manager. 'How long had Brand been staying here?'

'Five nights, Friday through to Wednesday. He'd prepaid the whole amount.'

As if what was important was that the hotel got their money.

Thomas turned up fifteen minutes later when the forensic investigation was in full swing.

'How nice of you to let Charlie call the entire circus for a suicide,' he said.

I didn't tell him that it was as much for my benefit as Charlie's.

That I was hoping the pathologist or the forensic scientists would find something to suggest this wasn't a suicide.

It was only too obvious what had happened, and I didn't like the obvious answer in this case. I told Thomas to check everything and I would come and see the pathologist in a couple of hours.

Chapter 6

'What was the time of death?' I asked. I could tell he had been dead for at least twelve hours, but I wanted to know for sure.

Baker, the pathologist, didn't make eye contact but looked down at her notes. 'More than twenty-four hours ago. Between twenty-four and twenty-six hours.'

I quickly did the sums in my head. That meant he would have died between 7 and 9 a.m. yesterday. 'That can't be right.' The words escaped from my mouth before my brain could get into gear.

Now Baker did look up. 'Doubting my work, Detective Meerman?'

I shook my head. 'Sorry, of course it can be right.'

What time had I seen him? What time had it been when I'd decided not to talk to him?

It had still been dark, I knew that. Ingrid had called me to go to the crime scene at around 5.15, and it had been about 6 a.m. when I was out there waiting for her. I wasn't entirely sure how much time had passed between then and the man turning up. We had looked for CCTV cameras and then she'd made that phone call.

It could have been any time between half past six and seven.

Then he would have had to go back to the hotel, and that was probably a half-hour walk away from the Lange Niezel.

'Had his body been moved after his death?'

'No, the decay was all in line with the position he was found in.'

I nodded, but still thought the earliest boundary of the time of death was off. I didn't think he could have been dead at 7 a.m.

The anger I'd felt when I'd seen him in the hotel flashed up again. He'd told me to speak to him and instead he'd killed himself? It didn't make any sense.

'Are you sure this was a suicide?'

'Well, it looks like suicide. The medicine in the bottle matches the opioid in his bloodstream. The actual cause of death is asphyxiation, of course, but that's absolutely as would be expected with an opioid overdose. There was heavy scarring on his right leg: a sign of substantial surgery that happened at least twelve months ago. Do you want to see?'

'No, that's okay,' I said. 'I trust you.'

'That could well have been when he was first prescribed the opioids. This is only a guess, of course.'

'Any fibres—'

'In his nostrils? No, nothing. Nobody held a pillow over his face, if that was what you were thinking of. The only thing is some bruising around his eye socket.'

I shook my head, because he'd already had that when I met him. I didn't say it out loud. 'That would have nothing to do with asphyxiation,' I said instead.

'Exactly. No marks around his throat, either.'

'Water in his lungs?'

'Nothing. We wouldn't have missed that. He died from the pills by his bedside. There's no bruising or marking around his mouth, or anything else that would indicate he was forced to take them. No sign of a struggle, either in the room or on his body. Why are you asking this?'

If I hadn't met the man yesterday morning, we would have done very little with this apart from notify the family and the necessary legal departments. Instead I was asking her questions. 'It's just that Charlie wants to know,' I said. 'It's his first case and he seemed disappointed that there isn't anything to investigate.'

The pathologist smiled. 'You've got a suicide, Detective Meerman. Congratulations on not adding to the Amsterdam crime statistics.' She gave me a copy of her preliminary report and a bunch of photos. Normally I liked working from photos, but this time the images were heavy in my hand.

As I walked back to our office, I couldn't help but think about the timing again. I wondered if I'd been the last person to speak to this man.

At my desk, I opened the folder that Edgar Ling had given me and took out the photos from the hotel room. I looked at Theo Brand's face. Examining these photos was different from looking at his body when we found him. Because I was no longer in his presence, I could do my job; I could study him as I should have done then. As I would have done if I hadn't met him a day beforehand.

There was bruising around his left eye. If I had to guess,

54

I would say a single punch. The kind of bruising that should have been on Peter de Waal's face if his assault had happened the way he said. I scanned the pathologist's report, then looked at the victim's phone. There'd been no fingerprints on the device apart from his own. Maybe it would tell me if there was a next of kin I should contact.

The truth was that I was interested to find out whether he'd told anybody else he wasn't dead. I checked the last call he had made. That morning, at 6.43 a.m., he'd talked to someone called Laurens for eight minutes and twelve seconds. So at least we knew he'd still been alive at that point.

I tried to remember everything I could about yesterday morning, but I couldn't be sure if I'd spoken to him before or after 6.43 a.m.

I hoped it had been before.

I paged through his diary. He'd come to Amsterdam less than a week ago, and since then had arranged to meet with, in order of dates, Laurens, Julia, Harry and Daniel. Underneath each name there was an address and a telephone number. Theo had obviously been a meticulous person. I thought of the man I'd met yesterday morning: his smart clothes and long woollen coat matched that image.

I put a call in to the hotel and asked them if they had checked what time Theo had come back to his room yesterday. They told me it was 8.37 a.m.

At least an hour and a half after I'd talked to him.

He must have taken the overdose just after he'd got back to his room. Come back and seen the bottle of pills. Somehow that made it seem like a more impulsive act. Spur of the moment, not necessarily long-planned.

Why did that make it feel worse?

'Our new team member here wants Forensics to investigate everything because he thinks this suicide looks suspicious,' Thomas said as he and Charlie came into the office. 'We've got a limited budget and limited resources and we can't waste it all on obvious suicides.'

'There was no note,' Charlie said. 'The man died of asphyxiation.'

'That's perfectly normal for an opioid overdose. You stop breathing.'

It sounded as if they had been having this discussion for the last hour or so already.

'There was bruising on his face,' Charlie said. 'Around his left eye.'

'It could well have been old,' Thomas said.

I could have told them that it had already been there yesterday morning, but I kept my mouth shut. The full pathologist's report would tell us more. Still, a bruise around the eye wasn't related to asphyxiation, and I would have disregarded it even if I hadn't seen it earlier.

I opened the diary again and looked at the meetings Theo had arranged. If these were people he'd met with to say goodbye, it would be a good thing to contact all four of them: Laurens, Julia, Harry and Daniel.

Julia.

Andre Nieuwkerk had had a sister named Julia; I remembered it from the newspaper article I'd read yesterday. Surely not.

I dialled the number underneath her name. The phone

rang four, five, six times. Then a woman answered. 'This is Julia Nieuwkerk,' she said.

I clutched my phone tighter in my hand. 'Good afternoon,' I said. 'This is Detective Lotte Meerman from the Amsterdam police.'

'Is this about that guy?' she said.

Her response surprised me. 'What guy?' I asked. I had to work hard to make my voice sound calm. To sound normal.

'That guy who came to my house a few days ago,' Julia said. 'That nutter claiming to be my dead brother.'

Chapter 7

Julia Nieuwkerk's flat was in the Watergraafsmeer, an area of Amsterdam where low rows of houses gave the impression of being part of a village instead of the capital city. As Charlie parked the car, four small children stopped playing in the street, not to avoid being hit but out of curiosity to see who we were. I waved at them, and that made them decide that their game was infinitely more interesting than these two strangers in their street.

The flat took up the ground floor of a house. Three bicycles were parked right outside the window, and one of them, a child's pale blue tricycle, had fallen over. Julia opened the door. She wasn't young, probably only a few years younger than me, but she had an elfin quality about her. Her long blonde hair was tied back in a messy ponytail, and she wore a dark-blue jumper with wide sleeves that were embroidered in white around the cuffs. She asked to see our IDs, scrutinising them carefully. When she was finally satisfied, she opened the door wider and invited us in.

A bright orange safety jacket and a builder's helmet were hanging from hooks on the wall. Mud-covered sturdy boots stood by the door. They looked far too big to be Julia's: she would be swimming in them. Also, the safety jacket didn't seem to go with her checked skirt and the slippers with bows on the front.

The kid's tricycle and at least one of the other bikes outside must have belonged to the upstairs neighbours, because as soon as I was inside, I could tell that this was a single person's studio flat. There was a kitchen and a long table at one end of the room, and a large double bed occupied the space by the window on the other side. Even though the place was small, it was warm and full of light. The owner of the builder's gear didn't seem to be here.

'I thought it was a very tasteless joke,' Julia said before I could even ask a question, 'but I didn't think it was illegal.' She pulled out a chair at the kitchen table and sat down. Charlie and I took seats opposite her. Freckles touched the skin on her cheekbones and the bridge of her nose, even though it was winter. She must have spent a lot of time outdoors. 'I was pleasantly surprised when you contacted me, and then I got a bit suspicious. Sorry that I was being paranoid, but I thought maybe you were in it with him.'

So that was why she'd looked at our IDs so closely.

'In it with him?' Charlie asked. 'In what way?'

'I've had trouble in the past,' she said. 'Reporters coming here, or some of those true-crime writers. All wanting to talk about the story of the Body in the Dunes.' Her voice was sharp. 'For them it is a story. For me it's my brother.' She swallowed down the words to stop herself from saying more.

'It was all so strange,' she said after a pause. 'That's why I thought that maybe it was an elaborate set-up.'

'When exactly did the man come here?' I asked.

'Saturday evening,' she said. 'I think it was about six, because I was going to have dinner with a friend and I was just getting ready to go out.'

'Did he phone you beforehand?'

'No, he just showed up. If he'd called, I would have told him not to come.'

'What did he say when he got here?' Charlie asked.

'He asked if he could come in. At first, I just thought he was trying to sell me something, or was a religious nut, so I said that no, he couldn't. Then he said he was my brother Andre. That he was alive. He said he was really sorry for what had happened.'

I looked for sadness on Julia's face, but saw none. There was only annoyance. It was the same emotion I'd had, but it bothered me to see it on someone else's face.

'You didn't believe him,' I said.

'Of course I didn't.' She frowned at my question. 'My brother was murdered thirty years ago.'

'You didn't think the man looked like him?' I asked. 'Or like your father?'

'Like my father?' A laugh escaped from her mouth as if that was the funniest thing she'd heard all day. 'No.' The word was conclusive. 'He definitely did not look like my father.'

'You were young when you last saw your brother.'

'I was twelve when he went missing. I wanted him to come back every single day. Even when the police came four years later and told us he'd probably died, I still didn't believe it.' She rested her elbows on the table in front of her. 'Do you know when I finally accepted that he was really dead? It was when that bastard killed himself. Even if he only did it because he got kicked out of the church, still, that was when I knew that he'd not only abused him but also murdered him, and that Andre was never going to come back.'

I remembered seeing the photo of Paul Verbaan and his family being publicly stopped from going into the church on Sunday morning. That was the photo that had made it to the front page of the paper, the one where Paul Verbaan had been only too easy to identify.

Julia's voice started to sound more heated. 'So when someone turns up on my doorstep with a crazy story, asking to be let in, of course I don't believe him.'

'How long did you two talk for?'

'Not long. It was five minutes at most,' Julia said. 'As soon as he said he was my dead brother, I tried to close the door on him.'

'Did he speak to you in English?' I asked.

'No,' Julia said, 'he spoke in Dutch. I'm sure he was Dutch.'

'Dutch?' Charlie said. 'We thought he was British.'

'Well, he spoke Dutch to me.' Julia looked down at some typed-up notes on a piece of paper in front of her. She must have prepared for our visit. 'What are you going to do about him? He knows where I live. It's because I'm in the phone directory, I know that. I'm easy to find. But I don't want him to come back here. It's really disgusting that he's pretending to be my brother.'

'He won't come back,' I said. 'He died yesterday morning.'

She leaned back on her chair and smiled, but immediately

bit her lower lip to keep the smile hidden. I had seen it, though. I'd seen that she was happy that this man had died.

I wanted to grab her by the arm and shake her.

I wanted to tell her to show some respect.

'What happened?' she asked.

'We think he killed himself,' Charlie said. 'We found him in his hotel room.'

'So we're just trying to piece together what happened,' I added. 'Why he'd come here. What was he like when he talked to you?' I tried to keep the harsh edge out of my voice.

Julia rubbed her face. 'Whoever he was, he was really good. Really convincing.' She slicked her fringe back. 'He had tears in his eyes. I felt a bit bad for him; I feel bad now, but what was I supposed to do? Should I have gone along with his crazy story? Even after I'd shut the door, I heard him banging, pleading with me to listen to him. He said he was so sorry. He kept saying it over and over again.'

I exchanged a glance with Charlie, then made a note. *I'm sorry.* What could he possibly have been apologising for? I drew a large circle around the words, then wrote, *Should I have gone along with his crazy story?*

'Then what happened?' I asked.

Julia sighed. 'This place doesn't have a back door, so I couldn't leave. I felt trapped. I didn't want him to see me, so I stayed in my bathroom. He was outside for at least ten minutes, banging on the door. Finally I got fed up with it and shouted: "Leave, just leave." And he did. I was surprised, but he actually went away. I was quite shaken up and thought I should get the police involved, but he hadn't threatened me.' She laughed. 'I could hardly report a man for apologising, now could I?'

'Were you scared of him?' I asked.

'It just felt wrong.' Julia pulled the piece of paper closer to her. 'I know my brother was murdered a long time ago,' she said, 'but sometimes something happens that brings it all back, and I'll feel overwhelmed. That's why I didn't want him here. I wanted him to go away. I didn't want my brother's death to be shoved in my face by this man.'

I nodded, because I understood only too well how everyday things could remind you of grief.

I'd been there.

I tried to stop being angry at Julia and to put myself in her position instead. Theo's visit must have been surreal, a stranger knocking on her door claiming to be her dead brother. As she had said, it must have been a reminder of what had happened all those years ago that she could have done without.

I looked down at the notes I'd scribbled. *I'm sorry. Should I have gone along with his crazy story?* They were Julia's words, but my sentiments too. I folded up the piece of paper and put it in the back pocket of my trousers.

It also made me think about the effect Julia's reaction must have had on Theo. Initially I had assumed that he had been another victim of child abuse and that was why he'd identified with Andre Nieuwkerk. I was beginning to realise that this assumption had been wrong, and that he hadn't used the name to expose another crime; it was possible that he had believed he really *was* Andre Nieuwkerk. If that was the case, he must have expected a very different response.

63

What had he thought was going to happen? Maybe he had hoped his sister would welcome him with open arms. It was all speculation, of course, but either way, I didn't think he would have expected to be doubted. Was that why he'd killed himself?

'Did he offer you any evidence for who he was?' I asked. 'Did he say he could prove his identity or anything like that?'

'No,' Julia said. 'Nothing. What could there have been? He wasn't my brother.'

'I know you're sure he wasn't,' I said it carefully, 'but we would like to rule it out.'

The doorbell rang. Julia looked at me. 'Can I answer that?'

'Of course,' I said, and she went to the door.

'You bitch!' I heard an angry voice yell. I turned around to check what was going on. Over Julia's shoulder, I could see her visitor. He was probably her age. He had a thin moustache with a hint of a matching goatee beard, and wore a baseball cap backwards. He was too old to be wearing a cap like that. His dark hair reached down to the furry collar of his thick green coat. His face was pale and intense, and his fists were balled. 'Did you know?' He lowered his voice. 'Have you always known?'

I got to my feet, because a soft voice worried me more than shouting.

'Did you know he wasn't dead?' he said. 'Don't you feel guilty? My father killed himself.'

Julia threw me a look over her shoulder and pivoted until her back was against the wall. Her fingers gripped the material of the orange safety jacket. It was as if she'd been pushed back by his words.

'You did know!' He took a step forward. 'You and your fucking family knew and said nothing. My father died!'

I squeezed past Julia and pushed the guy away from her front door. He didn't fight the pressure of my hand but let me guide him into the quiet street. I kept one hand on his shoulder and used the other to show him my badge. Charlie's substantial presence at my back was comforting in case this was going to escalate. Based on what he'd said, I had a pretty shrewd idea who the man was and why he was here.

'Calm down,' I said.

He pulled his arm free, then tore the baseball cap from his head. 'The police.' He glared at me. 'You're only here to cover up for your mistakes.'

I looked behind me and saw Julia still standing in her doorway.

'I'm guessing you're Paul Verbaan's son?' I said.

'Yeah, that's right.' His voice was defensive, as if in his mind he was adding: what of it? He put his cap back on, the right way around this time. 'I'm Daniel. Daniel Verbaan.'

Daniel. The fourth name in Theo Brand's diary.

'We'll come back later,' I said to Julia.

'No,' she said. 'Come on in.'

The neighbours in the houses on either side were at their windows, trying to catch every second of this unusual spectacle in their quiet street. I wanted to get this guy away from their prying eyes.

'If you want to talk to me, I'll talk to you,' Julia said. She stepped back and pulled the door open wide.

That took me by surprise. Daniel stepped forward and crossed the threshold. I followed him. I felt less in control than I wanted to be, but I couldn't help thinking that this conversation was going to be very interesting.

I checked Julia's face as I went back in. She seemed calm and collected, and I wondered if I'd completely misread her emotions when she'd backed away from the door. Had she always intended to ask him in? Why would she do that – greet the son of her brother's murderer?

The thought popped into my mind that maybe Daniel was right and she'd known all along that her brother wasn't dead.

'Would you like tea or coffee?' she said as calmly as if one of her friends had turned up. Daniel was a full head taller than her, but she looked him in the eye and didn't back down.

He shook his head. 'Nothing from you,' he replied.

Julia shrugged as if his answer was uninteresting and sat down at the table. Whatever her emotions were, I couldn't see any evidence of guilt. 'That man was a fraud,' she said.

Daniel sat down opposite her and I took the seat next to him, ready to physically interfere if I needed to. 'So why are you willing to talk to me?' he said.

'I talked to you last time too. As I said then, what your father did wasn't your fault. Daniel, look, I know why you want to believe him, but that man wasn't Andre.'

'We talked for a long time,' Daniel said. 'I filmed our conversation.'

The skin on my arms broke out in goose bumps. 'You filmed him?'

He ignored me. 'I remember him from school. It's him, Julia.' He grinned at her. 'You can't fool me. The guy who came to see me is your fucking brother.'

II

The Troublemaker

Chapter 8

On the screen, I saw the man I'd seen yesterday morning. He was as neatly dressed as he had been then, almost someone ready to go to work rather than a man from London visiting Amsterdam for pleasure. Had he seen his trip here as work? Was he wearing a suit and tie because this was important to him and he'd dressed for the occasion? I couldn't figure it out. He looked so ordinary: dark hair speckled with grey, small glasses, and a carefully groomed beard; once again it proved that it was hard to read people's histories from their features. His eyes were squarely and confidently aimed at the camera, as if he was ready for his confession. The footage was paused.

Daniel had given us the recording, and once we'd got to the police station I hooked it up to the bigger screen. Daniel had said it was probably for the best if Julia didn't see it. She hadn't argued and neither had I. She had maintained that this man couldn't possibly be her brother.

I had a printout of Andre Nieuwkerk's photo in front of me: the school picture that had gripped me this morning. Had this awkward kid grown up to be the man I'd met yesterday? The way the three of us were sitting here – me,

Charlie and Daniel – with Theo Brand projected large made it seem that he was in the room with us, so real on the screen that he was impossible to avoid. I would think of him by this name until we had evidence to the contrary.

'What made you think this man was Andre Nieuwkerk?' I asked. 'It isn't immediately obvious to me.' I held the photo up next to the screen. 'I can't really see a likeness.'

'It was something he said.'

'You knew him well, then?' Charlie asked. It was an interesting question.

'Not him per se . . .' Daniel took off his baseball cap, rubbed his head, and put the cap back on in reverse. His face looked vulnerable now that it was no longer shadowed and protected by the peak. A tuft of dark hair escaped over the adjustable strap and stood up straight. As if there was a teenager still hidden inside the middle-aged man. 'He said something about Julia. We used to be classmates.'

'You and Julia Nieuwkerk?' I thought nothing could surprise me any more, but I was still taken aback that Daniel's father had killed the brother of his classmate. I looked at the man with the too-youthful baseball cap in a new light. I could only imagine how horrific this must have been for him.

'Yeah, we were classmates in primary school and then went to the same secondary school. So I knew her well and I knew her brother a bit.'

Julia's assertion that she'd always been willing to talk to him, that he wasn't to blame for what his father had done, suddenly took on a different meaning. I had misread the situation from the beginning: when she'd stepped back, it had been to let him in, and that wasn't because she'd known that her brother wasn't dead but because this man used to be her friend at school.

'The secondary school you went to, was that the school where your father was a teacher? The same school Andre went to?' Charlie asked.

'Yes.'

'And the man who came to see you – let's call him Theo, to be clear – he knew you?' I said.

Daniel nodded. 'He said, "Hi, Daniel, it's been a while. I last saw you when you and my sister used to cycle to school together." I got the feeling that he said that because it would convince me.'

I nodded. That made sense. I'd cycled with a classmate to school too. My mother had arranged it with another mother, so that we had company for the twenty-minute ride. It was a big step from walking to primary school to cycling to secondary school.

It just didn't seem like fireproof evidence to me.

'Wouldn't lots of people have known about that?' I asked. 'Any of your classmates, for example?'

'No, because Julia didn't want to be seen with me. She'd make me wait at the last bicycle tunnel, around the corner from the school, for exactly three minutes. It was only for a couple of months anyway, and then my mother told me I had to go by myself.'

I looked at the photo of Andre again. I looked at Theo on the screen. I understood why Daniel had let the guy in, even if they looked like different people. If nothing else, he was someone who had clearly known the family well.

Daniel pointed at the screen. 'Can we just watch the footage? I'm sure you'll have questions for me afterwards.'

That pulled me up. I nodded at Charlie, who was the one closest to the laptop. He pressed play, and the frozen face started to move again.

'Are you sure about this, Daniel?' Theo spoke in the same lightly halting Dutch that he'd used with me. 'Are you sure you want to record this?'

'You're not dead. This is evidence that my father wasn't a murderer.' The footage wasn't quite steady, but moved ever so slightly. It only showed Theo's face. 'Where have you been hiding all these years?'

'I live in London.'

'Living a happy life.' Daniel's voice was bitter.

Theo grimaced. 'I try my best.'

He would kill himself the next morning, so it was clear that his life hadn't been that happy.

'Did you think about us?'

'About you? Why would I? I was too busy trying to survive.'

'You didn't feel guilty that you let everybody think my father was a murderer?'

'He wasn't a murderer but he was an abuser,' Theo said.

'Don't lie.'

'I'm not lying. You know I wasn't the only one. Others came forward. He'd been doing it for years.' His mouth moved as if he was fighting to keep the emotions inside, but he stayed calm as he spoke.

'They retracted their statements.'

'And you know why they did that.'

'Because they were lies.'

Theo shook his head. 'I know that's what you want to believe. But you went to the same school. You know what that place was like. They would have put huge pressure on the kids to withdraw their statements, not to get the school involved. Especially after your father's death.'

'My dad killed himself.'

The term 'dad' was unusually endearing. I was more used to abusers' and murderers' families creating an emotional distance from the perpetrator.

'He was accused of having murdered you; that's why he killed himself.' I could hear tears and anger in the voice, even though I couldn't see Daniel's face on the screen. But I could see it here, in the room, and could tell that he was fighting to hide those emotions from us.

Paul Verbaan's suicide had been interpreted as a confession of guilt by the investigating team. But he'd left no written confession behind.

Theo leaned forward and Daniel must have moved back in response, as the footage shook. 'Don't you think all those years of abuse were worse than murder? All those boys whose lives he ruined? Don't you think that was why he killed himself? Because now everybody knew what kind of man he was.'

Everybody seemed to have a different opinion as to why Paul Verbaan had killed himself. I understood that Theo probably wanted to think he'd committed suicide out of guilt over the abuse. Julia had said he'd killed himself because he'd been barred from the church.

Personally, I thought that the press and the police were

culpable too. Not just for the pressure that they must have put on the man, but also for his name getting out.

'Didn't you feel sorry for us?' Daniel asked.

'You know what?' Theo folded his arms. 'I mainly felt sorry for me. For being abused by your father, for being kicked out of my parents' house when your mother came to confront me.'

His parents had kicked him out of the house? I remembered that as students we had been surprised that it had taken his parents four days to report him missing, but nobody had known this bit of information. I made a note of it, because I couldn't decide if it made things clearer or more confusing.

'My mother knew about you?'

'Is that news to you?' Theo smiled, but I could see how his mouth moved with another emotion as well. 'Yes, she walked in on us.'

'That's a lie.' Daniel's voice was tight.

'She didn't tell you? It's what started it all. She believed your father was the victim. That I had come on to him. Forced myself on him. That I was sucking him off because I loved him so much.' His voice was bitter and sarcastic at the same time.

'You fucking queer!'

Daniel must have dropped the phone at that point, because suddenly the screen showed the ceiling of the room and a corner of a lampshade. I heard a thump. I heard someone cry out.

'Get out of this house,' I heard him say. 'Get out now.'

The phone moved again, Daniel recording the aftermath

of his violence. Theo was holding his face. His hand was over his left eye.

I threw a glance at Charlie, because it explained the bruising he'd noticed earlier, and which I'd seen the previous morning. I looked down at Daniel's hands and noticed the telltale marks on the knuckles of his right hand.

On the screen, Theo was on his feet and grabbing his coat. The footage showed his back as Daniel followed him with the camera until he left the house and the door closed behind him. The recording ended.

'I tried to call him,' Daniel said. 'After he'd left. I left him a whole bunch of messages because I wanted him to make an official statement to the police.'

My head spun with questions that this clip had raised. 'Did you know his parents? Julia's parents?'

'Not well, but yes, I'd met them. Why are you asking me about them?'

'Theo said they kicked him out of the house.'

'I could believe that. It's quite possible. They were very religious. Very strict orthodox Calvinists.'

'But their own son . . .'

'"If your right eye causes you to sin, pluck it out and throw it away."'

I recognised the Bible quote, but that didn't make it any easier for me to understand what they'd done.

'I think he was telling the truth about that,' Daniel said, 'and that made it even more likely that my dad didn't kill Andre. I wanted him to tell you what he told me, but he wouldn't answer his phone. I didn't know where he was staying. That's why I went to Julia's. She's in the phone directory.'

'You hit the guy and then you were surprised that he didn't answer his phone?' I couldn't keep the sarcasm out of my voice.

He took his baseball cap off again. 'I shouldn't have, I know that. It was just . . . the language he used, seeing him alive. And he didn't seem to feel bad about lying all those years.'

I counted to five slowly to get myself under control. Anger wasn't going to help.

'But I felt I should show you all of it,' Daniel continued. 'I haven't edited it at all. You can check that, can't you?'

'You did the right thing,' I said.

'What Theo talked about in this footage,' Charlie said, 'how much of that were you aware of?'

'None of it.'

'Well, you knew that other boys had come forward,' I said, 'because you knew they'd retracted their statements.'

'Yes, that I knew. But the other bit . . .' he folded the peak of his cap double, straining the cloth between his fingers, 'that bit about my mother, that she'd walked in on them, that she'd gone to his parents . . . I didn't know about that. My mother died two years ago. She never talked about any of it much.' He let go of the cap and shoved it away as if it was to blame for him ruining it.

'Was it around that time that she told you to stop cycling to school with Julia?'

'I don't know. I'm not sure.'

I knew I shouldn't be angry with the guy for what his mother had done. I didn't know if the man in this footage even was Andre Nieuwkerk. I didn't know how much of what he'd said was true. It was also unfair to expect Daniel to remember exactly what had happened thirty years ago. 'Let's go back to what you talked about before this recording. Did Theo say anything about why he'd come to see you? Why now?'

'He said that he wanted to tell me in person because soon everybody would know.'

'Everybody would know?'

'Something like that. Afterwards, I thought that maybe he was planning on writing a book or going on TV. He's probably going to try to make money out of it.'

Everybody would know. I wrote the words down because, as it stood, nobody knew.

The man Daniel had punched in this footage would be dead the next morning. If he'd been planning to let everybody know, why had he killed himself?

'You should talk to him,' Daniel said. 'Trace him and find out the full story. Surely now we can prove that my father didn't murder him.'

That pulled me up. I hadn't realised he didn't know. There was no reason why he should have known, of course; we hadn't talked about this at Julia's. 'There's no need to trace him,' I said. 'We know where he is.' I scrutinised his face to read his reaction from his features. 'I'm sorry, but he's dead. He died yesterday morning.'

'He died?' Daniel slumped back in his chair as if I'd just

pulled the rug from under his feet. The only emotion I could see was disappointment. 'He can't have done. That's so unfair. Then what was the point of all this?' He pointed at the screen. 'He talked to me just to stir things up?'

Chapter 9

If I'd learned anything in my long experience as a police detective, it was that it was better to keep your boss informed of what was going on, so I went to brief Chief Inspector Moerdijk.

I was concerned he might have left for the day, because he liked to run home. It was all part of an extreme health regime that bordered on the fanatical. The crazy amount of exercise he did made him too thin, and even though he was less than ten years older than I was, his face was shot through with wrinkles that showed the patterns his skin would form depending on his expression.

His door was open, though, and he was obviously pleased to see me, the smile lines on his face deepening. 'Congratulations,' he said in a jokey voice. 'Trust you to have been in the right place at the right time.'

That was very different from the 'What the hell have you been up to?' that I had been expecting. 'What do you mean?'

'The commissaris just called me. He said that getting the guy who assaulted Peter de Waal could be a real break-through for these cases.'

My mouth went dry.

'Of course,' the boss continued, 'I bragged that Ingrid used to work for me too. That DI Bauer should count himself lucky that I let her go to his team.

'Are you talking about Erol Yilmaz? For Peter de Waal's assault.'

'They think he might have links to the people who carried out the other attacks too. That he's been in some way involved. The method looks similar.'

I rubbed my forehead.

The boss frowned. 'You don't look happy.'

'What did they get?'

'What do you mean?'

'Well, did they find CCTV footage? Another witness?'

'I don't know. I suppose so, I didn't ask. Anyway, well done.'

'Do you want us to officially help Ingrid and her team out?'

'No,' the boss said. 'I think they've got it under control at the moment. To offer help now would make it look as if we're trying to steal their glory.'

I felt she could do with all the assistance I could give her. I didn't like the turn this had taken. But seeing as the boss was in a good mood, I might as well bring up the other thing. 'We may have a problem.'

'With Yilmaz?'

Well, that as well, I thought, but I knew better than to voice that before I'd spoken to Ingrid. Maybe they'd found new evidence. Maybe it had been him after all. 'The man who committed suicide in his hotel room yesterday morning claimed he was Andre Martin Nieuwkerk.'

The boss sat back in his chair. 'The Body in the Dunes? There's no way. He can't have been.'

I knew why he didn't want it to be true. It had been such a high-profile case, and solving the murder after the name-less skeleton had been found had been an enormous success story. The police commissioner at the time had been only too happy to talk about the force's excellent work in cracking a case that had seemed unsolvable for so long. I could understand why he'd been proud. Even today, with modern forensics, it would have been hard to identify the skeleton. They had narrowed down who the dead man was by looking at the shape of the skull and comparing it to photos of men who'd gone missing at the time. Now it seemed possible that they'd got it wrong.

I didn't say any of that to the boss. 'Whoever he was, there was something odd about him. He was travelling on a British passport but he spoke to Nieuwkerk's sister in Dutch. She's pretty sure he *was* Dutch.' It was a good thing we'd met with Julia, so that I could put my observations into her mouth. 'He also met Verbaan's son. Daniel Verbaan recorded the conversation.'

'Ah shit.' It was unlike the boss to swear. 'We can't have any of that getting out. We can do without endless specula-tion about police mistakes.'

'We're doing a DNA test. Just to rule it out.'

'Good, that's good. What method did he use?'

'OxyContin overdose. We found the tablets; they were in his name.'

'Could it have been accidental?'

'I'll double-check that in the pathologist's report, see what the amount in his blood was.'

'Good, good.' He took his reading glasses off and rubbed his eyes. 'We'll decide what to do when we know more. There's no way he was Andre Nieuwkerk, so it will all be fine. How's Charlie doing?'

'He's okay.' Apart from arguing with Thomas, of course.

It will all be fine. I repeated the CI's words to myself as I walked back to our office. What did that even mean? A man had killed himself. A man who had told me that he wanted everybody to know he was still alive.

More than ever I understood that I really shouldn't tell anybody I'd spoken to him that morning. That I'd dismissed him to take Peter de Waal's statement instead. I was glad I hadn't mentioned it to Thomas or Charlie, and was going to make sure I kept it that way.

By the time I got back to our office, Thomas and Charlie had gone to Julia Nieuwkerk's to take a DNA sample. After watching the footage, that had seemed the sensible thing to do. She had agreed to it without any pushback. 'It will be the quickest way to rule it out,' she'd said. 'It will put an end to all this.'

Left alone in the office, I worked my way through the list of the people Theo Brand had met with. I dialled the number for the next person.

'This is Laurens Werda,' a man said.

I took a note of the surname. 'I'm Detective Lotte Meerman. Do you know Theo Brand?'

'Theo? Yes, he's a good friend. Why?' His voice was calm.

A good friend. That was very different from how Julia and

Daniel had seen him. Also, Laurens was the first person who had actually known him as Theo. This was great; someone who had talked to Theo on Tuesday morning, and who had been a good friend, would know what his mental state had been. 'We'd like to speak to you.'

'When? Now?' There was still no real concern in the man's tone. I could hear a number of voices in the background. He was probably in a busy office.

'If possible.'

'Of course. Let me go somewhere more private.'

'I meant in person.'

'Oh, I see. Yes, yes, of course. Can you come here?' He gave me the details of his place of work.

I looked up the address. It was close to the Amstel station. I told him I'd be there in half an hour.

After disconnecting the call to Laurens, I dialled the final number.

A woman answered. 'Hello, this is Katja.'

Katja? That name wasn't in the diary. There was only Laurens, Julia, Daniel and Harry. 'This is Detective Meerman from the Amsterdam police. Can I speak to Harry, please?'

'You've dialled the wrong number.'

I read it out to her. 'Isn't that your number?'

'There's no Harry here.' The voice was resigned, as if she got these calls a lot.

'Do you live on Frankstraat 12?' That was the address in the diary.

'Yes. But there's nobody named Harry living here. As I've said, you've got the wrong number.' The call disconnected with a dry click.

Whoever Katja was, she had hung up on me.

Maybe Theo had had an old number for someone, and an old address. The number in the diary was a landline, not a mobile, so that was possible.

I got on my bike and cycled along the Singelgracht until it hit the wider water of the Amstel. Here, modern buildings stood uncomfortably side by side with eighteenth-century canal houses. Where I lived, on the canal ring, Amsterdam's houses looked like a real-life history lesson. Around the Zuidas, all the buildings were modern and entirely new. Here it was different. Historical houses were preserved, but any space around them had been used to build modern flats and offices until the new towered over the old, taking precedence.

And wasn't that exactly the thought I'd had yesterday morning? At that moment, it had seemed the obvious choice to go with the urgent over the historical.

No, I corrected myself. Yesterday I'd made the decision to go with the practical over the potentially crazy. It was because he'd said he was Andre Martin Nieuwkerk that I'd dismissed him. It was because that had been too outlandish to believe.

I crossed the Berlagebrug and put my bike in the large stand on the left-hand side of the Amstelplein, then located the building where Laurens Werda worked. He'd told me he was on the eighth floor. There was security downstairs and they made me sign in before I could go up, even after I'd shown them my badge. I had to go through glass turnstiles of the kind that could snap your leg off if they shut before you'd reached the safety of the other side. I was glad we didn't have those at the police station; ours was a more old-fashioned entry that was metal and actually rotated. None of this snapping business for us.

I pressed the button for the lift. I was the only one here: 4.43 was obviously not a popular meeting time. I guessed that if you arrived on the hour, it would be busy. It was the kind of place that sucked people in and chucked them out exactly when the large hand of the clock hit twelve.

The lift pinged to let me know it was ready for me. I got in and hit the button, but just as the doors started to close, someone approached from the outside. I did the right thing and pressed the button to keep the doors open. I was ready to say good afternoon to the person getting in when I found myself looking straight into a familiar face.

I'd known that Erol Yilmaz had an office job, but I'd never imagined that he'd work in the same building as Laurens Werda.

Yesterday, Erol had worn jeans and a black T-shirt. Now he was smartly dressed and clean-shaven. The one thing that hadn't changed was his attitude. He still radiated the same aggression as before. He threw me an angry glance as if he suspected me of having come to his workplace to question him. It was uncomfortable being in such a small space with him. It put us in closer proximity than I would have liked.

He pressed 5. At least he wasn't going to the same floor as me.

'What are you doing here?' His voice was as inhospitable as it could be without actually sounding as if he was up for a fight.

'I'm going to the eighth.' I pointed at the button I had pushed, to make it clear that I had not come here for him.

'You people should just leave me alone,' he said. 'You've already questioned me.'

What I'd seen yesterday morning was the only reason I thought he was probably innocent. Nothing else, neither his attitude nor his answers, would have given me that feeling. I could imagine him beating me up, let alone someone he actually had a personal grudge against. But facts were more important than feelings. Just because he didn't like the police, that wasn't a good reason to think he was guilty.

'Did you take a photo of your hands?' I asked. 'With something specifying the date, and with a witness?'

I wished I wasn't in a confined space with someone giving off those vibes.

He frowned and held his hands out in front of him to examine them himself. 'Why?'

'Please just do it.'

He turned to glare at me.

There was no way I'd be able to take him in a fight. Not that there was going to be a fight: we were in his place of work and he was going to get out of the lift in a few seconds. I wanted to take a step back – I had space behind me to retreat further into the corner – but I stood my ground. Why was I even bothering trying to help him? By now it was a day after the assault. Still, if he'd beaten up Peter de Waal, there would have been marks left on his hands, as there had been on Daniel's. A photo now wouldn't be as conclusive as if he'd taken one straight away, but it would still give reasonable doubt.

The lift arrived at the fifth floor and the doors opened.

'Just do it,' I repeated, but I was talking to his back as he walked away.

The doors closed and I continued to the eighth floor by myself. The lift suddenly felt twice the size.

The company that Laurens worked for was called Alliance First. Even though I had never heard of it, judging from the offices, with their separate reception area, it was a large firm. The girl behind the desk tried to contact Laurens Werda for me, but he was on the phone just now and would I mind waiting?

I wasn't a big fan of the conversation I was about to have – telling someone his friend had died – so I didn't mind waiting at all.

I wasn't sure what line of work the company was in, but the walls of the reception area were covered with photos of happy people doing healthy, fun things. That didn't narrow it down per se. It seemed to be the way everything was advertised today.

Eat our food! Become healthy and happy.

Join our gym! Become healthy and happy.

I took a seat in reception. There were no leaflets around to read, so from the nice-to-look-at-but-uncomfortable-to-sit-on sofa, I googled the name on my phone. Alliance First was an insurance company.

I remembered that Erol Yilmaz also worked for an insurance company. Maybe Alliance First had offices on the fifth floor too.

Maybe Erol had thought I was going to talk to his boss. Or to HR. That was probably why he'd been so annoyed.

I hoped he would still do what I'd suggested. He must understand why I'd said that, mustn't he? I couldn't really spell it out for him, because I didn't want to hinder Ingrid's case, but I did want to make sure that someone who hadn't attacked the victim in the way described did not get falsely accused. Was Erol Yilmaz innocent? Who knew? But he hadn't punched Peter de Waal in the face with his bare hands, I was sure of that. I trusted Ingrid, but I knew what the pressure could be like, and maybe she wouldn't be able to control what the powers that be wanted. If Erol could prove his innocence, I wasn't hindering her investigation; I was protecting Ingrid from that pressure.

I looked at the posters again. Even knowing what the company did, I could not figure out what this advertising campaign was trying to say. Use our insurance and you'll never be in an accident? If that was true, they were really amazing.

It was a good thing I wasn't in advertising. I would have gone with a picture of a car crash and the caption: *You never want this to happen, but if it does, we'll pay for everything.* Surely the point of advertising for an insurance company should be to remind people that bad things could happen? These posters seemed to suggest that life was puppies and sunshine all year round. If that was true, nobody would need to get insurance.

I stopped looking at them. I knew I was only thinking about these things to avoid thinking about the reason why I was here. I had the unpleasant duty to give Laurens Werda terrible news. It brought my mind back to Theo's death, and the role I might have played in it.

A man had died of an opioid overdose in a hotel in Amsterdam. I knew what assumption I would have made normally, but there wasn't anything normal about this situation. If the man hadn't talked to me that morning, we would probably just have called it an accidental overdose to make it easier on the family, especially as there was no suicide note, and that would have been the end of it.

Now I was left with a lot of questions that hopefully Laurens Werda could help me with. Maybe he could tell me what Theo had been like and why he had come to Amsterdam, but I would have to tread carefully.

I'd been waiting for ten minutes when the door at the back of reception opened and a man approached. He was a decade or so older than Theo, in his mid fifties, and was wearing a combination of navy-blue jacket and red trousers that did nothing to hide the fact that he was overweight. The flesh of his neck strained against the collar of his shirt, and his tie only just allowed him room to breathe. His hair was thinning, but he'd made no attempt to conceal it. The shine of his balding pate made his head seem even wider.

I could imagine that he'd been friends with Theo Brand. In fact, I could imagine that he'd be friends with a lot of people. He'd probably even be friends with Erol Yilmaz if Erol would offer to buy him a glass of red wine.

Only I couldn't imagine him having even the slightest interest in doing that.

The man greeted me with a handshake, then cleared his throat as if he had to work up the courage to speak. 'I'm Laurens Werda,' he said. 'You wanted to talk to me about Theo?' His voice sounded slightly thick, maybe from nerves, or perhaps he had an inkling of why I was here. I was sure that he understood that being visited by the police wasn't a good thing, but at least he wasn't ready to beat me up.

The eyes of the receptionist were on us and she was actually leaning forward so that she wouldn't miss a word of what we said. 'Can we talk somewhere private?' I asked.

Laurens threw a glance at the receptionist, but she shook her head. 'All the meeting rooms are taken,' she said without even checking.

I tried to guess how strongly he might react to the news I was going to give him, but I realised I couldn't. 'You don't have an office?' I asked.

'No, it's all open plan.'

'Okay. Well at least let's go through here,' I said, and pointed at the double doors behind us, the way I'd come in, which opened on to the corridor leading to the bank of lifts. Nobody had come through them in the ten minutes I'd been waiting on this uncomfortable sofa, and even if someone walked past, they would only catch bits of our conversation and not the entirety.

The receptionist looked annoyed, as if I'd spoiled the most interesting part of her day. She shouldn't have listened in so blatantly. If she'd put headphones on, even if she hadn't been listening to music, I would probably have talked to Laurens right there.

Instead I waited until he'd followed me out and we were standing outside the lifts before I spoke. As I'd expected, there was nobody around. 'I'm sorry to give you bad news,' I said with the sound of the whirring of lift cables behind me, 'but Theo Brand is dead.'

He stared at me, then swallowed. 'What happened?' he said eventually.

'We found him in his hotel room.'

Laurens jerked his head back and looked at the ceiling. He put his hands on his hips to keep his balance and took a few deep breaths.

I gave him time.

He rubbed his right hand over the bald centre of his head, as if that would wipe away the image. 'You're sure it's him?'

I nodded, keeping a close eye on him because I wasn't sure I'd be able to carry his weight if he collapsed. 'I understand this has come as a shock to you,' I said, 'but can I ask you a few questions? Or do you need a moment?'

'Go ahead.' His face was pale but his voice was steady. He reached for the wall as if he needed support.

'Do you want a drink of water?'

'Let's get this over with.'

'Okay.' I got my notebook out. 'When did you talk to him last?'

'We had dinner on Friday and then he called me yesterday, early in the morning.'

'How did he sound?'

'Fine, I thought.'

They had spoken at 6.43 a.m.. Theo had come back to his room at 8.37. By 9 a.m. he had killed himself. I was surprised that he had been fine two and a half hours earlier. 'What did you talk about?'

'He called me to thank me for dinner, and we chatted. Nothing special.'

Did he mention meeting me? I wanted to ask. Did he tell

93

you I didn't believe a word of what he'd said? 'It was very early for a call like that,' I said instead.

'I'm always up early. Theo knows that. Knew that,' he corrected himself.

'You had dinner with him the first night he was in Amsterdam?'

'Yes, he called me a few weeks ago to tell me he was coming on this trip and asked if I had time to meet up.'

What if Laurens had talked to Theo before Theo had met me? What if he really had been fine before he spoke to me? 'Was there anything in particular that he wanted to discuss?' I asked. 'Did he seem distressed about anything? Depressed?'

'Was it suicide? Is that why you're asking that?' He shook his head. Not to disagree with what I was saying, I thought, but out of shock at the situation. 'It was really strange,' he said. He fell silent.

'What was?' I prompted.

'That he came to the Netherlands in the first place.'

'Why do you say that?'

'He hated being here. He had a British passport, but he was Dutch originally. I don't think he'd been to the Netherlands in twenty years or so.'

'How do you know he hated it here?'

'I know I said when you called that we were friends.' He rubbed his hand over the bald part of his head again. 'But really he was my ex.'

'Your ex.' The last person Theo had spoken to was his ex-partner.

Unless the last person he had spoken to was me.

I could picture the two of them together, even if the man

94

opposite me was a fair bit older than the man who'd died. Or maybe the partial baldness and being overweight made him seem older than he was.

'We met in London. We lived together for over a decade. I returned to the Netherlands a few years after we split up.'

'When was this?'

'I came back to Amsterdam in 2012. Left London just in time to avoid the Olympics.'

'And you stayed friends?' I would have no interest in meeting my own ex for dinner, but then our separation had been rather acrimonious. I couldn't tell if this had been a happy enough relationship while it lasted, or if it had been painful but time had rubbed away at the sharp edges until it had all been smoothed over.

'We lost touch for a bit and his call came out of the blue, I have to admit. But it was great to see him again.'

'Why did he have a British passport?'

'He no longer wanted to be Dutch. He made a really big deal of it. Even though he didn't need to because of the whole EU thing.' He smiled at the memory. 'He said it made him happy not to be Dutch.'

I automatically nodded in return, even if it was a sentiment I didn't understand.

'Theo hated this country,' Laurens continued, 'and everything to do with it.'

'The people in the hotel didn't realise he was originally Dutch.'

'That would have made him very glad.' He smiled again. 'We never spoke Dutch to each other, not even at home.'

Theo's Dutch had been awkward when I'd first met him,

not because he didn't speak the language fluently but probably because he hadn't used it in such a long time. Add that to the fact that he'd hated this country for some reason I could only guess at, and it all made much more sense.

'So why he would come here for a visit was beyond me,' Laurens continued. 'There are so many other places he could have gone instead.'

At that moment the lift closest to us made a pinging sound and the doors opened. Laurens had been about to say something else, but instead he had to exchange greetings with the people who came out of the lift.

'Do you have the details of Theo's family? Is there anybody else I should inform?' It was a leading question. I waited for Laurens to tell me about Theo's past.

'He wasn't in touch with any of his family. They'd had a big falling-out. I don't even know if his parents are still alive.'

'Do you know anything about them? Did Theo talk about them much?'

'He never really wanted to discuss it. All I know was that he went through some tough times. His childhood was very unhappy and he would sometimes say that, because of that, he wasn't wired for happiness.'

An unhappy childhood. It reminded me of my original assumption, that Theo had been abused as a child and that was why he identified with Andre Nieuwkerk. There was no point in speculating; the DNA test would show what the truth was.

'I don't know if he ever attempted to kill himself,' Laurens said. 'I hope not.' He rubbed his face. 'It makes me feel really sorry for him. If only he'd mentioned how he felt, maybe there was something I could have done.'

'Do you have his UK address?'

'Let me look it up.' He scrolled through his phone and read the address out. I made a note of it.

'And when he changed nationality, he kept his Dutch name?'

'Yes, because he was lucky with his name. Brand works in both languages. Werda was always much trickier.'

I looked at Laurens Werda, scrutinising his face, but nothing showed other than sadness over his ex-partner's death. 'When you saw him, did he tell you why he'd come here?'

'No, not really.'

'What did you talk about when you had dinner? Did he say anything out of the ordinary?'

'He seemed to be doing well. We chatted about his flat in London, his job, some of our old mutual friends. It was all really normal stuff.'

I nodded. 'What about the Body in the Dunes? Does that mean anything to you?'

'No.'

'Theo never told you anything about that? Or about Andre Martin Nieuwkerk?'

'No, never. Who's that?'

I didn't respond to his question. 'That's all for the moment,' I said.

'That's it?' Laurens seemed relieved that I didn't have any further questions. He probably wanted some privacy to think about his friend.

'Thank you for your time. We'll get back in touch if there is anything else.'

I watched as he walked back to the reception area.

I took the lift down. I rested against the back wall and felt tired. These conversations were draining.

Had Theo not given any thought to what was going to happen after his death? He must have known the effect it would have on everybody he had talked to. He'd raised questions in their minds and then died before he could give them answers. It seemed a spiteful thing to do.

I thought back to the man I'd met the other morning. He hadn't seemed the spiteful type. I was sure he had wanted me to believe him. What was it he'd said? That he thought it was important that everybody knew he was still alive? Julia had said that he had kept repeating that he was sorry, over and over again. Unless he'd been apologising for what he was going to do – taking his own life – it didn't make any sense.

I knew that this wasn't always how it worked, though; that a person's existence could get so black that there was no space to think about the consequences.

We would know much more once we'd got the result of the DNA test; we'd be able to say for sure if this man had been Andre Nieuwkerk. Julia was certain that he wasn't, Daniel was certain that he was. I was in two minds, some-where between the two. Like the tide, coming in and going out, my opinion about Theo Brand kept changing.

At first I'd thought there was no way that he was Nieuwkerk, that he was only using the name. Then I'd thought, after talking to Julia, that maybe he was crazy after all. That it was a delusion. After seeing the footage that Daniel had recorded, it had struck me that he'd known a lot about the Nieuwkerk family. That didn't mean he was Andre, though; he could have been one of his close friends.

It was possible that he had been another of Paul Verbaan's abuse victims. Someone taking a different type of revenge by making life difficult for Verbaan's son.

I didn't want him to be the real Andre. I didn't want him to be this dead man come alive again. Because it would be awful if he'd come here to tell people he hadn't died, only to end up killing himself.

Chapter 10

I looked at the cards in my hand but there were none that I could get rid of, so I had to take one from the pile in the middle. It was a ten of spades. I sighed. I already had one of those, and now I had that useless card twice.

My mother sat at the head of the table and I was in the seat opposite her as we played our Wednesday-evening game of cards. I used to sit next to her, but when we first played at my flat, I became suspicious when she insisted on having that same seat. It had only taken me thirty years or so to understand this advantage that my mother had had all along: peeking at my cards when I wasn't paying attention. I used to think she was just better at the game than I was. After a few months of meeting at mine, we had now returned to my mother's place. It was probably because she didn't like my cat. The feeling was entirely mutual.

'How's Mark?' my mother asked as she added another queen to the set of three already out. It was easier to talk when you had something else to concentrate on.

'He's very well. He said hi.' I took the queen of spades from the set of four and put it in front of me.

'Don't mess this up,' my mother said.

I knew she wasn't talking about the cards. 'I wasn't planning on it.' I added the jack and the ten of spades to the queen, then sat back and folded my free hand around my mug of tea. The mug with the smiling clown was the same one I'd had since I was five. If things weren't broken, there was no reason to replace them.

We'd always been together at Sinterklaas and now I was going to change that. I didn't want my mother to be upset about being by herself. Even if it was mainly a celebration that kids loved, I hated to think of her being alone. I couldn't bring myself to start the subject and decided to talk about work instead.

'I was wondering,' I said, 'what was it like, growing up in Elspeet?'

She threw me a quick glance before examining her cards again. 'What brought this up?' She took one from the stack. 'Something you're working on?'

'Can't I show interest in your life?' I looked at the cards on the table and those in my hands, as if studying them deeply would hide the fact that she'd seen right through me.

'So it is something you're working on.' She had little flesh on her and you could see every bone. Her cheekbones were so sharp that they looked as though they could cut through the wrinkled skin that hung off them. I really needed to get into cooking and enjoying my food, otherwise when I got to her age I would be as skinny as she was.

In my head, I immediately corrected myself. It would be different for me. I wouldn't live and eat alone. Mark would still be cooking for me.

I reached out, took a card and added it to my hand. I

managed not to smile even though the nine of spades was useful. Julia's words came to mind. 'A woman told me today that someone killed himself not because of guilt but because he got barred from the church.'

'In Elspeet?'

'Yes.'

'Things have changed, even there. Everybody's got access to the internet now; the church no longer controls what people are supposed to think.'

'This happened in the nineties.'

'Ah, okay, well that's different. Still, one thing doesn't rule out the other.'

'What do you mean?'

'You said he killed himself not because of guilt but because of being barred. It could be both, or maybe it's the same thing. The church is your conscience. Being barred from the church means that your conscience, your religion, is telling you that what you've done is beyond the pale. Beyond forgiveness and redemption.' She picked up a new card from the stack and grimaced, then slid the blue-backed card between two red ones. The backs of both packs were equally faded, the red cards now the colour of my mother's cracked lips, the others the shade of her eyes, bleached by age from sky to duck-egg blue. We always used this double set; not a single card had been lost in over twenty years of playing. Another thing that didn't need replacing.

'He was barred on a Sunday morning, in front of the whole congregation.' That was what I'd seen in the news-paper photo: the shocked faces of the other people around, the preacher stopping the man from entering the church. If they'd thrown tar and feathers over him, it couldn't have been more obvious.

'And everybody knew what it was about?'

'I would have thought so: it had been in all the papers that he'd murdered his student.'

'You're talking about that school teacher. That Body in the Dunes case.'

'Do you remember it?'

'I remember you asking the same questions at the time as well. Wasn't it your university project?' She picked up her mug, her other hand holding her cards close to her chest. I hoped the heat would warm up her fingers, with their swollen knuckles. 'That was the one you worked on with your friend, wasn't it? What was her name? Karin something?'

'That's right. I'm surprised you remember.'

'I remember because she stole your work.'

'What are you talking about?'

'Didn't she hand it in as her own? Then you had to write about another case.'

I shrugged. 'She didn't really steal it.' I'd been too happy that I could share my interest with somebody to really care about that.

'You had to work all night. Don't you remember? Till five or six in the morning, days in a row. Wasn't there a deadline for the project?'

'You probably cared more than I did, because the light kept you awake.' It hadn't been a big deal; it was supposed to be an individual project, not a group one, and she had handed it in instead of me. 'Whose turn is it?'

'Yours. Just pick a card.'

I looked at the large handful I had. I couldn't seem to get rid of any of them so had to pick up a new one, a three of clubs. I counted how many I had in my hand. 'Fifteen. That's more than I started with.'

'If you checked properly,' she said, 'I'm sure some of them must be in a set. You're not paying attention.'

'What about you? You're just as bad.'

She scanned the cards on the table, as if it would cause sets to miraculously form.

'Was it hard for you to move from Elspeet to Alkmaar?'

'It's Elspeet.' Her voice was defensive. 'It's a town, not a tiny village, not like Staphorst.'

'But you left your church behind.'

'I didn't leave anything behind. I joined another church.'

When I was a kid, we would still go to church twice on a Sunday. I stopped going when I was a teenager, and, to be fair, my mother never pressured me into coming with her. She said I was old enough to make my own choices. My own mistakes, I think she called it.

'Hold on,' she said. 'I think there's something I can do with those cards.' She took three runs, hearts, spades and diamonds, and rearranged them into three sets of the same numbers. The cards moved over the table with the sound of old hymnbooks being opened. Her smile bunched up the skin on her cheekbones.

I split up some of the half-sets I had and put down a run of four, including the three of clubs. Eleven cards left, finally fewer than I'd started with.

'See,' she said. 'I could tell you weren't paying attention.

Your mind is on your work. That school teacher, I feel sorry for his family.'

'I met his son earlier today. He's turned into a very angry man.'

'Everybody in Elspeet must have known who he was. All his friends, his classmates. He probably went to the school where his father taught.'

'He did. He was in the same class as the victim's sister.'

'It must have been terrible for him, to find something like that out about his own father.'

He'd still referred to him as 'Dad', though. He still wanted to believe that his father had been innocent. 'He knew the victim. The murdered boy. He used to talk to him.'

'Ah yes, it was a boy, wasn't it? I wondered if that was why he was thrown out of the church.' She took my three of clubs and added two more threes from her hand.

'Because it was a boy?' I worked hard to keep my voice under control. 'It would have been okay if he'd abused and murdered a girl?'

'No, you're right. Of course not. How old was the boy?'

'Fourteen when the abuse started. Fifteen when he disappeared.' I added another three to the set that my mother had just formed. 'That's messed up. That you think he should have been allowed to stay if he'd had sex with one of his female pupils and killed her. That the homosexuality was what made the church act.'

'I meant that the fact that it was a boy made it worse. Made it abhorrent in the eyes of some of those orthodox churches.'

Hearing those words come out of my mother's mouth

seemed strange. I was reminded of the man in Daniel's recording recounting how his parents had thrown him out of the house. 'You don't think that,' I said. 'Do you? If I'd been gay, would you have shown me the door?'

'Of course not. And just because you're a member of a church, that doesn't mean you have to agree with every single thing that's being said.'

'Doesn't it? I thought that was the point.'

'There were a lot of things that didn't sit well with me. I didn't just leave that church because I married your father. My parents didn't just leave over the polio vaccinations. I remember talking to my father about it. He cared deeply about individual freedom, and the preacher coming around on Sundays to check what channel they were listening to on the radio really bothered him. Being told how to live every second of his life rubbed him up the wrong way.' She added a six to the set on the table. She only had two cards left in her hand. 'But that it was a boy does make it worse, don't you think?'

'Why?'

'The teacher was married, and had a kid. That meant he'd lived a lie all his life. If you prefer men, you shouldn't get married to a woman.'

'It's not as straightforward as that. For me, the worst thing was that the boy was his pupil. If he wanted to be with a man, he could have slept around with grown-ups. You know, above the age of consent.'

'And he killed him . . .'

'It's possible he didn't.' As soon as the words left my mouth, I wondered when I'd started to believe that. At what point it had become possible for me that Theo really was Andre.

'Did he do all those other things?'

I thought of Theo talking to Daniel. Of telling him exactly what had happened. About the wife finding out. 'Yes,' I said. 'I'm pretty sure he did all those other things. He sexually abused his pupils.' I reshuffled the cards in my hand and formed a run of high clubs. I put them on the table, hoping that she could use my cards to get rid of her last two.

'Pupils? More than one?'

'Some other students came forward who later retracted their statements.'

She sighed and picked a new card from the stack. 'It's terrible, the things that people do.' She held her last three cards between her fingers as she checked the ones on the table. Then she put them face down on the table and took a sip of tea.

I slotted a ten in the middle of a run. We were both silent for a bit.

'Still, that poor family,' my mother said before laying out the three cards in one set: a run of diamonds from seven to nine. Her gesture had a sense of finality about it, as if the last word about this case had been said.

She'd proved that she could win, even without cheating.

I threw my handful of cards on the table. It wasn't that she was better at this than I was. I hadn't been able to concentrate. Nor had I brought up the subject of Sinterklaas, so I'd just come here and maybe ask Mark to join us.

'Oh, there was something I wanted to talk to you about,' she said. 'Sinterklaas.'

It was as if she'd read my mind.

'Richard asked me to come to his. They're having a big family do. Kids, grandkids.'

'Nice. Meeting the kids, are we?' I still hadn't been introduced to this Richard; I just knew of his existence, that was all. When you were my mother's age, meeting the kids was probably the equivalent of meeting people's parents when you were younger. 'That makes it sound serious.'

She blushed.

I laughed. 'Go and spend Sinterklaas with them.'

My mother handed me a present. It had the shape of a thick paperback, but I knew it wasn't a book.

'Can I open it?'

'You know what it is anyway.'

Of course I did: it was the traditional chocolate letter in a cardboard gift box. When I was a kid, it had always seemed that a chocolate L for Lotte was smaller than something like the M for Mark. Even if the box said they were all the same weight, it never looked like that. It would have meant changing my name, though, and that would have been too much effort just to get a larger piece of chocolate once a year. 'I haven't got yours yet.'

'It's okay, I don't eat that much chocolate any more. You can get me something else.'

She didn't say what she'd want instead, but I was pleased that we'd sorted out Sinterklaas without me having to bring it up. I gave her a hug and said goodbye. Now all I had to do was buy Mark some presents.

As I cycled home in the dark, I thought about the fact that, for my mother, it had all been about the family. Then

I saw Theo as he had been yesterday, vehemently telling me that he was alive and that he should let people know about it. I had ignored him. I had looked at my watch to make it clear that he was wasting my time, and he had been embarrassed.

If only he hadn't committed suicide when he had, I could have asked him questions. I could have asked him why he was here, why it had taken him so long. Why not five years ago, or ten years ago, or even as soon as he realised that the police had misidentified the body? What had kept him out of the country all this time? What had made him take a different nationality?

I hadn't asked any of those questions. Instead, I had turned away from him to help Ingrid take the statement of a man who hadn't told the truth. I realised I no longer doubted that Theo had been Andre Nieuwkerk. Even though his sister didn't believe it and his ex-partner didn't know any-thing about it, deep down I felt that he had been telling the truth. Watching the footage that Daniel had recorded had convinced me.

Andre Nieuwkerk had come back to Amsterdam to let everybody know that he wasn't dead, but had ended up killing himself.

Chapter 11

As soon as I walked into the office the next morning, before I'd even taken my coat off, Charlie started talking. 'It was him,' he said, as happy as a child with a particularly nice Sinterklaas present, or maybe a dog with a new bouncy ball. 'It was definitely him.' When he saw that Thomas wasn't smiling, the grin dropped from his face.

'What the DNA test showed,' Thomas corrected him, 'was that the dead man, Theo Brand, was definitely Julia Nieuwkerk's brother.'

'So he *was* Andre Nieuwkerk,' I said. I wasn't surprised at what they were telling me.

'Theoretically, there could have been another brother.'

'There's no evidence of another brother,' I said. I'd checked the birth registers beforehand.

'I know. I'm just telling Charlie what conclusions we can officially draw.'

I knew he was just nit-picking to be annoying.

I wanted to check a couple of things before we went to talk to the boss about it. Maybe my conversation with my mother last night had influenced me, but I was struck by the way Paul Verbaan's family had been hounded by the press.

Daniel had only been thirteen years old when Andre had gone missing, but by the time the skeleton had been found and mistakenly identified, he'd just turned eighteen and was therefore fair game. He'd been photographed at his father's funeral, a young man in mourning, in a dark suit, standing all alone at a graveside. There was no sign of his mother, the woman who according to Andre had known all about the sexual abuse and blamed him.

They must have taken this photo with a telescopic lens, because Daniel seemed unaware that he'd been observed. I couldn't even begin to imagine what must have been going on in his head.

Or what he must have felt when Theo turned up on his doorstep. Not Theo, I corrected myself. Andre. Daniel had hit him. Had anything happened afterwards?

'Do you think that maybe it wasn't suicide?' Charlie asked, as if he could tell the direction in which my thoughts were going.

'There's no evidence of that,' Thomas said.

I found exactly what I wanted on one of the front pages: a photo of Andre and Julia Nieuwkerk's parents, taken at a press conference to say how grateful they were to the police for finally finding their son, so that, even though their hopes had been dashed, they now at least knew what had happened to him. The father had a rough-hewn farmer's face with a large nose and ears. He could have come straight out of Van Gogh's *The Potato Eaters*. I understood why Julia had laughed when I'd asked if the man who'd come to her door had looked like her father. There seemed to be no greater contrast than between the well-dressed man I'd seen that morning and this man in his old-fashioned clothes. The mother had tears streaming down her face.

The abused kid had been thrown out of the house by those parents, fled to London, made a life for himself and then came back to Amsterdam thirty years later, only to kill himself. Daniel's words, that he'd wanted to stir things up, kept going round in my head. It could so easily be true. He could have come back to cause trouble for his abuser's family.

'He met with Julia Nieuwkerk and with Daniel Verbaan and told both of them that he was Andre. Don't you think it's suspicious?' Charlie said. 'Daniel punched him when he came to his house and was careful to film him leaving. When he came to Julia's flat, he was very angry. He was convinced Andre's family had known all along that he wasn't dead.'

'You've watched too many movies,' I said, but I didn't mind him throwing theories around. I wanted him to think. 'Daniel would want him alive, so that he could clear his father's name.'

'He had the recording,' Charlie said. 'Surely that's enough.'

'He would want Andre to withdraw the abuse claim too—'

'Let's go.' Thomas interrupted us as if he knew that I was procrastinating. 'Let's talk to the boss.'

But before he had even got up, Ingrid came into the office, closing the door behind her. 'So did you hear?' She said it softly, as if she wanted to make sure that nobody else who had any interest in this case could listen in. She sat down at my old desk.

I didn't know what she was talking about. 'What happened?'

'It's spiralling out of control. Bauer thinks we've got grounds to arrest him.' Detective Inspector Bauer was her boss. 'And then the commissaris got word of it and was over the moon. He insisted on scheduling a press conference straight away. I only just managed to stop him.'

I didn't have to ask her who she was talking about. I threw a glance at Thomas, who pretended to be interested in what was on his screen. 'Bauer didn't even try to stop him, I guess?'

Ingrid shook her head.

'That figures.' I'd worked with DI Bauer on a case before. I knew exactly what he was like and where his priorities lay. 'So now what?'

'I persuaded him to just call Erol in for questioning,' Ingrid said. 'We've got no evidence.'

'I know what the pressure's like.'

'It's a mess. But you know, maybe Yilmaz did it. It's a possibility.'

I shook my head. 'Don't go there. Not just because you need to make arrests.'

'He could have beaten up Peter de Waal, you know that.'

'Sure, if de Waal had said someone had beaten him with a baseball bat, I might have believed it was Yilmaz. But even then it would have been his word against Yilmaz's and we couldn't have done anything. Not without a witness or CCTV. Not without any forensic evidence. I'm guessing you haven't found any traces of blood on Yilmaz?'

'You know we found nothing.'

'Has Peter de Waal changed his testimony at all?' Thomas asked.

'Nope, he's still sticking with what he originally said.'

'That he came out of a bar, heard someone say his name, turned around, and Erol Yilmaz punched him in the face?'

'Yup, that's it.'

'What time was that? Around three a.m.?' I said.

'That's right.'

'I'm guessing he was far from sober.'

Ingrid stayed quiet for a bit, then nodded and tapped the armrests of her chair with both hands. 'Thanks, Lotte.' She got up.

'Shouldn't we help her?' Charlie said as soon as she was out of earshot.

'You can help her by not talking about this to anybody,' Thomas said.

Charlie grinned and drew his finger across his mouth to indicate that his lips were sealed. His suggestion made me think, though. There was a thin line between helping and interfering, and I would do Ingrid an injustice if I stepped over it. She would ask if she needed more concrete help, as she had done that first morning, when she'd called me to the crime scene in the Lange Niezel.

I knew that whatever my motivation was, it didn't matter a great deal to CI Moerdijk. Just because I thought something was important didn't mean that he was automatically going to agree. I'd worked for him long enough. There were some real advantages to not changing teams and not changing reporting lines.

'I heard,' was the first thing he said when I came through the door of his office.

'What are we going to do?'

'You'll want to investigate,' he said. The other advantage was that he knew what I wanted to do too.

'Do you disagree?' Thomas asked.

'Not necessarily,' the boss said. 'The story is going to come out, I know that. As soon as the press get hold of it, we'll be on the back foot. We can't be seen to be doing nothing. We made a terrible mistake all those years ago.'

Of course it had been a miscarriage of justice, but watching that footage of Theo telling Daniel about the abuse made the fact that the abuser had been falsely accused of murder feel less important. That said, I'd never before been so pleased to be involved with an exercise to cover our backs.

'We need to be seen to be making amends for that, and of course we're the right team for the job. I just don't know how much we can do, and you have to be careful what you say to the families.'

'Andre Nieuwkerk wasn't the Body in the Dunes,' Thomas said, 'so someone else has been murdered. We should start with the same list of missing men. Check if any of them have turned up.'

I hadn't thought of that. I'd been so preoccupied with Andre and with Paul Verbaan's family that I'd almost forgotten that a young man really had been killed.

That there was another victim out there.

115

'You do realise that you don't have anything we didn't have in the early nineties?' the CI said.

'We've got improved forensics,' I said. 'We can raise the skeleton and do a DNA test.'

'You didn't check?' the CI said. 'How unlike you. The remains don't exist any more. The family cremated the body.'

'Ah shit,' Thomas said.

'We can—' I started, but the boss interrupted me.

'I'm serious,' he said. 'Don't assume that you're going to be able to solve this just because you've got more modern techniques. We need to prepare ourselves for failure.'

'Even by your normally optimistic standards, that's quite something,' I said.

'You know what I mean. Go through the motions, keep the families happy, especially Paul Verbaan's.'

Verbaan's family, the abuser's family, needed to be pacified now that it was certain he'd been incorrectly accused of murder. I understood it, but I didn't feel good about it. 'I'll see what I can do. Try to get the commissaris to talk about this instead of those assaults.'

'Talk about a police failure?'

I shook my head. 'It's talking about a failure or creating another one. Peter de Waal is a very unreliable witness. Nobody else has come forward.'

'Don't interfere, Lotte.'

'I don't want to interfere.' I paused and looked at CI Moerdijk. 'The victim was drunk and the assault clearly didn't happen in the way he described.'

'We need to show some progress, after all those interviews the commissaris did.'

116

'He's making a problem for himself. He doesn't need to do those interviews; it's not as if he's an elected official or something.'

The CI gave me a long glance. Before he could make a decision either way, his phone rang. As if he'd known we were talking about him, the commissaris was calling. He'd heard about the Body in the Dunes, and could we come and speak to him about it?

The commissaris looked busy behind his desk. 'Give me a second,' he said. 'I just need to finish this and then I'm all yours.'

I didn't mind. It gave me a chance to mentally prepare. This was the first time I'd spoken to him in person. He'd only joined us a month ago. His sleek hair reminded me of an otter I'd seen in a nature documentary the other night. It was combed back, with a side parting. I remembered that on the morning I'd first met Theo – Andre, I corrected myself – the commissaris had done that interview and wearing his cap hadn't even ruffled his hair. I imagined that if I touched it, it would be hard, slicked down with a mixture of gel and hairspray.

He was dressed in his uniform. In my jumper, I felt at a disadvantage, as if my casual clothes diminished me. I wondered if the CI felt like that even though he was at least wearing a suit. He sat down and I took the seat next to him. Thomas had smartly made himself scarce and escaped. He was going with Charlie to give Julia the news. I would have preferred to be the person doing that, but I'd got stuck with the official bureaucracy.

Behind the commissaris, a row of framed photos lined the wall. It was a cabinet of high-profile criminals that our police force had apprehended. Many of them were posing in front of their house or car, or with a powerful person. I knew why those particular photos had been chosen. They said that no matter how wealthy or well connected you were, you could not get away with breaking the law.

What was more interesting was that they were exactly the same photos as the previous commissaris had had on his wall. The new guy hadn't changed them at all. These were all cases that had been solved before Commissaris Smits had even been in Amsterdam. Was he trying to take credit for his predecessor's work, or did he just not really care what his office looked like?

I wished I knew. It would give me a useful insight into his character. It was strange to sit here and really have no idea how this man was going to react to what had happened.

That he was new should work in our favour: if I were him, I would want to reopen the case and make amends. He could put the blame on the old team of twenty-five years ago and promise to do a better job.

'Right,' he said, and turned away from his computer screen to focus on us. It was odd to have a commissaris who was this young. He couldn't be more than a few years older than me. 'So, you've unearthed a huge police failure and miscarriage of justice.'

'I wouldn't put it like that.'

He waved his hand. 'I'm not blaming you, I'm stating the

facts. This is how it's going to look. We misidentified a skeleton and the man who was under investigation for the murder committed suicide. Have I got that correct?'

'He wasn't an innocent man.'

The commissaris raised his eyebrows. 'He was innocent of murdering Andre Nieuwkerk, because Andre was still alive.'

'He didn't murder him, but he sexually abused him. Andre was his pupil at school, only fifteen at the time. And there seems to have been evidence that he wasn't the only victim.'

'Fine.' He made a few notes. 'A sexual predator, but not a murderer. That means there'll be fewer complaints.'

'Complaints?'

'If we can avoid any "hard-working teacher killed himself under wrongful police pressure" headlines, that will make things easier.'

I thought back to Daniel's attitude yesterday. 'His son might not accept the "sexual predator" label.'

He picked up his pen and crossed out what he'd just written. 'Why not?'

'I don't know the exact details, but the son, Daniel Verbaan, sent us footage of a conversation he'd had with Andre Nieuwkerk on the day before he died. When they talked about the historic abuse, Daniel pointed out that the other boys withdrew their statements after his father killed himself. Nieuwkerk did describe the sexual acts, though, and he also claimed that the teacher's wife knew about the abuse.'

'Send me a copy of that footage. I want to see it.'

'Of course. But to be honest, I don't think we should talk about that. We don't need to go on the attack. We should just be open and upfront about what happened.' We should let everybody know that Andre Nieuwkerk had been alive. We should fulfil his wishes. 'We could just say that improvements in forensic technology have allowed us to correct a previous mistaken identity. And we should inform the press. They'll find out anyway.'

'What about raising the skeleton? The original Body in the Dunes?'

'I heard that they cremated the body,' I said. 'But I haven't been able to check that yet.' I threw the CI a glance, but he remained silent. It was unlike him to be so tongue-tied. I wondered what it must be like for him to report to some-one younger than he was.

'Okay, so find out what the deal was with the guy.'

'Andre Nieuwkerk?'

'Yes. Where he'd been, why he didn't come forward. Why he had a British passport. Things like that.'

'Sure, we'll do that.'

'He definitely committed suicide?'

'There's no evidence of foul play.'

'Could it have been accidental?'

'That's what we'd like to call it, of course. There was no suicide note. I spoke to his ex-partner, who talked to him the morning he died, and he said there'd been nothing to suggest he was going to take his own life.'

'Prescription painkillers?'

I wanted to smile and praise him for being well informed, but I didn't of course. 'That's correct,' I said. His short sentences made me fall into a similar pattern.

'Okay,' he said. 'I think I'm all set with that.'

'So you'll schedule a press conference?'

'If we can get the family to agree. Nieuwkerk's family. There's a sister, right?'

'Julia. Yes.'

'We need to show a united front.'

I nodded. 'I'll talk to her. Sir, can I say something about Peter de Waal?'

His eyes shot from his paper. 'What about him?'

'His witness statement isn't credible.'

'It's not Yilmaz?' he asked, but he didn't seem overly surprised. Maybe he'd been aware all along that Bauer was stretching the evidence so that he'd get an arrest and improve his closure rate. I wished I'd spoken to him as soon as Ingrid started to voice her concerns.

'I don't know. All I'm saying is that it would never stand up in court.' There was no need to throw Bauer under the bus. 'If there's no evidence apart from de Waal's statement, we shouldn't focus on Yilmaz.'

'Fine. I'll take it up with Bauer. Thanks, Detective Meerman.'

For a second I thought of saying that he should call me Lotte. But that would have been weird.

Chapter 12

I looked at my watch. It was just after 4 p.m. I was tired and thought it would do me good to get some fresh air, even though it was almost dark outside. I shut down my computer, put my coat on and was going down the stairs when I bumped into Ingrid.

Her voice dropped to a whisper. 'I went back to the hospital,' she said.

'When?'

'After we talked. I wasn't happy with de Waal's statement. As you said, if Erol Yilmaz had punched him, I would have expected some marks on his hands. So I went to ask more questions.'

I felt proud of my ex-teammate. 'You did the right thing,' I said.

'I looked at him, you know, really checked him out to match up his injuries with what he told us. To be honest, his face didn't look as if it'd received just the one punch.'

'I know.' I remembered that from when we'd both been to see him. His right eye socket had been badly bruised. His nose had been broken. He'd had a split lip. His entire face had looked purple against the white of the pillow.

'I asked him again what happened, and as I was talking, I studied the cuts on his face. The skin around his eye socket wasn't broken. It hadn't been a knuckleduster. He was adamant that it had been Erol Yilmaz. That he'd heard his name, turned around and then Erol had punched him.' She rubbed her head, making her short hair stand up in spikes. 'His wife was there as well. She clearly didn't like my questions and said that the police were to blame for this. That she'd told us Erol was violent but that we'd just ignored her.'

'There had been recent threats?'

'No, nothing recent. It all seemed to line up with what Erol said: that he'd stopped harassing the couple. I asked him what he was wearing,' Ingrid said.

'Who?'

'I asked Peter de Waal what Erol had been wearing. He said he wasn't sure, that he'd mainly looked at his face. Then I asked him about his hands.' She gave me a meaningful glance. 'We both noticed there were no marks on Erol's hands when we interviewed him. So I asked him: bare hands or gloves.'

'What did he say?'

'He said he was absolutely sure about that one: his assailant had had bare hands.'

'Peter de Waal had been drinking heavily, he heard someone shout, then he turned around and was punched in the face by a man with bare hands.' A very drunk man was not a credible witness.

'Funnily enough,' Ingrid said, 'I can almost believe that the assault happened like that. It fits with the pattern of the attacks so far. Some of the other victims said a similar thing:

that they heard someone shout behind them, turned round and then got their lights punched out. I think he just saw a man and assumed it was Erol because he'd been harassing him.'

And after he'd said it, it became hard to back out and harder with every time he confirmed it. I'd seen that before: that the more people said something, the more they believed it themselves. But another possibility also crossed my mind. 'Maybe he's setting him up,' I said. 'Maybe he's accusing him on purpose.'

'Why would he do that?' Ingrid said.

'Because he can? Because the guy had been harassing him and now Peter is using this to get his own back? To make Erol's life difficult for a bit?'

Ingrid nodded slowly. 'Then he might not back down. Can you come with me to interview one of his younger colleagues? He's been very hesitant to talk to me and I want to follow up.'

'Seriously? Me?' I looked around, but there was nobody else in the corridor. 'What about Bauer?'

'I don't want to go with him. He's telling me to stay away from . . . well, from anything negative.'

'Really.' I looked at my watch and then back at Ingrid. 'Now?'

'Just half an hour,' she said. 'Please?'

I didn't want to go, but somehow I found it impossible to ignore her plea.

We went down the stairs to the basement car park and Ingrid drove us to the premises of the place where Peter de Waal worked. We were shown to a meeting room. A young man stood up from one of the seats at the large white table. 'Hi, I'm Frank Termeulen,' he said. He had slicked-back hair and he looked too small for his pinstriped suit and pink shirt. The sleeves of his jacket came down to halfway over his hands. Almost as if he'd borrowed his father's clothes. 'I'm sorry, I should have met with you sooner,' he said.

Ingrid held out her badge, but Frank waved it away as if he wanted her to keep it hidden. We took seats next to each other on the opposite side of the table from him.

'Thanks for talking to us,' she said. Her voice was dampened by the wallpaper. At the far end of the table a projector was ready to beam a presentation onto the wall.

I was going to let her run with this. I picked up one of the pencils marked with a small golden crown and the words *Konings Markt*.

'You work for Peter?' she asked.

'He heads up this office.' Frank nodded as he spoke, as if he would seem more honest if he agreed with himself. 'He's my boss's boss.'

The door of the meeting room opened and a smartly dressed man poked his head around it. 'Sorry to interrupt,' he said. 'I thought I'd check if you wanted any coffee? Tea? Anything?'

'Yes please,' I said. 'I'll have a coffee.'

'I'm okay with just water,' Frank said.

The man left.

'That was my boss,' he said with an apologetic smile.

'I know,' Ingrid said. 'I talked to him yesterday.'

Frank opened one of the bottles of mineral water that stood in the centre of the table and filled a glass. His hands

125

were shaking. He looked almost too young to work. Maybe the nerves and the fright had taken a few years off his face.

Did you get coffee yesterday? I wrote on my notepad and pushed it to Ingrid.

Nope, she wrote back as Frank filled glasses of water for us as well.

'You were with Peter that evening, weren't you?' Ingrid asked.

'Yes, I was. It was a company do. Our whole team had to go because the big boss had come over from the States to visit clients here in Amsterdam.'

'And you went straight from work?'

Frank nodded again. 'Yes. We had meetings until five then came back to the office. A group of us were supposed to go to the restaurant together. We had dinner at six.'

'It's a restaurant that you go to a lot?'

'Yeah, it's close to here.' The nods that accompanied every syllable were beginning to get annoying. It must be a nervous tic. 'Sometimes there's a band playing. It's a pretty cool place.'

As if Ingrid was asking the questions to get a dinner recommendation.

'Peter joined you later?' Ingrid said. She must have heard that from the other people she'd interviewed. I had the feeling that some of her questions were for my benefit.

'That's right.' His eyes dropped down to the table and he picked up his glass and turned it round in his fingers.

'Tony told me that you were late turning up at the restaurant.'

As if he'd heard his name, Frank's boss came back in with

126

my coffee. It was only too obvious that he was doing this to eavesdrop; perhaps to make sure that Frank wasn't telling us anything we shouldn't know. The apparent control made me more interested in Frank's story.

Frank didn't say anything whilst his boss was within earshot but answered my question as soon as the door had shut behind him. 'I was waiting for Peter and the big boss. We'd all agreed to meet downstairs but they didn't turn up.' The nodding stopped. 'I waited fifteen minutes.' He sounded as if he was explaining his actions to a headmistress who'd caught him misbehaving.

'And then you left.'

'No, I called Peter on his mobile a few times. Went straight to voicemail. But he knew where we were, so I left him a message to join us there.'

'They arrived how much later?'

'About an hour or so.'

'Did you ask him where he'd been?'

Frank guffawed. 'He's not the kind of man to answer those sort of questions.' He drank some of his water. 'I didn't even ask,' he said more quietly.

'Okay, so you had food and then went on to the bar in the red-light district?'

'Yeah, that's where they wanted to go. Some people went home but I think there were six of us who went to the bar. I'm not much of a drinker, but I thought I'd go with them.'

'You stayed in the same bar for the rest of the evening?'

'Yes,' Frank said. 'Until about half ten or so. Then the big boss said he'd had enough and called it a day. I was quite relieved. I need my sleep in order to function. Tony took the boss back to the hotel. It was on his way home anyway. Plus he probably wanted to chat to him about something. I don't know.'

'This was at half past ten?' I asked. 'You all left then?'

'Well, most of us. Tony had told us beforehand that we should keep it tidy. The big boss apparently doesn't like it when people get too drunk, and we had an important meeting here at nine the next morning.'

'So it was almost frowned upon to stay, but Peter didn't come with you when you left?'

He nodded in response. 'Yeah, that's right. He stayed.'

'Was anybody else with him?'

'Nope.'

I looked up from my notebook. 'He was by himself in that bar for the next five hours?'

'Yup.'

'Didn't you think that was strange?' I asked.

'He . . . erm . . .' Frank scratched the back of his head, then picked up a pencil.

I let the silence last.

Finally he filled it with 'He refused to come.'

'He refused?'

'I tried to get him to leave.' He gestured around him. 'A bunch of clients were supposed to come here for a presentation.' The pitch of his voice was rising. He opened the bottle of water in front of him and filled his glass again. After he'd drunk it, he sounded calmer. 'So yes, I really tried to get him to leave, but he became aggressive. Started shouting that I wasn't his mother, that he could look after himself.'

'Was anybody else still there?

'Tony had left with the boss, but a guy who lives around the corner from the office tried as well, said he had to go home to his family and that Peter should go home too, but Peter wasn't having any of it. We tried for half an hour and then we left him there.' He filled the glass again.

I looked at Ingrid.

'I was waiting for him to show up the next morning, and when he didn't, I called him. I was sure he was still in bed with a hangover, but I spoke to his wife and she told me he was in the hospital.' He swallowed. 'As soon as I found out, I called the clients to cancel. The big boss was angry. Maybe we should have gone ahead with the meeting – Peter wouldn't have said much anyway – but I panicked. I didn't know what to do.' His voice had a note of anger. 'I shouldn't say this, I'll probably get sacked when he gets back to the office, but he always does this. He stays out late and I have to do all the work the next morning.'

'He can't stop drinking?'

'I guess so.'

I looked over at Ingrid. 'So on the night he was assaulted, he'd been drinking a lot, he was argumentative and he was refusing to go home.'

Frank nodded with a miserable look on his face.

'And all his colleagues left that bar five hours before he was beaten up.'

He nodded again.

'Thank you,' I said. 'You've been a great help.'

The guy looked as if he already regretted talking to us.

Chapter 13

It was Thursday evening, the evening that Mark would normally come to my place. This time, we decided to go out for a drink and something to eat. Thursdays were good evenings to go out: the city centre was lively but not jam-packed. Plus my cooking was terrible. It was a good solution all round.

We chose one of the many bars that specialised in home-cooked-style food, where they might only have one or two dishes. Like many of my favourite things in my beloved home town, this café warmly embraced its past but also acknowledged that time had irrevocably moved on. What had been a greengrocer's in a previous life was now a light and spacious bar called Groen. Behind the large windows where fruit and veg would have been displayed, an elderly couple sipped their beers in silent contentment. The café had retained many of the original features, which gave it a quirky trendiness, such as the cubicles behind the bar that had once held pots of herbs and spices and now housed glasses of different shapes and sizes. A pregnant woman sat at a table by herself, looking at her glass of water as if she hoped it would miraculously turn into wine. The evening was quiet and peaceful. It was just after 6 p.m. and already pitch dark, but a few people sat on the bar's large terrace, wearing their winter coats zipped up all the way to their chins, convinced by their need for nicotine that it was a good idea to be outside.

Mark and I were at our usual corner table, which gave us privacy. Unless someone wanted to use the toilet, of course, because then they had to walk behind Mark to get to the stairs. I liked this bar. I liked our evenings here. Two middle-aged ladies in colourful tracksuits were sitting a couple of tables along. We had exchanged greetings when they'd come in; they were often here on Thursdays too.

Mark tucked a strand of hair behind my ear, careful to keep his arm high over the small tub of mustard in the centre of the table. I reached out, held his hand in place and ran my thumb over the inside of his wrist. I felt his heartbeat. Or maybe it was mine. Not being able to tell seemed more intimate than a kiss.

'I love you,' he mouthed silently. The words brought a smile to my face. I mouthed them back.

Through the open door, a gust of wind brought in the sound of the Line 10 tram rattling past. It also brought in a group of women, one of whom I recognised.

Julia Nieuwkerk saw me too. She said something to her friends and then came over to our table.

'I'm sorry to interrupt,' she said.

Not sorry enough not to have done it.

'It's such a mess in my head,' she continued, 'and I'm really worried.'

'What are you worried about?' I said.

'I'm worried about me.' She laughed. 'Okay, that sounds weird. It's just that I feel as if I'm standing on quicksand. Everything I believed about myself and my life has turned out to be wrong, and I don't know what to do.' She took a chair from the table next to us, turned it round and sat down. 'I know that DNA test wasn't wrong, but it feels so strange.'

'He was your brother,' I said.

'My brother.' She shook her head. 'It's as if we're talking about a complete stranger. I'm his only family, I should probably arrange his funeral, but the more I think about it, the more I realise I didn't know him at all. So why do I have to do it?' She looked at me. 'Does that make sense?'

'It does,' I said. I could have said: he's got travel insurance, let them deal with it, but I could tell she wasn't here for advice. She was here to talk and I could listen. I hadn't listened to her brother.

'It doesn't feel as if he was anything to do with me. He was a man I met once, for about five, ten minutes. Who scared me.'

One of her friends came over and handed her a large glass of white wine without saying anything.

'I've already done this once. I've already helped arrange a funeral for my brother. The thought of doing it again, a second cremation, a second service, it just sends my head into a spin.' Her hands started to shake and she had to put the glass down on the table to stop her wine from spilling. She tucked her hands under her legs. 'I'm not sure what's real and what isn't, and that really worries me.' She didn't sound like a woman my age. She sounded like a frightened child, scared now that the dead had come alive. Alive and then dead again.

I wasn't surprised that it had messed with her head.

'It was all so tidy,' she said. 'Very sad, but tidy. I'd long ago figured out how to feel about it. My brother had been murdered but his body had been found and his murderer was dead. That was my story. That was who I was: the brave younger sister of the murdered teenager. Now I have no idea how to feel.' Her voice was starting to sound angry. 'My brother wasn't murdered; he just abandoned us. And then a man who was a stranger came to my front door and I was angry with him and he killed himself and now I have to organise his funeral.' She suddenly opened her eyes and looked at me. 'Does any of this make sense? Because it doesn't make sense to me. I feel as if all my anchors have been cut off and I'm cast adrift.' She lifted her glass to her lips and took a big gulp. 'The story I've been telling myself has been all wrong and I have no idea who I am any more.'

I understood. There was a story I had been telling myself as well. That I had made the right choice that morning.

'Daniel told me that you two used to be classmates,' I said.

'I used to have this major crush on him.' She smiled at Mark. 'When I was about ten. Andre always teased me about him.' The smile dropped from her face. 'Before everything changed.'

Before the abuse started, probably.

'Andre reminded Daniel about the two of you cycling to school together. That's why he believed him.' Why Daniel believed him when no one else had.

'He said he filmed their chat, didn't he?'

133

I nodded. 'He did.'

'That's only barely legal.'

'Andre knew about it. It was with his permission.'

'Did he say anything . . .' she lifted her glass of wine to her lips again, 'anything about my parents?'

I thought back to how Andre had phrased it, what exactly he'd said. 'He seemed to imply,' I picked my words carefully, 'that your parents had been aware of the abuse.'

Julia put her glass down and pressed her hands against her eyes.

Mark looked at me and very slowly shook his head, warning me to stop.

'Is that how you remember it?' I asked.

'They knew Verbaan,' Julia said. 'He was a married man. His wife blamed my brother. My parents believed her.'

Anger rose up from my stomach to my eyes. 'He was only fifteen.'

'They kicked him out of the house.'

I tipped my head back to look at the ceiling.

'They didn't think they'd done anything wrong until years later when the preacher barred that bastard from the church after the other kids had come forward. Before he could even be convicted of murder. That's what pulled them up. The fact that the preacher condemned the man whereas they'd condemned their own son.'

'I'm so sorry,' Mark said.

'What happened then?' I asked, trying to keep Julia's focus on me. To keep her talking.

'Then Verbaan killed himself on the evening the story was

in all the papers. That was the end: the case was closed and the family moved away.'

'How much did you know about this at the time?' There was a hard edge to my voice. 'When your parents threw your brother out of the house, I mean.'

'I knew my brother was in love with Paul Verbaan. Or thought he was anyway.' She drank more wine. 'Half the school was probably in love with him, and he had his favourites. All boys.'

I grimaced. That hadn't been love. That had been grooming. 'But did you know why your parents kicked him out?'

'Yes.' She rubbed her eyes. 'I overheard. I knew. Sorry. I can't talk about this any more.' She got up.

I didn't stop her, but watched as she joined her friends.

Mark followed her with his eyes. 'Are you allowed to do that?' he asked as soon as she was out of earshot.

'Do what?'

'Question her.'

'I wasn't questioning her. I was asking her a few questions. That's a very different thing.' I smiled at him. 'Plus I had a witness.'

'It didn't seem right to ask her all those things. She's in shock. Shouldn't you have cautioned her?'

'She's not a suspect, Mark. I've been wondering about why Andre never contacted his family, and now I think I know. That chat was very useful.'

'Useful for you, but not for Julia.'

'I'm trying to do my job here.'

'And she was out with her friends because she's upset and confused.'

'A lot of the people I deal with are upset and confused.'

'So shouldn't you be more understanding? I think her brother behaved very selfishly—'

'Selfishly?' I couldn't keep the sarcasm out of my voice. 'Please explain.'

'Coming here, talking to all those people, getting everybody upset all over again and then killing himself.'

'The son of his abuser hit him; his sister didn't believe him.'

'Neither did you.'

A small noise escaped from my mouth. It sounded like a laugh but felt like a sob. 'You're right.' I nodded. 'You're right, neither did I. And I'm making up for that.'

'By punishing his sister? Are you angry with her because you're angry at yourself?'

I raised my eyebrows. 'I'm punishing her? Really?'

'She was only twelve at the time. She wasn't the one who kicked him out of the house.'

'She didn't stop her parents either. What do you think happens to fifteen-year-old boys who are sexually abused and end up on the street? Do you think they go back to school, finish their education and live happily ever after?'

Mark opened his mouth.

'No, they don't,' I continued without giving him a chance to speak. 'They're the ones who are killed and buried and their bones found after five years.'

'But Andre wasn't killed.'

'He was lucky. He seemed to have made a good life for himself in London. Can't you see how this makes it all so much more devastating? And you say he was selfish? I'm sure he wanted to make amends.'

136

'But he didn't make amends, did he? People confess in order to feel better about themselves. They don't think about what it does to the people who have to listen to their confession. And then he killed himself. That seems pretty selfish to me.'

'People get so depressed that they don't think rationally.'

'But he stayed silent all these years. He didn't tell his parents, or his sister, that he was still alive. Can you imagine what it must have been like for them?'

I shook my head in bewilderment. 'Did you hear a different conversation from me? He was raped by his teacher, and when his orthodox religious family found out about it, they kicked him out on the street.'

'Raped?'

'Fifteen, Mark. He was fifteen. That's statutory rape. The man was more than twenty years older than him. He was his teacher.' I remembered looking at Andre's school photo and thinking that he was the kind of kid who would stay quiet. 'That was rape,' I repeated. I stood up abruptly. 'Do you want another drink?'

Mark seemed confused by the sudden change in subject. 'Sure.'

I walked over to the bar, away from the discussion. I got him a drink and paid our bill. I put the glass on the table. 'I'm going back to work,' I said.

'Lotte, don't be like this,' I heard him say as I walked away.

As soon as I went out through the door, I saw Julia smoking a cigarette. She saw me too.

'You didn't do anything wrong,' she said. 'I overheard what he said,' she gestured with the cigarette in Mark's direction, 'about you questioning me. But don't worry about it. I knew what you were doing. It's fine.'

'Thanks.' I didn't know what else to say.

Julia took a drag of the cigarette, and the end lit up bright in the dark November night. 'I'm a social worker,' she said. 'I understand how these things work.'

That made everything easier. 'The commissaris wants to do a press conference,' I said. 'He wants you to join him.'

'Me? Are you kidding?' She laughed. 'He wants me to sit there and say how great everything is? No thank you.'

Pippi was happy when I got home. She meowed and demanded to be fed. I filled her food bowl and rubbed her little head and then remembered I had to feed myself too. I should have waited until after we'd eaten before I stormed out in a huff. If only Julia had arrived later, this wouldn't have happened.

I went into the kitchen and got out a ring binder covered with food stains. Mark had said that I needed to eat better. I needed to look after myself. He'd given me the cooking course as a birthday present. The fact that it was called *Cooking for One* had an irony to it that I'd liked at the time. Now it didn't feel so good.

I followed tonight's recipe. Step 1: chop the onion. Step 2: fry it for fifteen minutes until brown at the edges. I set the timer on the oven clock. I filled the kettle and put it on. The great thing about the course was that it had made me realise that if you just followed the recipes to the letter, you would end up with something edible. I appreciated that this wasn't like real life, where you could follow all the rules, set your priorities correctly and still find yourself in a total mess. In cooking, you fried the onions for fifteen minutes and they would have a brown edge. You boiled the pasta for twelve minutes – or ten for al dente – and it ended up perfectly cooked. You added half a teaspoon of oregano to the tomato sauce and suddenly it tasted wonderful. Miss out a step – like not adding the salt, as I had done the other week – and it was a disaster. Stick to the rules and you had a nice dinner. It had been a revelation to me.

I had tried to explain that to Mark and he had just laughed. Cooking isn't like that, he'd said. It's an art, not a science. It was a science in my experience. I'd now made every recipe in my ring binder at least twice. Maybe, after cooking the same fifteen recipes ten times or more, I would know them by heart, but at the moment, the laminated pages were my Bible, and their steps were rituals that had to be obeyed.

The kitchen clock announced that the pasta was cooked. I drained it and put it on a white plate. I poured the tomato sauce on top. I fished a fork out of the kitchen drawer and started winding the spaghetti around it. It tasted good. In five minutes, it was all gone. I gave the plate a rinse and put it in the dishwasher. I filled the tomato pan with water to let it soak. I hadn't left the kitchen. It seemed extravagant to lay the table for one person. It was just as easy to eat stand-ing up.

Once everything was tidied away, I went to my study and clipped a fresh sheet of paper to my architect's table. It was one of the items the previous owner of my flat had left behind. She'd been an interior designer who'd needed the money; I'd needed furniture and a place to live. I'd taken over everything she had. The only thing that had changed recently was that some of Mark's possessions had turned up, things he'd brought here so that he didn't have to shuttle them back and forth with each visit.

I hadn't thought the table would be useful, but it had turned out to be a great tool. I now used it for every case I worked on; it gave me space to sort out my thoughts, away from the office and in the privacy of my own home.

I tilted the table.

What I most wanted to make sense of was what Andre Nieuwkerk had been doing whilst he was in Amsterdam. I drew a long horizontal line on my paper. I marked in the days he had been here: Friday through to Tuesday.

On Friday evening he'd had dinner with Laurens Werda.

On Saturday evening he'd gone to Julia's place.

His talk with Daniel had been on Monday afternoon.

On Tuesday morning he'd called Laurens. He'd met me. I had refused to talk to him. He'd killed himself maybe an hour later.

The words stared at me from the page and I tore the paper from the table.

What did this tell me? Nothing apart from that he didn't meet anybody on Sunday. What had he been doing? Somehow I couldn't believe he'd spent the day in church.

This wasn't even the right thing to focus on. Thomas's reminder that there had been another victim, that another young man had been murdered thirty years ago, stuck in my head.

That might be a much more interesting angle to look at. After all, suicide wasn't a crime.

Daniel might think Andre could be blamed for his father's death, but really he couldn't be. When people killed themselves, that was their choice. Their responsibility.

What someone else might have done leading up to it was completely irrelevant.

As I drew another horizontal line on a fresh piece of paper, I accepted that I didn't actually believe that.

Don't think about it, I admonished myself. Focus on the person who was murdered thirty years ago. Think about the family of that young man, a family who needed to know what happened to their son. Julia Nieuwkerk had thought she'd scattered her brother's ashes all those years ago, but it had been someone else's brother. Someone else's child.

I would work on what I could control. There was nothing I could do to turn back time to Tuesday morning. I could not meet Andre again, I couldn't stand in the red-light district and have a long chat with him instead of going to the hospital to talk to Peter de Waal.

What I could do was try to find out who had been murdered. I could give a family some answers, and thinking about what Andre Nieuwkerk had done while he was in Amsterdam wasn't going to help me with that.

Instead I should go through the boxes that were coming up from the archives and find out where the original investigating team had gone wrong.

That would be my job for tomorrow.

I put the cap back on my marker pen, picked up my phone and WhatsApped Mark. *Sorry*, I wrote. *This case is getting to me*. It wasn't entirely truthful, but it was as good an explanation as any. What I should apologise for was letting my boyfriend see what my job actually entailed. Giving him an insight into my mind. *I shouldn't have taken it out on you.*

My phone beeped a reply. *I'm sorry too.*

I stared at the screen to see if there was going to be a follow-up message to tell me what he was apologising for.

It didn't come.

That night I dreamed of Andre Nieuwkerk. He was standing on the bridge at the edge of the Lange Niezel with a pot of pills in his hand. I told him I didn't care. I told him I didn't believe he was going to take them. I told him I had more important things to do, and stood in the darkness of a November morning and watched him as he swallowed the pills. In my dream, I waited with him as he lost consciousness and died.

Then I walked away.

Chapter 14

When I got into work the next morning, I saw that the files had been brought up from the archives. I opened one of the boxes and spread the photos out in front of me. They were all of the remains that would become known as the Body in the Dunes. Close-ups of the bones and the skull featured prominently. All that forensics at the time had been able to say was that the dead man had been between fifteen and twenty-five years old, based on the bones in the wrist. The cause of death had been ruled as strangulation, based on the fractures of the bones in the neck. On the desk next to mine, I put down the photos of Andre Nieuwkerk. I was eerily reminded that this was probably exactly what the original team had done over twenty-five years ago: they had also compared these photos. Based on the shape of the skull and the length of the bones, they had decided that it was Andre Nieuwkerk's body.

Now we knew that they had been wrong.

I looked at the photos. If this young man wasn't Andre Nieuwkerk, then who was he?

The detectives at the time didn't think he'd been killed where he'd been found. They thought he'd probably been transported to the dunes in a vehicle. The burial site hadn't been that far away from a path that would have been easily accessible by car. The theory was that the murderer had gone there in the middle of the night, dug the grave and dumped the body, which had been stripped of its clothes. I nodded in agreement as I read the report. The body had been found downhill from the path. That made sense. Dead bodies were heavy to carry and nobody would have wanted to go uphill in the dunes if there was a convenient hollow nearby.

There had been nothing on the body to identify who he was. I totally understood the difficulties in solving this case. Today we would have taken a DNA sample and compared that to the DNA of the families of the missing men. Even now, though, we still found bodies that we couldn't identify, especially if the person in question had not been reported missing. A couple of years ago, there had been a drive to unearth unidentified bodies from a number of cemeteries, to see if, with modern technology, we could now find out who they were. Give them a proper burial and give the families closure.

With the Body in the Dunes, we hadn't done that. After all, hadn't we identified him? Hadn't the police closed the case? The Nieuwkerk family had held a funeral for their son. Their brother. Had cremated him. Had closure. A false closure.

After the police had decided that this was Andre Nieuwkerk, they'd also decided that he'd most likely been murdered on the day he'd gone missing. That had been four years before the remains were found.

I took a blue marker pen and walked up to our white-board. I drew a horizontal line to represent the timeline. The skeleton was found in April 1993. Given the stage of decomposition, the young man must have died between three and five years before then. So between 1988 and 1990. I marked those dates with my pen. Andre had been reported missing in February 1989, so that was comfortably within the timeline. I drew a cross in the middle of the section.

Charlie came in. 'What are you doing?' he asked.

I pointed to the whiteboard. 'This is when Andre went missing. The police decided he'd been murdered the same day.'

'That makes sense,' he said as he took his coat off and hung it over the back of his chair.

'Right. But there was no evidence really to suggest that he had been murdered at that point. There would have been a fourteen-month window after he went missing.'

'Plus we know he definitely wasn't murdered then,' Charlie said, 'because he was still alive. Can we go to the place where the skeleton was found?'

'Do you want to go to the place where he was found?' Thomas said. 'We should look at the site.'

I put down the page I was looking at and nodded. Getting out of the office wasn't a bad idea. We waited for Thomas, and together we set out on the thirty-kilometre drive to the dunes near Haarlem.

Time changed things. It changed how we looked at this case. What had been an astounding success for the police had now been revealed to be an abject failure. Time had also changed the landscape around me. At first glance, you might think these dunes had been there for ever, that the white sand that peeked from between the green marram grass was the same as it had been twenty-five years ago. Like then, these rolling hills stretched all the way to the beach. But I could see the changes as I looked at the photos the team had taken at the time.

Decades of wind and rain had changed the landscape. The wind had blown sand from one place and deposited it in another. The path that had been a narrow red-brick track twenty-five years ago had now been asphalted. As far as I could tell, it was taking the same route, but I couldn't be entirely sure.

The width of the dunes would have changed; how far in the sea came would have altered. The wind whipped my hair around my face and a sand stream moved like water around my feet. With every step I took, I was destroying a piece of the dune as well as creating a new one. This particular part was not open to the public, the fragile landscape protected. It had already been a protected area when the body was found. It was the main reason that it had lain here undiscovered for years, until it had decomposed to a skeleton.

My mobile rang. It was Julia. She apologised for bothering me again, but she had realised that she had to deal with the situation. She was going to go to London to look at her brother's flat and sort out his belongings. But she was worried about going alone; could I go with her?

I didn't let my annoyance show about being used as a babysitter. I told her she was doing the right thing but it wasn't really in my remit to go along with her. I suggested she take a friend because I appreciated this was going to be hard for her. She sounded disappointed when she said that she understood and disconnected the call.

I went back to looking at the photos. I could tell that marram grass had grown above the remains by the time the skeleton was unearthed. The block of vegetation was particularly lush, having had access to far more nutrients than would normally be found in the white sand.

'They thought the murderer drove here, probably with the body in the boot of his car,' Charlie said. He was holding another set of pages in his hand. The paper flapped in the wind and he needed both hands to keep it still. 'That makes sense, doesn't it?'

'Yes, it does,' I said. 'I think he was carried from the car to the nearest spot in the off-limit zone that couldn't be seen from the road.' From where we were standing, a dune top obscured our view of the road, but even though it was a gloomy morning, I could still see a few people on the walking paths, out with their dogs.

'Okay,' Charlie said. 'Can we assume he was murdered somewhere else, driven to the dunes and buried here?'

'That's what the police thought when they still believed Andre had been murdered. That Paul Verbaan had driven him here at night.' I shrugged. 'It seems the logical explanation. During the day, too many people would have come along the road, as it takes you to the beach.' A woman with a dog looked in my direction, obviously curious as to why three people were out walking in a restricted part of the dunes. 'Even on a day like today, there's no way you could carry a body from a car and not get noticed.'

Charlie studied the pages again. 'It was a shallow grave. The person was in a hurry.' He glanced from where we were standing to the path higher up. 'He rolled the body down.'

'Or carried him,' I said. The body would have decomposed quickly in a shallow grave. If the sand had been dry, the body would have been preserved better, but in the Netherlands, it rains a lot. Part of the reason why the dunes were a restricted area was that they contained large sand-filtered reservoirs that supplied drinking water to most of the coastal towns. The rainwater would have seeped through the sand, speeding up decomposition.

'It's a two-hour drive from Elspeet,' Thomas said.

'At one point, they speculated that Verbaan was still meeting with Andre after he'd left Elspeet. That maybe he had actually been killed closer to here: Haarlem or Amsterdam.' I rubbed my eyes. I'd had a restless night and had been relieved when it was morning and I could go back to work.

'Do you think they would actually have convicted Verbaan for the murder if he hadn't killed himself?' Charlie asked.

'Probably not,' I said. 'Without knowing what day or even what year Andre was killed, it would have been virtually impossible to prove.' The original team never found the car the murderer had used, but then what traces of evidence would there have been four years later? The lack of evidence hadn't bothered them, and they'd decided the car would have been easy to get rid of.

'Did you see the paper this morning?' Thomas asked.

I nodded. A newspaper had been lying on the doormat in our communal area as I'd left home. *Political correctness gone mad*, the headline screamed. *Turkish attacker with restraining order not arrested by the police.*

I'd scanned the article. The journalist had clearly talked to Peter de Waal and his wife.

I saw who did it but the police won't believe me, victim says. They treated me like the criminal.

'No mention of the fact that Peter de Waal was drunk,' I said, 'or that it all happened in a second.'

'Of course not; that would make the story far less interesting.'

I tried to push it out of my head. I had enough problems dealing with Andre Nieuwkerk's case. With the Body in the Dunes. 'Let's just focus on this,' I said.

'The boss said he thinks it's pointless,' Charlie said. 'That it's just an exercise in covering our backs.'

Thomas had filled him in on our conversation then, as they were going to Julia's.

'Maybe it is,' I said. 'To be honest, from looking through these reports, the previous team did a pretty decent job. Apart from misidentifying the victim, of course. A lot of the cold cases that get solved are because of the improvements in forensics, sure, but even more are solved because of things like this.'

Charlie frowned. 'Things like what?'

'The kind of thing that drove Andre to come back and talk to people. We still don't know why he did that, but maybe he felt guilty.' I looked at an empty sweet wrapper that was being blown about in the wind. 'Guilt can be a very strong driving force. As can fear.'

I looked around me. The answers wouldn't be found here,

I was sure of that. I made my way out of the dunes. It was heavy going as my feet kept sinking down into the loose sand. Slowly I made my way up the hill, then back down to the road. With solid asphalt under my feet once more, I wiped the sand off my boots.

I looked through the file for the original missing persons report. The name on it pulled me up: Andre's disappearance had been reported by his sister. Julia Nieuwkerk, his twelve-year-old sister, was the one who'd gone to the police four days after he'd left.

Of course, I knew now that there were a lot of details missing: there was no mention of the blazing row Julia said her parents had had with her brother the evening he disappeared. The evening they'd thrown him out of their house. Nothing about Paul Verbaan's wife coming to the house.

According to the report, Julia had said he'd just gone missing that evening. Had walked out of the house and hadn't come back. She'd said there'd been no reason for it. She'd said she didn't understand what had caused it.

I put the page down. It was hard to read.

I decided to check a different angle. If Andre had gone to the UK, he must have had a passport. There must be a paper trail of him giving up Dutch citizenship.

A paper trail that the police had missed.

I could see how this could have happened: the information had all been there, but they just hadn't looked. They'd identified a young man who'd gone missing four years earlier and they'd never checked to see if there had been any signs of him abroad. The police could have looked into that when his sister had first filed the report, but this was before everything had been computerised, and he had fallen through the cracks. With runaway teenagers, it was often the parents who insisted the police continued to check every detail. In Andre's case, that pressure wouldn't have been there. His parents hadn't even considered their son 'missing', as they had shown him the door. The police would have stopped investigating very quickly, and probably well before Andre had changed his nationality.

I could also see how Andre might not have realised that his sister had reported him missing. He had probably thought: they wanted me to go, I've taken my stuff. What did they think I was going to do?

It was even more plausible that, being thrown out of the house, with nowhere to go, he hadn't thought at all.

Had his parents expected him to come back a few days later? Was that why his sister had gone to the police when he hadn't returned? I turned back to reading the files.

What evidence had there been against Paul Verbaan? I looked for the reports on his questioning. The answer was: not a great deal. Yes, more boys had come forward about abuse, as Andre had said on that recording. The rumours were there.

Verbaan had said that it was all lies.

The police of course had not believed him. The newspapers hadn't believed him and had put pictures of him on the front page. The reverend had kicked him out of the church.

And then he'd killed himself and nobody was going to believe him ever again.

I realised that none of the police work from twenty-five years ago was going to be useful to me. This had been an investigation into a murder that had never happened. I might as well tape up this box again and send it straight back to the archives, because it was all pointless.

We had to start from scratch with identifying the victim.

I sat back in my chair. Andre's family had cremated the body, as if they wanted to erase him totally from the face of the earth. All the forensic advances we'd made in the twenty-five years since this case was originally investigated were useless, because we had nothing. There was no evidence left apart from what was in these boxes.

If we wanted to reopen the case, we'd have to do it without a body, without a proper time of death – or even a year of death – and without knowing who the victim was.

It was impossible.

So why did I still want to try? Why did I feel I had a duty to investigate?

If I'd taken Andre seriously that morning, I could have asked him things. I could have asked him what he'd known. Whether he'd just run away from difficult parents or if there was more behind him leaving the country. I could have asked him why he'd been so adamant about changing nationality and why he'd hated the Netherlands so much. I could have asked him why he'd come back, why now; why he had tried to talk to his sister and to Daniel.

But I hadn't taken him seriously, all the talks he'd had with people had gone very differently from what he'd expected, and he'd killed himself.

It wasn't just that, though. There was also this feeling that twenty-five years ago the police had committed . . . well, not a crime, but at least a miscarriage of justice. A mistake that we had touted as a huge achievement. Clearly I wasn't responsible for that, but didn't I owe it to all involved to at least have a go? Try to investigate?

Thomas stared at the timeline I'd drawn on the whiteboard earlier. 'We should look at missing young men again. We should check anybody who disappeared during this time.' He tapped with his marker pen on the section that I'd marked out earlier.

'We need to check three years' worth?' Charlie's voice was that of a child being told to do his homework.

He probably wished he'd stayed with the traffic police.

Looking at this paperwork, especially the missing persons report, made me think about Julia's phone call again. I called her and said I wanted to talk to her. She told me to come over to hers. I asked her to give me half an hour.

Chapter 15

The orange builder's jacket and the boots were no longer in Julia's hallway. I wondered what had happened to them but didn't ask. We sat down at the big table in her kitchen. I was facing her bed at the other side of the room. This was the problem with studio flats: when someone came to visit, you displayed parts of your life you probably wanted to keep behind closed doors. I didn't necessarily want to know what colour bedsheets Julia had, or that she hadn't straightened the duvet since she'd got out of bed.

'Do you mind if I smoke?' she asked. She had her back towards the bed. Maybe she didn't want to see her own messy room either.

'We're in your flat; you can do what you want.'

'What's up?' she said.

'Remember that request from the commissaris? He wants to do a press conference about your brother and he'd really like you there.'

'I bet he would. He needs me to back him up, right?' She rummaged through her handbag until she found her lighter. 'I'm there to show that I'm not pissed off with him. What if I say no?'

'The press conference will still go ahead. It won't look good for the police force if you're not there.'

'I've got no reason to help him.'

'But what happened wasn't his fault. Misidentifying your brother wasn't his fault.'

She took a drag from her cigarette. 'I know, I know. I'm just so pissed off. At the time, it seemed so amazing that after all those years they'd managed to identify my brother. That Verbaan got some punishment.'

It hadn't actually been the police who'd done that, but I knew better than to say it was the church who'd judged the man.

'That it was all wrong has just hit me really hard. I can't believe they messed it up so badly.'

'This was before DNA was widely used. Plus we all make mistakes, don't you think?' I had definitely made my share of them. I couldn't imagine that Julia had always been right either. We were human, after all, however much the general public wanted to think otherwise.

'I understand that,' she said, 'but what is this press conference going to be about? What do they want me to do?'

'The commissaris is going to say that the police got it wrong twenty-five years ago, that the Body in the Dunes was misidentified, because . . .' I paused.

'Because my brother came back and then died.'

'Yes.'

'I know how these things work, Lotte, remember? No need to wrap me in cotton wool.'

'He was still your brother.' I said it kindly. 'However much

155

you're used to this sort of thing from work, I know it has come as a shock to you.'

'Sure.' She tapped the cigarette against the ashtray. 'He can go ahead with it, but I won't be there.'

'He wants to put up a united front.'

'You can tell your commissaris that I have the utmost faith in the police force to get it right this time, but I don't want to be involved. I didn't recognise my own brother. I'm probably more to blame for this debacle than the commissaris is.' She took a deep drag from the cigarette and looked at me through the smoke.

I thought again about the papers I'd seen this morning, the ones that told me she'd been the one who'd gone to the police. She'd reported her brother missing against the wishes of her parents.

'I know you refused before.' She hesitated when I stayed silent, but then continued. 'Please come to London with me, to look at Andre's flat. I was given his things from the hotel; I have his keys, I have his address. I know I should go, but I really don't want to do it by myself.'

Previously I'd said no because I had been annoyed with Julia. Now I knew that she'd reported her brother missing. She'd done what she could at the time.

What had I done?

Deep down inside, I knew I was more to blame for Andre's death than either Julia or the commissaris. 'When are you going?' I said.

Chapter 16

After I'd left Julia's, I didn't go home but drove north, to Alkmaar, to have a chat with my father. He'd still been a policeman when Andre's murder case had been going on. I felt pulled in too many directions, all of which set me on a straight collision course with my ultimate boss. I wasn't sure what to do about Peter de Waal's case. Part of me wanted to just trust Ingrid, but I also knew that she was junior in her team and that her boyfriend would be keen to do what his boss wanted. I'd worked with her for long enough to know that she had integrity and would want to do the right thing, but being pushed from two sides might make her go in a direction that she wouldn't normally.

All there was between Amsterdam and Alkmaar was a stretch of entirely flat land. A few small villages broke the monotony of the landscape, their churches the only mountains in sight. In the flat land, there was nothing to slow the wind down as it drove across the country, rushing straight from the sea. A strong gust grabbed my car and pulled it sideways. I had to steer against the wind. It seemed to get stronger by the hour. It had been windy yesterday, but today it felt more like a proper storm.

It was quiet on the road, though not so long ago rush hour had filled the grey tarmac with colourful cars. The land all around seemed pushed even flatter by the wind. Storms ruled the country at this time of year, when westerly winds brought rain, easterly winds frost, southerly winds sunshine and northerly winds all three together. The wind might not be your friend, but it was your constant neighbour.

I hit Alkmaar's roundabout and then there were only a few turnings before I was at my father's house. I parked behind his BMW. Every time I visited him, I thought that no ex-detective should live in a house this big. It had at one point made me wonder where he had got his money from, but now I knew it was all my stepmother Maaike's. I rang the doorbell, which made an old-fashioned sound like a bicycle bell.

Maaike opened the door and greeted me with a big smile. She might technically be my stepmother, but it was weird to call someone that when you were already in your forties. She'd insisted I use her first name and I had been only too happy to comply.

My father came out of the kitchen.

'Hi, Dad,' I said.

He gave me a kiss on the cheek. 'Hi, Lotte, how are you?'

'Fine, I'm fine.'

'You sit down,' Maaike said, 'and I'll finish making dinner. And no work talk,' she added.

I smiled and made a zip sign across my lips. I did have other topics of conversation. It was just that when I was with my father, we often ended up talking shop. There weren't many people who understood the ins and outs of police work as well as he did. I waited until Maaike had gone back into the kitchen before I turned to him.

'How's work?' he asked.

I grinned, because I wasn't the first one to ignore Maaike's request. It made me feel as if we were co-conspirators. 'I'm stuck,' I said, 'and I really don't know what to do.'

'That doesn't sound like you.'

'Well, it's a truly delightful mix of things. I've got an unsolvable case where the police did everything wrong, and a case where we're doing too much wrong at the moment. You'd think we hadn't learned our lessons from the past.'

'People want us to find answers,' my father said. 'They're used to watching crime shows on TV where the answers are hard to find but at the end there will be a solution to the riddle. It's good in a way. They trust us.'

'I get that,' I said. 'I totally do. But what's the point in giving the wrong answers just for the sake of saying something? Isn't that worse than saying nothing at all? We now know we misidentified the Body in the Dunes. Do you remember that one?'

'Of course I do,' my father said. 'They got that wrong? That's a terrible mistake.'

'But I can understand how it happened. Even considering the old-fashioned thinking and the way they went about identifying the remains, the police didn't necessarily do anything wrong. Apart from allowing the press to find out about the suspect, of course.'

'You think they did the best they could with the techniques available to them at the time?'

'Yes,' I said. 'Unfortunately, they were totally wrong. It's a mess. And I'm even more worried about what to do with these assault cases.'

'Are you working on that?'

'I'm not, and that's part of the problem.' I sighed. 'Ingrid asked me to help her out with one of them. As it turned out, the problematic one. The guy woke up and said he knew who'd done it. His wife's ex-husband had been harassing him for a while, had a restraining order and, according to the victim, had now punched him in the face.'

'You're talking about the Turkish guy?'

'The Turkish guy. That's exactly it.'

'I saw that.'

'You think he was guilty too, don't you?'

'It sounds plausible and everything fits.'

'Doesn't it just. Only when we went to talk to the guy an hour later, he had no visible wounds on his hands. Not a single scratch. Not a bruise. No marks at all.'

My father raised his eyebrows. 'You're sure about this?'

'Yeah, absolutely. I was surprised too. Anyway, Ingrid went back to the victim to ask if maybe his attacker had been wearing gloves or used some kind of weapon. But no, the guy was adamant it was a bare-handed punch. Then we talked to one of his colleagues about what had happened that night, and it seemed that he was extremely drunk and argumentative.'

'And you have no other witnesses?'

'No witnesses, no CCTV.'

'Well, then you can't arrest your suspect. The testimony of a drunken guy is going to count for nothing. Plus he didn't look as if he'd done it.'

160

'And his car hadn't left the car park outside his flat.'

'Oh well. Back to square one.'

'I don't know what to do,' I said. 'I want to trust Ingrid and the commissaris to do the right thing.'

'You don't trust the commissaris?'

'He's very cosy with the press. I saw him give an interview about all these assaults on the morning that Peter de Waal was beaten up. And in the meantime, we've got this old case where we've clearly misidentified the body. Seeing as the victim wasn't actually dead.' I rubbed my face. 'No, that's wrong, he died two days ago.'

'What happened to him?'

'Suicide. Overdose of prescription painkillers. He'd lived abroad for a long time and came back to Amsterdam to tell people that he was still alive. I think he'd expected his sister to welcome him with open arms, and the family of the guy accused of his murder to be happy that he was here to set things straight. Instead everybody dismissed him. Or was angry with him.'

'It's terrible,' my father said. 'Nobody knew he was still alive?'

'No. I had a long chat with his sister this afternoon. She's really shaken up. All this time she'd thought her brother had been killed.'

'And he'd just gone abroad instead?'

'According to his sister, his parents threw him out of the house after they'd found out he'd been abused by his teacher.'

'They threw him out?'

'Strict orthodox family.'

'How old was his sister at the time?'

'Twelve. There wasn't a big age gap.'

'But even if this guy was still alive,' my father said, 'there really was a victim, I assume?'

'Yes, but the remains were cremated, so we can't use forensic science. It would have been so much easier if we'd had DNA evidence.'

'This wouldn't have happened if they could have used DNA tests at the time. We didn't have any of that. So you've got an unsolvable case, and you've got evidence on another case that everybody hates.'

'Yup,' I said. 'That's it in a nutshell.'

'Maybe you should run away,' my father said jokingly. 'But do let us know you're all right.'

His words stuck in my head all the way through dinner and during my trip back to Amsterdam along the quiet dark motorway.

Chapter 17

I got to Schiphol the next morning with not much time to spare before my flight. This was on purpose. I had no desire to spend a lot of time at the airport and had cut it as close as I'd dared. I'd checked in online at the same time as I'd bought my ticket, and didn't see Julia until I got to the gate when the plane was ready for boarding. She had a seat a couple of rows in front of me and I could mainly see the back of her head, her hair fair and thin like a girl's down her back. She was wearing the same blue jumper with the white embroidery that she had worn when Charlie and I had first come to her door.

It was Saturday and the plane was full of people going to London for a fun weekend: the theatre maybe, some shopping, seeing the Christmas lights. We were going to look at the flat of a man who'd died. As everybody else was placing their wheelie bags in the overhead lockers, pushing and shoving for space, I slid my handbag underneath my seat. Going only for a day was expensive, but at least you could travel light. I didn't think I'd be able to claim the money back. In fact I was sure the chief inspector would have preferred that I didn't go, but sometimes that wasn't what was important. This weekend I didn't have to work, so I could do what I wanted.

My phone beeped with a message, but we were getting ready for take-off so I switched it off, put it away and settled down to sleep for an hour. It had been an early start.

I woke up when we landed at Gatwick. My brain was still half asleep as we trundled off the plane like a bunch of docile sheep. Not thinking was the best way of dealing with airports, and I went with the stream of people around me to get to passport control. I put my passport on the scanner, the computer matched up my face with my photo and the gates opened. I didn't have to engage with a single human being.

When Andre had first come to London, it would have been different. He would have had to show his passport to an actual person. But then it was very possible that he hadn't flown. If I'd been a teenager, running away from home, I would have gone by bus and boat. Flying was much more likely to get you stopped. I didn't know how old you had to be before you could fly alone. And where would he have got the money to buy the ticket in the first place? I didn't know exactly when he had arrived here, as it was of course very possible that he'd lived in the Netherlands by himself for a while after his parents had kicked him out. But if he'd travelled by bus, he probably wouldn't even have had to show his passport. Nobody would have stopped a fifteen- or sixteen-year-old from going to London.

Julia waited for me at the other end of Customs.

'Had Andre ever left the Netherlands before?' I asked her.

She extended the handle of her wheelie bag and started walking towards the signs for the train without responding.

I was that outcast again: I should have talked about something else first, maybe asked her if she'd had a good journey, or if she was feeling okay about going to her brother's flat.

But she paused and let me catch up with her. 'You're wondering if he had a passport?' she said. Her thinking was along the same lines as mine.

I nodded. 'Exactly.'

'I don't think so. I first got mine when I was seventeen or so and we went on a school trip to Germany. We never took holidays abroad when we were kids. We went to the coast in a caravan, that was it.'

That didn't surprise me.

We walked through the airport to the train station together and bought tickets to London from a confusing machine.

'Get a ticket to Putney,' Julia said. 'That's where the flat is. I looked it up. We have to change at Clapham Junction.'

It was so expensive that I double-checked we hadn't bought first-class tickets by mistake. We stood on the chilly platform, alongside all those other people from all over the world. Again, not having luggage was an advantage. I should always travel like this. It was fortunate that we got seats next to each other. I let Julia sit by the window.

Outside, the countryside rolled by. The ticket had probably been so expensive because Gatwick was nowhere near London. This long a journey would have taken me from Amsterdam to Rotterdam with time to spare. Opposite us, a man was concentrating on his newspaper.

'I saw the missing person report on your brother,' I said. 'I noticed you were the one who went to the police.' Speaking a language that nobody around us spoke provided us with a certain amount of privacy. I couldn't have had this conversation on the Amsterdam–Rotterdam train.

'My parents were angry with me for that,' she said, her face turned away from me. 'They said I should leave it, but I was worried about where he was. Where he could have gone. When they kicked him out, I really thought he was going to be back in a couple of days. They would have let him back in, I'm sure of that. They were just angry. But he never came back.'

I wasn't so sure, but I didn't question it. I just let her talk. It was what she had wanted to do the other night, but I'd cut her short and asked her questions about what I wanted to know. It did interest me what her opinion was a few days after Andre had been identified. I could only imagine that she had been turning this round and round in her head.

'We didn't talk about him for four years. Didn't pursue where he might have gone. It was as if he was already dead to my parents. But when we heard he'd been murdered, they felt so guilty. Everything changed when the church barred Verbaan. Then they started to question what they'd done.' She turned to look at me. 'Up to then, they thought it had been the right thing, casting their sinning son away from their doorstep.'

'What did you think?'

'It's so hard to remember. Hard to think of those years when we were silent about what had happened. Even though I knew about the sexual relationship that Verbaan had had with my brother, I never told anybody. I don't know what I was thinking. Everybody loved Verbaan. He was such a popular teacher. And maybe people thought differently then. I definitely didn't argue with my parents over what they'd done. Teachers, the school, they were all such figures of authority, beyond questioning.' She looked out of the window again. 'As my parents were,' she added, more to the glass than to me.

'Apart from reporting him missing.'

'I guess so. But when the reverend said Verbaan had been in the wrong, had been abusing his pupils, that his wife had condoned the abuse and had been covering for him, it was as if my eyes were opened. That was when I realised that what I'd accepted was actually immoral.'

'How old were you?'

'Seventeen. I finished school, I left home, became a social worker.' She shook her head. 'A psychiatrist would have a field day with that. I couldn't stop my brother being abused, I couldn't even stop my parents from throwing him out of the house, so now I'm trying to stop that happening to other children.'

My phone beeped again, but I ignored it. 'That's a good reason,' I said. 'There's nothing wrong with that.'

'My parents found all of it hard to live with, but we never really talked about it. It was this great cloud that hung between us, the words not said, the topic not discussed. Then my father died almost ten years ago and my mother three years ago, and now we'll never talk about it. But maybe it's a good thing they're no longer alive. Sorry,' she said. 'I'm rambling on. I think I'm quite nervous about what we're going to find in Andre's flat. I'm all over the place. I didn't sleep at all last night.' She closed her eyes, shutting me out as effectively as if she'd picked up a newspaper like the man opposite us.

I could well imagine how she felt. Even I wasn't sure what we were going to find, and I had plenty of experience of going into the houses of people who'd died.

Getting from the station to the flat was an interesting experience, especially with cars coming from all directions. The people who lived here must have trouble with that too, as it was painted on the streets which way you had to look before crossing the road.

Even Amsterdam wasn't as complicated as this.

Andre's flat was in a quiet road. The houses were small and old, painted in colours ranging from white to a steel grey. The neighbours had a family of pottery Dalmatians in their front window. I didn't know anything about London so I couldn't tell what kind of an area this was. The neat paintwork seemed to suggest that the people who lived here at least had enough money to keep their houses tidy and done up, even if the houses weren't very big.

Up to this point, my main focus had been on helping Julia, but now it was starting to feel like part of an investigation. I stepped aside as she opened the front door with the keys that Andre had left in his hotel room. I hadn't actually questioned if those keys would open the door, and it struck me that I should have contacted the Metropolitan Police about coming to London. I had no jurisdiction here. This was just a day trip. It was definitely *not* part of an investigation, I kept telling myself.

The house was divided into two flats. I found it interesting that Andre had lived in a very similar type of place to his sister, as if there had still been a connection between them. Putney reminded me of Watergraafsmeer: both in big cities but a little way out of the centre.

We went up the stairs to the second floor, and as I followed Julia, her brother's life gained a new reality for me. He'd had a whole life outside of the Netherlands. Someone had to inform his friends and colleagues about his demise.

At Andre's front door, Julia looked through the bunch of keys to find the correct one for this lock. It suddenly came to me that if Andre had a burglar alarm, we would set it off. I breathed a sigh of relief when the door opened to silence.

The flat was a mess, as if Andre had left in a hurry and hadn't had time to tidy up. There were papers on most of the surfaces. Old newspapers, discarded magazines and unpaid bills fought for space on the coffee table. The room was dominated by a green sofa that would seat three people and took up more than half the space. A few bits of paper had fallen onto the floor. I picked up the one closest to me. It was a leaflet for pizza delivery. Others were cards with taxi numbers on them and postcards with information from estate agents.

I wondered why Andre had kept these. Surely, like in my place, the mail must come into the communal area, so why was all this rubbish inside his flat?

I wasn't sure what London apartments generally looked like, but this was smaller than I'd expected: only a little bigger than Julia's studio flat and definitely not as big as my own place on the canal. Places that weren't lived in were always a little eerie, even if they had only been shut down because the owner had gone on holiday. It had been over a week since Andre had closed the door to his flat behind him to go to Amsterdam.

I normally cleaned up before I went on holiday because I hated coming back to a messy apartment. Andre must have been different. Julia dropped her overnight bag on the floor, picked up some of the bills and put them in a small pile. I could tell that she was thinking how she was the one who was going to have to deal with them.

I checked the rest of the flat. A door off the hallway opened to a bathroom. It had carpet on the floor. That was a terrible choice. Unlike the front room, it was tidy. Toiletries were tidied away in a glass-fronted cupboard. I would check everything later, after I'd finished the first scan. The bedroom to the right was filled from wall to wall with a small double bed. The wardrobe door stood open and I could see that half the clothes were missing. The items Andre had taken with him to Amsterdam most likely.

I went back into the narrow corridor. When I opened the next door, I was greeted by another whirlwind of paper. A single bed was pushed up against the wall to show that this could be used as a spare bedroom, but it was dominated by a large red corkboard on the opposite wall crammed with printouts and pages of handwritten scribble. The state of this small study was reminiscent of what I'd seen in the lounge, but here all the papers were about the Body in the Dunes. I looked more closely at the printouts. These weren't newspaper articles that had been kept for decades. He must have printed them in preparation for his trip.

That was interesting.

I took my phone out to take photos of everything. Here was evidence, if I needed it, that Andre had prepared before coming to Amsterdam. I'd known that he had looked into his own murder case – even just that thought was odd – but being confronted with it like this made it seem different. He had found many of the same articles that I had been looking at over the last couple of days. What must it have felt like to know that it was all wrong? Incorrect? But also, what must it feel like to read about your own death over and over again?

My phone beeped again, but my eyes were glued to a photo in the bottom left-hand corner of the board. It was of Paul Verbaan. Not the one with the black bar over his eyes, but a picture of him smiling in the middle of a group of schoolchildren. With that smile, it was obvious how handsome he was. Dark-haired, suave, top button of his shirt undone, one hand up in the air in a victory salute. What had Julia said earlier on? That everybody had loved him. I could see it in the faces of the teenagers around him: all eyes were on him, their faces turned towards him. If a kid had come forward to say that he had abused them, who would have believed them? Even Andre's parents had thought their son had forced his attentions on the teacher.

Next to that photo was the one of Verbaan and his family being barred from the church, cut from a newspaper printout.

The contrast between those two pictures hit me in the stomach. The family man and his hidden life as an abuser were here side by side. I could understand why Andre's parents had found it easy to believe Verbaan's wife.

I might have believed her too if I hadn't seen it before: those abusers hiding in plain sight, their so-called attraction and popularity a perfect camouflage. I'd worked on a case of domestic abuse early on in my career in which nobody had believed the wife because the husband was so nice, so popular, so successful. Surely he wouldn't beat his wife as soon as the front door to their perfect house had closed? There had to be something wrong with her to have driven this man to hit her. Or she must be lying. But I had seen her the day after she'd been beaten, and the truth, which none of their friends had wanted to see, was that he was a narcissistic individual who thought the whole world turned around him, who felt he was allowed to do whatever he wanted, and when anybody stood in the way of that – his wife, for example – he would get violent. But only when nobody else could see it, of course.

I looked at the photo of Paul Verbaan surrounded by those adoring boys and I could easily believe that here was some-one with the same character trait.

What must it have been like for Andre to look at these pictures? Why had he hung this photo of his abuser in his study?

I scanned the other photos. There was one of Andre's parents and Julia at the press conference where the police commissaris at the time had revealed the identity of the Body in the Dunes. It wasn't the one I'd looked at yester-day but it had been taken on the same occasion. The photographer had caught them at a bad moment, and I wondered if that was why the papers had liked this picture too. Andre's father wore an ill-fitting shirt, the collar only just coming down over the too-wide tie; his mother had her hair in a bun, her eyes large as an owl's behind her round glasses. They didn't look upset in this photo, unlike the one I'd seen yesterday. Instead they looked bewildered, as if they didn't understand all this attention that had been turned on them. As if they wondered why everybody was so interested in the murder of their wayward son. Or why their choices had turned out to be so wrong, a feeling I understood only too well.

I took a step back. I imagined Andre standing in this very spot, looking at these same pictures. Why put this photo up instead of the other one, the one in which his family were crying? What must have been going through his mind? Anger? Hatred, maybe? In light of the fact that he hadn't died, was their confusion easier to bear than their tears? Why have the photo in plain sight, in pride of place even, where he couldn't avoid it, where he had to see it whenever he came into his study?

The need to figure out why he'd come to Amsterdam gnawed like hunger in my stomach, along with a desire to understand what he had meant to do. He'd told Daniel that soon everybody would know the truth, that everybody would know he'd still been alive. That hadn't happened yet. It would once the commissaris gave his press conference, but had that been Andre's plan? I couldn't help but think he might have had something else in mind.

A large PC stood on a dark-wood desk. It was likely that he had done all his research online and hadn't printed everything out. I sat down at the desk. I had little hope of guessing a password, but I switched on the PC just in case it wasn't password-protected.

No such luck.

I pulled the keyboard towards me, thinking I could at least start with 'Body in the Dunes'.

I stopped the movement when it revealed a handwritten note on A5 paper that had been hidden underneath.

PEOPLE TO SEE, it said at the top in large underlined capitals. It was followed by a list of names. The first was Julia's. Then *Daniel Verbaan*, with a question mark, and *Laurens*. At the bottom of the list were two more names, only one of which I knew: *Robbert Brand + Harry*. Harry, who couldn't be reached on the address and number that I'd found in Andre's diary, and who might be vitally important.

If I hadn't moved the keyboard, I would never have found that piece of paper. It made these names seem even more significant that they'd been hidden from view.

Robbert Brand was the only new name. I didn't think I'd seen it in relation to the Body in the Dunes. After all my study, I would have remembered it. A thought popped into my head. Brand. Theo Brand. I pushed that thought, and what it could mean, back down immediately. I folded up the piece of paper and decided that I wasn't going to show it to Julia. I didn't want the same thought that had popped into my head to pop into hers.

I looked around the office for anything that could give me a hint as to who Robbert Brand and Harry were. I scanned the clippings on the corkboard, but I didn't see them mentioned there. I studied every handwritten note but found nothing about either of them. I closely studied every one of the photos, but the only people I didn't know were the schoolkids in the photo with Paul Verbaan.

I went in search of Julia. She was sitting on the sofa looking through a pile of what were really a stranger's papers. A stranger who had been her brother.

'Do you know a Robbert Brand?' I asked her. 'Or a Harry?'

She glanced up from studying what appeared to be a gas bill. 'Harry Brand? No, I don't think so.' She shook her head and went back to opening drawers and cupboards.

I hadn't made Julia's assumption that Harry would be Harry Brand, but it seemed to make sense. 'Did you know Andre's friends?' I asked.

'Like his school friends, you mean?'

'Yes.'

'I knew some of the guys at the school, of course. But outside school, not really.'

Just then, someone knocked on the door. Julia looked at me for a second, then went back to sorting through bills as if that was a safe occupation that had to be done anyway.

People often resort to practical activities when they don't want to accept reality. I could only guess that coming to her brother's flat had made this all terribly real for her.

I went to the door and opened it to a woman with grey-streaked dark hair and black-rimmed glasses.

'Is Theo in?' she asked.

'He's not. I'm sorry.'

'I heard footsteps up here and he should be back from holiday by now.' She rattled a set of keys in front of me that looked similar to the ones Julia had. 'I've been feeding his cat.'

A cat? I'd seen no sign of a cat. It was probably hiding. Then I realised I'd also seen no sign of food bowls or a litter tray.

I showed the woman my badge. 'I'm a police detective from Amsterdam,' I said. 'This is Andre's sister, Julia.'

'Andre?'

'You probably know him as Theo Brand,' I said. 'I'm sorry to tell you that he died a few days ago.'

The woman took her glasses off and rubbed her eyes. 'I told him he shouldn't go,' she said.

III

The Murderer

Chapter 18

'You told him he shouldn't go?' I asked. 'You knew why he was going?' My heart rate sped up. Here, finally, was someone who might have known what Andre's thinking was when he came to Amsterdam. I turned to Julia. 'Can I leave you here by yourself? I'm going to have a chat with your brother's neighbour.'

'Of course,' she said and went back to looking through Andre's paperwork.

'I'm Carol Reynolds,' the woman said as she walked down the stairs in front of me.

She opened the door to the downstairs flat with a key. A fluffy grey cat tried to escape. 'No, Ginger,' she said. 'Stay here.'

I didn't understand why you would call a grey cat Ginger, but I didn't comment. It was probably a British thing.

'He's Theo's cat,' Carol said, 'but I thought he was probably lonely all by himself in that flat, so he's been sleeping downstairs.'

Well, that was one mystery solved. 'Did you know Theo well?'

'We got quite close over the last year. Have a seat.' She

gestured towards a sofa. Unlike Andre's flat upstairs, this place was immaculate. It still wasn't big, but as it wasn't cluttered, at least there was a sense of space. 'So you're from Amsterdam? Like Theo? He spoke such wonderful English,' Carol said. 'So do you,' she added with a beaming smile, as if it was a special compliment.

'Thanks,' I said, doing my best to keep the sarcasm out of my voice.

'We talked a lot after he got into a really bad accident last year.'

I thought about the scars the pathologist had pointed out on his leg. 'What happened?'

'He was taken out by a lorry on a roundabout. He was on his bike. It was really nasty. He was in hospital for weeks.'

'And they put him on strong painkillers,' I said.

Carol nodded. 'He didn't realise how addictive they were. I guess that's what killed him?'

'Yes.' It was interesting that she'd automatically known it had been suicide.

Tears started to roll down her face and she covered her eyes with her hands.

My phone beeped. 'Sorry about that,' I muttered, and switched it off. I was struck by how his downstairs neighbour had so far been the only one who'd cried for Andre. Julia had been angry with him at first. Daniel had hit him and left him a slew of messages.

'When he first got home from hospital, it was very hard for him to get up the stairs with his crutches, so I ended up helping him a lot. We started chatting.'

'You said you thought he shouldn't go to Amsterdam?' I wanted to get her to talk about that.

'He was having a tough time stopping taking the painkillers. He wasn't feeling well.' Carol wiped her face with the palms of her hands and took a deep breath. 'I didn't think digging up all the stuff about his past was a good idea.'

'Did he tell you about his past? Or what he was planning?'

'Well, he told me something weird about a month ago. I bumped into him near the shops and he seemed out of it a bit. I said: how are you? And he said: not great really. He said he was shaken up by his mother's death.'

I frowned. Julia had told me that her mother had died three years ago. Had he only just found out? Given the state of his relationship with his parents, I was surprised that he'd been upset. It must have been the realisation that he would never be able to make amends. He'd had thirty years to get back in touch and tell them he hadn't died. Maybe the shock was because he'd waited too long and missed the opportunity. 'When exactly was this?' I asked.

'Oh, I don't know. Late September, I think?'

'He really didn't know before?'

'I don't think so. He was very upset. He had no reason to lie to me.' She smiled, but tears started to stream from her eyes again. 'He was going through a tough patch anyway. He'd lost his job after the accident because he couldn't go to work for so long, and it probably all just got to him.'

I could see her point.

'He said he should find out what had happened.'

'With his mother?'

'I think so. What else could he have meant? We talked

about it again a week later. I bumped into him at Water-stones and we ended up having a coffee together at the café.' She stroked the cat. Ginger purred, seemingly unconcerned that his owner was never coming back again.

'And that was when you told him he shouldn't go to Amsterdam?' I asked.

'He said he had to do something, but he wasn't sure what. That seemed a weird decision, or no decision at all. Now I think he wanted to say goodbye to people or something like that. To people and to places. Get closure. That was what he was going to Amsterdam for.'

I could see why she thought that, but it didn't feel right to me. He'd said to Daniel that soon everybody was going to know. 'Did he tell you that everybody thought he'd been murdered?'

'He'd been murdered? How could that possibly be the case?'

'And you didn't know that his name wasn't really Theo? That his real name was Andre Nieuwkerk?'

'No, I had no idea. People really thought he'd been murdered?'

I nodded.

Carol kept talking, as if to herself. 'I don't know what I would do if I thought I'd been murdered. Or that everybody thought I had been. I would probably go to the police and tell them I was still alive.'

'Thanks for your time,' I said. I probably didn't have any jurisdiction to ask questions here, so I wanted to make sure it would just be seen as a chat. I also wanted to walk away from her suggestion about telling the police, because that was exactly what Andre had tried to do and I hadn't listened to him.

I returned to Andre's flat. Before heading back to the airport, I took one final look around the study, taking photographs of every centimetre of it. I wanted to document what Andre had been thinking. Who were Robbert Brand and Harry, and why were their names on the list of people that Andre had been going to see? What was their relationship to the murder? Suddenly I was keen to get back to Amsterdam and do some digging. To find out if there'd been a real Theo Brand.

I said a quick goodbye to Julia. It wasn't that I wasn't interested in seeing anything of London; it was more that I needed to get back to Amsterdam as soon as I could, so that I could talk to Robbert Brand and find this Harry.

'Already? You could stay overnight,' she said. 'I saw that there's a spare room.'

Even if I hadn't wanted to get back to Amsterdam straight away, I couldn't have slept in that bed, right underneath all the photos of people that Andre hated.

'Let me at least walk you to the station,' she added.

Because she sounded disappointed, I gave in. The quiet little street ended in a park with tennis courts, and we'd only walked fifty metres or so before we came to the wide water of the Thames.

'The flat is worth a fortune,' Julia said. 'I looked it up online. Maybe even more than half a million euros.'

'That's crazy,' I said. In the distance I could see a bridge and red double-decker buses crossing it. Rowing clubs named after schools lined the river's edge, as well as, at the end, a bar called The Rowing Club. It wasn't very original, but then I guessed it didn't have to be. The boats were stacked on shelves as if waiting for spring to return. They looked like the eights that would cross the Bosbaan in Buitenveldert. Maybe Putney was more like Buitenveldert than Watergraafsmeer.

If house prices here were like those in Buitenveldert as well, then maybe Julia's estimate wasn't far out.

'You haven't found a husband, have you?' Julia asked.

'Who, me?' That reminded me: I really should buy Mark a present at the airport.

Julia laughed. 'No, not you. Andre. He didn't have a husband, did he? Or a wife? I mean, I am his next of kin, aren't I? There isn't anybody else who's got a claim?'

'As far as I'm aware, you're it,' I said. 'Unless he'd made a will, of course.' Maybe he'd left all his money to the cat. Stranger things had happened.

'At least you can say you've seen something of London now,' Julia said. 'Double-decker buses, black cabs, the river; you've been as much of a tourist as you can be in three hours.'

As much of a tourist as I wanted to be.

We turned off the riverside and along Putney High Street. I had the same thought as I'd had when I'd first cycled to Laurens Werda's offices by the Amstel station. Here was another part in another city where the old and new made uncomfortable neighbours. A seventies cinema, houses that looked at least a hundred years old, modern buildings, run-down shops all stood side by side in a hotchpotch as if unable to decide which was more important: old or new. For

Julia it seemed that new definitely beat old. She was more interested in the money she was going to inherit than in her brother's death.

Could I blame her? What was it she'd said? That he'd seemed like a stranger to her? So maybe he was a stranger who'd suddenly left her a lot of money. 'How long are you going to stay for?' I said.

'Just another day. I should see something of London, shouldn't I, now that I'm here. But I want to be back in time to sort out the funeral.'

I wasn't sure that Andre would have wanted to be buried in Amsterdam, in the country he'd left behind, the country that he'd hated, according to Laurens, but I also knew that graveyards and memorials were for the living, not the dead. Unless Andre had left specific instructions for his burial, he no longer had a say in what was going to happen to his remains.

Julia and I said goodbye and I boarded the train at Putney to go back to Clapham Junction.

The train to Gatwick was busy and people were standing in the aisles with their suitcases. In the Netherlands there had been complaints recently amongst commuters that they had to stand in the morning when they'd paid for a ticket and therefore surely were entitled to a seat. Here, everybody seemed to placidly accept that they were packed in like sardines. Maybe if you had no choice in the matter it was better to just go with it. Better to get to Gatwick tired and hot than not get there at all.

I held on to a metal railing with one hand and checked my phone with the other. There were a number of messages from Mark, asking me where I was and to get in touch. I called him but got his voicemail. I put my phone away. I'd talk to him later.

At the airport, I decided that I should buy something for him at the duty-free, ready for Sinterklaas. As I strolled through the aisles trying to find something suitable, I called Thomas. I knew he was working today.

'Can you look into something for me?' I said as I picked up a teddy bear with a Union Jack waistcoat. 'I need you to check the records for a Theo Brand. Father's name is Robbert or possibly Harry.' I put the teddy bear back. It was too childish. A tin of biscuits? Alcohol?

'Theo Brand?' Thomas repeated. 'Our Theo Brand?'

'Yeah,' I said. 'I think Andre took someone else's identity. The name and the date of birth on the passport should match.'

Thomas said he'd get on it straight away.

I filled the fifteen minutes I had before my flight boarded by looking through the nice shops. If I was going to get Mark something, I might as well get him something he'd like. As I was milling around, I responded to his texts, telling him that I was away today but we could meet up tomorrow. Then changed that to say that I really wanted to see him tomorrow. That was better.

I didn't want to think about Andre. I'd been feeling so guilty for not talking to him that morning. Not that I thought I'd driven him to suicide, but I could have stopped him, had I known. This guy who had been abused as a child, who'd had a tough life and had never got over what had happened to him

And now I was thinking that he had taken someone else's identity.

All I could hope for was that he'd just stolen a passport.

The flight home was uneventful – we seemed to ascend and then descend again almost immediately – and I stared out of the window watching the sun set over the thick layer of cloud.

As we prepared for landing, I saw the fields of glasshouses and finally the pastoral setting as we landed on the Polderbaan. Before today, I hadn't been on a plane for years, probably not since the Polderbaan had been built. Even when I'd had my long holiday, I hadn't left the country. It was embarrassing how little of the world outside the Netherlands I'd seen. I'd never had an interest in foreign shores, never been part of the global tourism that took people as old as my father to places as far away as Thailand for a whole month. I'd never been to London before, but now all I'd done was go to the house of a dead man. I hadn't even had any interest in seeing the sights. Once I'd realised that there really had been a Theo Brand, all I'd wanted to do was get on the plane back home.

The Polderbaan was in the middle of nowhere, a good fifteen minutes of taxiing, to keep the noise levels down. I looked out of the window and saw a cow next to the runway. The cow told me I was home.

There was an announcement telling us that we were allowed to switch our phones back on. As soon as I had a signal, my phone beeped to let me know that Thomas had left me a message.

I listened to it straight away.

He'd found them. Parents Robbert and Barbara Brand. Two sons: Harry and Theo.

Theo had been reported missing thirty years ago.

I nearly laughed. I'd argued with Mark about Andre, had defended him when Mark had said he'd acted selfishly by staying away all these years.

Mark hadn't been entirely right. It hadn't been selfishness. It had been something else.

Had I felt guilty over the suicide of a murderer?

Chapter 19

The darkness of the room was broken only by a circle of light thrown by a standard lamp next to the sofa. It made the space small and eerie, as if there was something hidden in the corners that shouldn't be displayed. I wanted to look for an overhead light switch so that I could illuminate every centimetre of this space instead.

Robbert Brand was sitting on a black leather TV chair. Behind him, the curtains were closed to block anybody outside from looking in. It was odd, those curtains. Normally people kept their curtains open to show they had nothing to hide. What would this man have to hide? He was in his early eighties, with shrewd grey eyes that belied his age. According to Thomas, who had picked me up from the airport to drive me to the other side of Amsterdam through thick rain that threatened to turn into sleet, Robbert was very keen to talk to us about a man who had come to see him the other day.

'You were easy to trace,' I said.

'Yes,' Robbert said. 'We never moved from here. We never changed our number. We wanted him to be able to find us. To be able to call if he ever wanted to get back in touch.'

'Tell me about the visit.'

'It was on Sunday,' Robbert said.

Sunday. So not the evening before Andre died.

'The man said he had something to tell us about Theo.'

'What time was this?'

'It was in the morning. Around ten o'clock, I think. Something like that.'

'And you had no concerns about letting him in?'

Robbert's hands gripped his knees. 'I would talk to anybody who had something to tell us about Theo.' He grimaced. 'We pretty much have over the last thirty years.'

'So what did he tell you?'

'He said . . .' Robbert swallowed. 'He said that he thought Theo was the Body in the Dunes. That he'd been murdered thirty years ago. It was weird.' He rubbed his face. 'I've always said I just wanted to know what had happened to Theo, but this really threw me. I knew about the Body in the Dunes, of course; the police came and talked to us when that skeleton was found, but I thought it had been identified. We followed the case at the time. I remembered that I was jealous of that family for having answers, but at the same time grateful that it wasn't Theo, because it meant we could still have hope.' He shook his head. 'I knew I was crazy for feeling both those things at the same time. I remember being torn inside, not knowing what I wanted. Anyway, the police ruled Theo out because apparently he'd moved to London. He'd renewed his passport there in 1991. October 1991, they said.'

Of course. That would have been enough to rule him out because it would have shown that he had still been alive at that point. But now I couldn't help thinking that it was Andre, not Theo, who'd renewed the passport.

'How old was Theo when he went missing?' Thomas asked.

'He was seventeen when he left home. Turned eighteen a month later. We talked on his birthday. We still talked over the next few months – he would call us every now and then – but then it stopped and we haven't heard from him since. That was thirty years ago.'

'When did you talk to him last?'

'I think it was May, early May of 1988.'

'What did you think had happened?'

'We really weren't sure. At first we thought he just needed some space; isn't that what they say these days?'

Thomas nodded.

Photos on the mantelpiece showed the Brands frozen for ever in happier times, when there had still been four of them. It was a typical family portrait, the boys standing behind the seated parents, and if it wasn't for the fact that Theo would never come home again, you would think it was a happy picture. Harry and Theo looked alike, both blond and with toothy grins.

'But when the silence lasted and lasted, when he never picked up the phone when we called, when he didn't even send a card on his mother's birthday, that's when we started to worry. We thought something had happened to him.'

'No arguments?'

'Of course we had arguments: what time we wanted him to be home, how much pocket money we were giving him, but they were typical run-of-the-mill things and they were largely in the past. Harry was always annoyed,' Robbert added with a smile. 'He said we gave Theo much more freedom than we'd given him at the same age.'

'What did you say to the man who came to see you?'

'I said that I didn't believe him because we all knew that the Body in the Dunes was Andre Martin Nieuwkerk. But then he said that was him. *He* was Andre Nieuwkerk and the body had been misidentified all those years ago.'

'Did he tell you why he thought it was Theo?'

'No,' Robbert said. 'He just said it was what he believed.'

Thomas and I exchanged a glance. We'd agreed that we wouldn't mention that Andre had been using Theo's identity. We were curious as to whether Andre had told the Brand family that himself. I also knew that telling them this would lead the family to conclusions that I wasn't yet ready to draw.

'Did he tell you why he believed it?'

'I asked him, but he refused to tell us. He just said: I thought you needed to know.'

I wanted to scream in frustration. All along Andre seemed to have told people things without giving any proof to back them up. He would tell them one thing but keep another ten things to himself. As if he was giving the answer to a quadratic equation without showing his workings. It was the kind of thing that would get you low marks on your maths paper in school. It was the kind of thing that made people wonder if they should believe you or not.

'Was he right?' Robbert said. 'Was the body misidentified?'

'Yes,' I said. 'The man who came to see you was definitely Andre Nieuwkerk.'

Robbert's face showed the struggle he had been describing before, between getting answers and not liking what those answers were. 'We should talk to him,' he said.

I shook my head. 'We can't. He died last week.'

Robbert raised his hands to his mouth. 'But we need to know.' There were tears in his eyes. 'Before I die, I need to know.'

I felt sorry for him. I wanted to rest my hand on one of his, which were gripping his knees so tightly. I wanted to give him the answers he so desired, but the bones of the Body in the Dunes had been cremated all those years ago and the ashes had been scattered.

The sound of the key in the front door stopped me from having to reply.

'Harry,' Robbert shouted into the hallway as the door opened. 'The police are here to ask about that man who came to see us.'

And again the thought popped into my head that Andre had made matters worse for everybody he had talked to. He had unsettled people, raised all these questions and never given them answers. He had never given them any closure at all.

Harry came hurrying into the room, still wearing his coat and with a sports bag over his shoulder. 'The police?' He was short and skinny, with blond hair that was going a washed-out grey at the temples. He was two years older than Theo would have been, in his late forties, and wore a red and white checked shirt under a blue jacket. 'What are you doing, sitting here in the dark?' he said, and flipped the light switch on the wall. Suddenly nothing in the room was

193

hidden any more. More photos were revealed, all over the room. All of Theo. Some of them also had other family members in them, but it was Theo who smiled at me from all corners. It was unnerving to see the central position he still took within his father's everyday existence.

Apart from the fact that his hair was blond and Andre's had been dark, I could see a slight resemblance between the two faces.

'I'm Detective Lotte Meerman,' I said. 'You were here when Andre Nieuwkerk came to the house?'

'Yes,' Harry replied. 'On Sunday. Did you speak to him as well? Was he a fake?'

'No, he really was Andre Nieuwkerk,' Robbert said before I could answer the question. 'Didn't I say at the time that I thought he was the real thing?'

'What difference does it make?' his son said. 'He didn't know anything about Theo.' He took a seat next to me on the sofa, on the part closest to Robbert in his chair.

'Did Theo know Andre?' Thomas asked. 'Were they school friends?'

'No, not as far as I know,' Harry said. 'It was all speculation.'

'They couldn't have been friends,' Robbert said. 'Andre lived in another part of the country completely. Wasn't he from Elspeet? I don't know how the two of them could have met.'

'Why do you say it was all speculation?' I asked Harry.

'All the man said was that he thought the body might have been Theo. He didn't have any proof. He had no reason to say it.'

No reason to say it.

That was a very interesting point to think about. What had been his reason? Surely he wouldn't have come to this family and told them he thought their son had died if he hadn't been absolutely sure. He hadn't planned to visit the parents of any other missing boy, only the Brand family. If he was just guessing, it would be too cruel.

'How did he seem to you when he said it?' I said. 'Nervous? Determined? Sad? What did you think?' I didn't even want to consider the fact that he might have lied.

'Gosh, I don't know,' Robbert said. 'He wasn't a young man, I remember thinking that. Probably the same age as our Harry. I would say that he was calm, not nervous.'

'Was he holding something back?'

'You mean you think he might have had more information than he gave us?'

'Something like that.'

'Well, we got annoyed with him for coming here. What was the point of saying those things about Theo and then just leaving without giving us anything?'

'Do you think Theo's dead? That he's really the Body in the Dunes?' Harry asked. 'Can we do a DNA test on those bones? That will tell us, won't it?'

'Those bones no longer exist,' Thomas said. 'Andre's parents cremated them and scattered the ashes.'

'You mean we might never find out?' Robbert said.

'I'll do whatever I can,' I promised. But I wasn't hopeful. 'Could you give me a couple of photos of Theo?' I wanted our forensics department to look at them and tell me if Theo and Andre had had similar-shaped skulls. Similar enough to explain the misidentification.

I chose two that showed Theo's face clearly but from different angles. I put them in my handbag and signalled to Thomas that we were done here.

As we left, I heard a voice call out to me.

'There's something else,' Harry said, catching us up by the car. 'I didn't want my father to hear.'

Chapter 20

'I'm really glad you came to see us,' Harry said, 'because I wasn't sure if I should call the police or not.' We'd walked to his house, which was only just around the corner from his father's place, and he led us through to the front room. Unlike at his father's house, here all the lights were on, but they only showed that the place looked quite sterile; the home of someone who didn't care about his surroundings. There were no family photos. There were no visual signs that anybody else lived here.

'I didn't know what to do after he'd been to see us,' he continued. 'I didn't know if he was crazy or if I should take what he'd said seriously.'

I could understand that. 'Did you believe him?'

'I didn't know what to think,' he said. 'I wasn't sure if I should believe that he was right, and that we would finally know what had happened to my brother, or if I should wish he was wrong and then I could keep hoping that Theo was still alive.'

'What exactly did he say?' I asked.

Harry looked at a pile of papers in the centre of the table, as if all the answers were written down somewhere within that stack. 'He asked if Theo had gone missing, and said he thought he was probably the dead boy.'

'Did he say why he thought that? How he knew?'

'No, he didn't. I asked him, but he wouldn't say.'

'Start from the beginning,' I said. 'He called you?'

'No, my ex-wife called me and said there'd been another nutter — her term, not mine — at the house.'

'Why did she say the man was a nutter?'

'We've had a lot of people contact us over the years. People who want to make money out of us, crazy people, swindlers. A lot of psychics,' he said with a hint of sarcasm in his voice. 'The number of people trying to take advantage of our grief never ceases to amaze me. A man came a month after we placed the first ad and claimed he was Theo.' Harry's voice was gruff. 'He was the right age. We believed him for a bit. We wanted to believe him, I guess.'

'Why did he contact you?'

'All he wanted was money,' Harry said. 'It was frightening in a way, how much he knew about Theo. He knew which school he'd gone to, he knew the names of some of his friends. He'd done his research. He even looked a bit like him. I wondered if that was what gave him the idea.'

'Did you report him to the police?'

'What was the point? We didn't actually give him any cash. We had dinner a few times; he came round to visit us.'

'And then he asked for money?'

'Yes. He was going to buy a house and asked us if we could help. Not with the mortgage, just a couple of hundred euros to help him furnish the place. But we got suspicious. Well, actually I already was suspicious.'

198

'Did you ask for a DNA test?'

'No, I just followed him for a bit. He wasn't particularly careful. I found out his name and tracked down his parents. He clearly wasn't Theo. I called him, told him what I knew and told him never to visit my father again. Katja thought that the guy who'd come to see me was another one of these.'

'Your ex-wife's name is Katja?'

'Yeah.'

That was the woman I'd talked to who'd told me there was no Harry living at that address. I could understand why she'd refused to let Andre in, but I thought she should have told me about that when I called her. It would have saved us a lot of time.

Maybe I should run Harry Brand's records to see if he'd ever been in trouble with the police. 'Are you still registered at that address?' I wondered why Andre had gone there if Harry no longer lived there. He'd found Julia and Daniel's details without any problems.

'We divorced not that long ago and I moved here.' He scratched his forehead. 'It's been good to live close to my dad, especially after my mother died.'

'Your mother? When did she die?'

'In September.'

The hairs at the back of my neck stood up. It wasn't Andre's mother who'd died but Theo Brand's. This seemed significant to me, even if I couldn't figure out why. He'd cried about the death of Theo's mother. Had he known her? Had he realised what he'd done to the parents of the man whose identity he'd taken? Had that been when he'd decided to come here and tell them . . . tell them what? The truth? A version of the truth?

'I created a family tree on every family history website I could find. I always thought maybe Theo would look there. At Mum's funeral, I kept looking for him. I kept thinking that maybe he was going to turn up. But he never did.' He looked down at his papers again. 'Only more scam artists got in touch.'

'That's why you didn't believe Andre.'

'Well,' he said, 'there wasn't much to believe. He asked if I knew about the Body in the Dunes and said he thought that might be Theo. And I said: but the police identified that body. That man was Andre Nieuwkerk. And he said, no, because *he* was Andre. That can't be right, can it? I can't believe that he's been alive all this time and never told his family.'

'It was him,' Thomas said. 'That man was definitely Andre. We ran a DNA test with his sister and confirmed it.'

'His parents buried the wrong body? They've thought all this time that their son died?' Harry shook his head. 'That's cruel, isn't it? I mean, him knowing that his parents believed he was dead and not setting them straight, that's . . . that's extraordinary. Are any of his family still alive?'

'Just his sister.'

'She must be ecstatic.' His voice held a hint of bitterness that might have come from jealousy.

'Andre's dead,' Thomas said. 'He killed himself four days ago.'

Harry leaned back. 'So we can't talk to him any more. We've got no way of telling if the dead guy was Theo.'

He'd cottoned on quickly to what the real problem was. 'We have no idea,' I said honestly. 'All I know is that Andre seemed to think it was possible, from what he told you. That's why I want to know exactly what he said. Why he thought it was Theo. Something must have given him that idea.'

'I wish I'd recorded the conversation,' Harry said. 'As far as I can remember, he didn't actually say why he thought that.'

'Was it possible that they knew each other?'

'We followed the case at the time,' Harry said, 'because Theo had gone missing. I'd never heard of Andre before then. I didn't know him. They hadn't gone to school together.'

So maybe they had purely been two runaways who'd met somewhere, and somehow one of them had ended up with the other's passport.

'And you met Andre just that one time? He only came here once?'

'Yes,' Harry said. 'He apologised. He said he was really sorry for what had happened.' He glanced down at his hands. 'I'm sure he wouldn't have come here if he thought Theo was still alive.' He looked up. 'My father has never given up hope. He still believes my brother is alive.'

'He told me he just wants to know what happened to him.'

Harry shook his head. 'That's what he says, but I don't actually think it's how he really feels. He still hopes that he just ran away, or that he was in an accident and lost his memory.' He rubbed his hand through his greying hair. 'Dad's had a lot of crazy theories over the years. It's what's been driving him all this time, following up on anybody who said they'd seen someone who looked like Theo in some part of the country. Once he even travelled to Portugal and met with this Dutch man, who was very nice about it.'

'What do *you* think happened to your brother? Not what you want to believe,' I added quickly, 'but how you feel, deep down, after having met Andre. What was your instinctive reaction? That can often be useful.'

Harry folded his arms as if he wanted to keep the answer inside, but in the end he didn't shy away from saying the words. 'I think maybe he spoke the truth. That it was my brother who was killed thirty years ago. That it was my brother whose body decayed into the Body in the Dunes. I didn't tell my father, but it sounded to me as if Andre had information about Theo's death. More than just guesswork. That's what I didn't want him to hear. It would be so hard on him.'

'What gave you that idea?'

Harry looked me in the eye. 'Why would he have come here otherwise? There were quite a few young men who went missing around the same time. He didn't visit anybody else, did he?'

I thought back to the list I had seen on Andre's desk. 'No, you're right. I found your name on a piece of paper in his study, but nobody else's.'

As Thomas drove us back, I wondered which was worse: thinking your brother was dead and then finding out he was still alive, or thinking he was alive and then realising he'd been dead all along. It wasn't actually a competition, of course.

It all depended on whether you preferred hope or closure. Both families were in the worst possible position right now. If they believed Andre, then Theo Brand's family had had their hopes dashed without finding any answers. Julia had found out that her brother had still been alive, but now he was dead anyway. I wouldn't wish their situation on anybody.

Deep down inside, I thought both families had been better off before Andre had come back to the Netherlands and talked to them all.

Chapter 21

'Are you going to tell me how you found out about Theo Brand?' Thomas said. 'You know how much I love finding out what's going on after the event.'

'Do you want to go for a drink?' I was tired. It had been a long day, and a beer would round it off nicely.

He looked at his watch. 'Sure, I can say my shift's finished for the day.'

'Or you can have something non-alcoholic and call it work.'

'I don't know. I've got a feeling I need a stiff drink for this conversation.'

This wasn't a particularly appetising part of town. Grey blocks of flats lined a busy road. On the other side of the street, across the four lanes and the tramline in the middle, there was a kebab shop that looked as if it would give you instant food poisoning. From the debris on the street, there must be a KFC west of here. Next door, a tiling showroom was already closed. Two doors down there was a bar with posters for upcoming gigs covering the windows. I suggested going there. There was something about being a police detective, and being accompanied by another police detective, that made you unafraid to drink anywhere.

It was only after we'd gone in that I realised we were probably the same age as the parents of everybody else in here. It wasn't dangerous – the vibe was pretty chilled – but it was mortifying to feel that I was an old person compared to the rest of the people here. The ceiling of the bar was low, as if the four storeys of flats above were pressing it down. Thomas and I exchanged a glance, agreeing wordlessly that the only thing more embarrassing than being in a bar filled with kids two decades younger than us would be to head straight out again. I walked up to the bar and ordered our beers. I wondered how many of these kids would actually be underage if we carded them. I also wondered what it was about this place that attracted them. There must be a university department somewhere close by.

The good thing about being old in the company of young people was that they all thought we were very uninteresting. When you're embarrassed, it's probably for the best that you're ignored. I was even more embarrassed when one of the kids by the bar got up from his stool and offered it to me. Not embarrassed enough to refuse the seat, of course. I was grateful for it. Even though I'd been sitting down for most of the day, on planes and trains, I was shattered.

Thomas stood behind me for a few seconds, until the kid on the next stool got up too. Thomas must have given him the kind of stare that could make people confess. And give up their seats.

He sat down on the vacated stool. 'How was your day?' he asked, as if we were two mates catching up instead of two detectives trying to make sense of what was going on. 'I'm guessing you weren't in London to go Christmas shopping.'

'No, but that reminds me: what are you giving your wife for Sinterklaas?'

'Nothing big, just the usual stuff.'

'What is she getting you?'

'I don't know, Lotte, it would spoil the surprise if I knew beforehand, wouldn't it?'

I paused as the barman put the two beers in front of us. 'What would you want her to get you?' I lifted the glass to my mouth.

'What's this about? You want to know what to get Mark?'

'No, not at all.'

'You're so obvious.' He laughed. 'What are you? Twelve? You were married before.'

'I know. It's been a few years, though. I want to get it right.'

'Okay, a chocolate letter, a book and something small and personal.'

'Like what?'

'Something he'd like.'

What *would* he like? Something to do with cooking, maybe. I'd seen a restaurant somewhere that did a knife-skills class, but that sounded like the kind of course that criminals would take. Maybe I should have got the teddy bear with the Union Jack waistcoat at the airport. I was beginning to understand why people bought tat like that.

'Just don't go overboard,' Thomas said. 'No big presents.'

'Okay. Got it. Something small that he'll like.' This was impossible. If only I had no time to think about it, I would probably do a better job.

'You didn't get him anything in London, then?'

'No, I went to Andre's flat with Julia.'

'Wait. What?'

'She asked me.'

Thomas shook his head. 'Only you would think it was a good idea to do that.'

'I'm not sure it was a good idea.'

'No kidding.'

'I thought I was helping this woman out, because it's been really rough on her. She was the one who reported her brother missing initially, not her parents, and in a way, she feels responsible for what's happened. I think that's why she's been feeling so conflicted.'

'And now?'

'And now I think . . .' I took a gulp of my beer to try to get my thoughts in order. 'Wait. Let me tell you what I thought before going to London. I thought Andre Nieuwkerk had left the Netherlands, and changed his name and his nationality so that he could never be found. That he'd been upset with his parents, that he was happy for his abuser to be questioned for his murder. Maybe he was letting it happen, and then when Verbaan killed himself, he couldn't go back on the lie he'd told. He certainly didn't make any effort to correct the mistake the police had made.'

'Yes,' Thomas said, 'I knew that's where your thinking was headed.'

'But now I feel that I've made quite a fundamental mistake. Now I know that Theo Brand wasn't a new name that Andre Nieuwkerk took.' I remembered what I'd thought when I'd first heard that Andre was using Theo Brand. I'd thought that it had been to indicate a Brand Nieuw, Brand new, identity. That's why I'd gone to the hotel with Charlie when the manager had called me.

'Now we know that Theo Brand is an existing person,' Thomas said. 'Or maybe he was an existing person to be more precise.'

'Right. Instead of Andre changing his name to Theo, he was using Theo's passport. He had taken Theo's identity. The identity of a person who the family has lost touch with over thirty years ago, a person who'd gone to London and changed nationality.'

'You think it was Andre who did that? Not Theo?'

'Wouldn't that have made him harder to trace? Or at least it made the family think that Theo had still been alive twenty-five years ago, when he did that. It was probably why Theo Brand had never been considered to be the Body in the Dunes.'

'You don't think Andre met him in London?'

I shook my head. 'No, I think Theo never left the Netherlands. I think Andre was right, and that Theo was the Body in the Dunes all along.'

'Two runaways met each other; one ended up dead, the other took his identity.'

I nodded. 'It makes you think, doesn't it?' In the corner, a group of young girls were laughing and shrieking as loudly as the flocks of parakeets that had invaded the Vondelpark.

Thomas narrowed his eyes. 'He could have killed him. Killed him, buried him, taken his passport and run away to London.'

I didn't want to think about this, but of course I could see the sense in Thomas's words. He was voicing what had been in the back of my mind ever since I'd found out that Theo Brand had been a real person.

'Yes,' I said. 'Yes, he could have done.'

Chapter 22

The next morning, I went to work early even though it was Sunday and my day off. I wanted to check everything we had on Theo Brand.

What I was interested in was whether there was another reason why the police had ruled out Theo as the Body in the Dunes, or whether it was based purely on his passport renewal.

I picked up one of the photos of Theo that his father had given me. The teenager was smiling widely. He shielded his eyes from the sun but was still squinting as he gazed into the light. He was wearing a pair of stone-dyed jeans. I remembered that I'd had a pair just like that when I'd been his age.

There could have been very good reasons why the initial team had thought the skeleton wasn't Theo's. I just had to find those reasons. The typed-up forensics report highlighted that the skeleton had no signs of previous fractures apart from those in the small bones in the neck that pointed towards strangulation as the cause of death. He was the same height as Andre. He was the right age.

In the files, I could find no good reason why the body couldn't have been Theo's.

The original investigation had ruled him out on the passport alone, but there was no way I could do the same.

I went down to the basement lab to talk to Forensics. I wondered what we would do today compared to the tools they had available twenty-five years ago.

Edgar Ling was typing up a report and seemed only too happy to be disturbed and asked about misidentified skulls. His blond hair showed the tracks of a comb.

'You're not distracting me. I like bones.' His face flushed pink. 'Sorry,' he said. 'That came out wrong.'

'It's okay.' I would sometimes say things like that myself, things to do with my work that in the context of normal conversation would make me sound like a very dangerous individual. I laid the photos down in front of him: the school photo of Andre Nieuwkerk, the photos of Theo Brand and the images of the skull that the initial investigative team had taken all those years ago.

'This is tricky,' he said. 'Do you have any other photos? Maybe from the side rather than full-frontal?'

I rummaged through the folder. Even though there were many photos of the skull and the rest of the skeleton from all angles, I couldn't find any more of Andre. His parents hadn't given the police much to go on. Four years after he'd left home, they might not have had any photos left. It was such a sharp contrast to the house of Theo's father.

'This is it,' I said.

He put the photos of the two teenage boys next to each other and studied them closely. 'To be honest, it could be either one of them.'

'If this wasn't an old case, would you feel comfortable opening a murder investigation into it?'

'That's a bit of a jump from wondering if it could be either one of these two. It's much easier to rule someone out than to think it's actually them. Especially from the photos. Look at this bit.' He pointed at the fringe on Andre's photo. 'With his hair like this, it's tricky to tell the shape of his forehead.' He shuffled through the photos of the skull, discarding them like my mother would discard her cards until he found one that had been taken from the same angle as Theo's photo. He put the two side by side and looked at them closely.

'I can picture the shape of people's skulls when I look at them,' he said. 'It's because I used to do forensic archaeology before I came here. I looked at a lot of skulls.'

'Can you see mine?' I joked.

He scrutinised my head. It was an odd sensation to watch his eyes trace my face's contours. 'If we find you dead,' he said, 'I'll know it's you.'

It made me laugh. 'If I decomposed to a nameless skeleton, you mean.'

'Exactly.'

'So these photos,' I said.

'It's really tricky.' He looked at them both again. 'No.' He shook his head. 'I wouldn't rule either one of them out. I'm really sorry.'

'You misunderstand.' I stood next to him and looked at the photos too. 'I don't necessarily want you to rule either one of them out. To know that you think both of them are possible is actually very interesting.' I pointed at the photo of Andre. 'We know it isn't him.'

'Oh, okay.'

'This is the man who killed himself the other week. Remember him?'

'The opioid overdose?'

'That's the one. Twenty-five years ago, they misidentified this skeleton. I now think it wasn't this boy,' I tapped on Andre's photo, 'but this one instead.'

Edgar nodded. 'I can have a look at the skull and check more photos and try and give you a better answer.'

'The skull no longer exists. All we have is those photos.'

'Ah. Okay. Well then the best I can do is to say that I wouldn't rule it out. It's possible. It's very possible.'

Back in our office, Charlie was standing at the whiteboard. Even he had come in at the weekend.

'We can wipe all of this, I guess,' he said.

'Why?'

'Thomas told me what you guys discovered last night.' He sounded disappointed to have missed the big moment. 'That Andre took Theo's identity. That Theo might be the Body in the Dunes. That Andre maybe killed him.'

I took the cleaner from his hand. 'Shall we find some evidence of any of this? Shall we actually try to make sure of it before jumping to conclusions?'

Charlie's eyes lit up. 'Do you think he didn't kill him?'

I took out my phone and showed him the photos I'd taken of the corkboard in Andre's study. 'This is all information that's in the public domain; what anybody googling Andre Nieuwkerk would have come up with. There isn't necessarily anything suspicious about any of these articles.'

Charlie looked through the images. 'Did it look as if he had been researching it for a while?'

I thought about that. 'Actually, no,' I said. 'It all looked new.'

Thomas came into the office. He threw a glance at what I was showing Charlie and then sat down at his desk. 'I've been thinking about this all night,' he said, 'and to be honest, Lotte, we might not be able to prove anything.'

'I know that, but I do think we should dig a bit deeper, don't you? We don't know anything apart from that Andre used Theo's identity and that there were two young men who looked alike enough to confuse our forensic scientists at the time.'

'But would it fit?' Charlie said.

I got up and went to the whiteboard, tapping on the horizontal timeline at the same dates that I'd pointed out to Charlie before. 'The skeleton was found in April 1993. They said that to have reached that stage of decomposition, the victim must have died between three and five years before then. Look here.' I drew a thick line from April 1990, the latest date of death according to Forensics, and February 1989, when Andre had been reported missing. 'Remember I said before that there was a fourteen-month window? Nobody ever tried to track Andre's movements after he'd gone missing, because they thought he'd been murdered.'

'In that time he could have met Theo,' Charlie said, 'and killed him.'

'Exactly. Nobody looked into that.'

'When did Theo's parents see him last?'

'It's a bit vague,' Thomas said. 'They believed he had gone to London, because he renewed his passport there in October 1991. They thought he was still alive then.'

I marked that date on my timeline too.

'But that's outside the time zone.'

'Exactly, so if Theo Brand is the Body in the Dunes, he was already dead at this point.'

'And Andre was using his passport,' Thomas said. 'Probably,' he added before I could say anything.

'Julia didn't think her brother had a passport,' I said, 'so if Andre and Theo met, it must have been here. In the Netherlands.'

'Or at least somewhere he could have gone without a passport,' Thomas said. 'He could have travelled from here to Paris, for example, and nobody would have checked.'

'I think it would have been tough to get into the UK without a passport.'

'But he got in on someone else's passport,' Charlie said.

'They looked enough alike for our forensic scientists to have got their identity wrong. I went down to the lab and checked with Edgar Ling just now, and he said he wouldn't rule out either guy as having been the Body in the Dunes. Of course he only had the photos, but there's no reason to assume the other team were incompetent when they misidentified him. The two of them looked similar.'

'And everybody thought Theo was still alive.'

'Right, so they didn't even know there were two guys who might have fitted that description.' I was thinking about how different the two young men looked because they had different-coloured hair. 'I guess Andre bleached his hair blond and could have passed for Theo easily enough, especially if the photo on his passport was a couple of years old.'

'That's a good point,' Thomas said. 'Theo was two years older than Andre.'

'Right, so the fifteen-year-old becomes an eighteen year-old. That must have made things easier for him too.'

'He was now legally an adult.'

'So you think Andre killed Theo at some point here?' Charlie drew a dotted line between the date on which Andre had gone missing and the end point of the decomposing window. 'That's roughly a year, sometime between February 1989 and April 1990.'

'If we could narrow that down, it would be helpful.'

Thomas nodded. 'If we could find out when he got to the UK . . .'

'We know he was there before October 1991, when the passport was renewed.'

'If Andre had killed him,' Charlie said, 'don't you think he would have gone to the UK immediately?' He shook his head. 'He must have been over the moon when he himself was declared dead. It meant he'd got away with murder.'

'And blamed it on his abuser,' Thomas added.

'Was that even true?' Charlie asked. 'Maybe he wasn't abused at all. Maybe all of it was a lie.'

'I'll look into that,' Thomas said. 'Didn't he tell Daniel that there had been other kids who had reported Verbaan?'

'But they withdrew their statements,' Charlie said.

Thomas shrugged. 'That's not that unusual. Sometimes people come forward to stop someone from abusing more victims. When that person is dead, the reason will have disappeared. They might no longer feel the need to go through painful memories, to go through something that is difficult for them to talk about. What I'll do is check the archives. The names of those accusers will still be there. We can follow up with a couple of them. It will be straightforward enough to confirm that.'

I went outside. The rain pummelled the little courtyard garden. This was one of those rare moments when I wished I smoked. A couple of my colleagues were huddling underneath a tiny awning to get their nicotine fix without drowning. A scream of frustration sat right at the bottom of my throat, ready to be unleashed towards the sky. Only the smokers stopped me from letting it out. They were already looking at me full of curiosity. I took another step forward and let the rain wash away some of my frustration. I stayed there until both my colleagues had finished their cigarettes. The rain plastered my hair against my skull. The coolness calmed me, but I would look a mess.

On the way back to our office, I popped into the ladies' and dried my hair with a paper towel. I stared at myself in the mirror. This was insane. I'd felt guilty for turning away a suicidal man, and now I was thinking that he might have been a murderer. I held my hand under the tap to cool the inside of my wrist. I had a brush in my handbag, but that was in the office. I pulled another paper towel from the dispenser and rubbed it vigorously over my head. I looked like a hedgehog. I combed my hair back with my fingers and tied it at the nape of my neck. It would have to do.

I thought I'd better talk to someone who had knowledge of Andre's London history. I put a call in to Laurens Werda.

Chapter 23

Charlie and I crossed Amsterdam to go to Laurens' house. It was Sunday morning. He was at home. There must be something good about having a normal job, because then you didn't have to work at the weekend.

'Thanks for seeing us,' I said.

'That's fine. At least I'm not one of those people who goes to church religiously.' He smiled at his own pun.

I put a polite smile on my face. 'What did Theo tell you about his life before you met? What did he do?'

'Are you still calling him Theo? He's Andre Nieuwkerk, isn't he?'

'How do you know that?'

'I read about it. Someone sent me a link to the story. I couldn't believe it at first.'

'You had no idea?'

'No, none. It was the name you asked me about as well, wasn't it? Andre Martin Nieuwkerk. When you came to see me.'

'Yes. Okay, we can call him Andre then. When you met him, he was already in London, wasn't he?'

'Yes, I met him in the late nineties.'

'What did he do?'

'He worked in a clothes shop. He was the manager. He loved clothes.'

'Had he worked there for a while?'

'Yes, he was very proud of that. He left school without any qualifications, started as a sales assistant in London and then worked his way up. He worked as a store manager and was one of their main fashion buyers by the time we split up, ten years later.'

I nodded. That made sense. 'Do you know when he moved to London?'

'I'm not sure. But I know that he became a British citizen in 1995 and I think you have to have been in the country for five years before you can apply for that. So maybe in 1990? Sorry, I'm really not sure of the dates, we didn't talk about that much.'

'Did he seem reluctant to discuss it?'

'Reluctant? No, not really. More that it didn't really come up as such. But I'm pretty sure he wouldn't have wanted to be buried here.'

'His sister is dealing with that.'

'His sister? Why?'

'She's his next of kin.'

'I don't think Andre would have wanted his sister to arrange his funeral.'

'Why do you say that? Did he say anything like that to you? Did he mention his sister?'

'No,' Laurens said. 'He didn't talk about her at all.'

'Did you know he even had a sister?' I asked him.

'Well, he mentioned he had, but that they'd lost touch. I

220

always thought she had something to do with his tough childhood.'

'Did you know that his family thought he'd died? Did you not know about that?'

'No, I had no idea. Even though he was often secretive, I'm surprised he'd have kept something like that from me.'

'What do you mean, secretive?'

'That was probably the wrong word. It's just that he was a very private person. He never talked about his parents much, or his sister. He didn't want to discuss his childhood, even though you'd think we'd talk about Dutch things together. I didn't think anything of it at the time. I knew his relationship with his parents was terrible, but that was all. I had no idea about the abuse or that he had been thrown out of the house.' He rubbed his hand over his head. 'Maybe I shouldn't interfere. I should let her get on with it. I'm sorry to have mentioned it to you,' he added.

Chapter 24

Julia called me the next day. She had come back to the Netherlands and told me that one of her old classmates had got in touch, a man who'd been in the same class as her and Daniel in Elspeet. He said he wanted to talk to her. He'd read about Andre and thought there were things she needed to know. I asked her if she remembered this man, remembered what kind of kid he'd been at school.

Quiet, she said. The kind of kid who wouldn't have talked.

It was when she said things like that that I was reminded she was a social worker. She was looking at things differently today than she would have done at the time.

I cycled to my flat to pick up my car. Last night, I'd gone to Mark's house to spend the evening with him. I'd told him about my London trip with Julia and how I'd talked to her and made amends. He said that he trusted my professional judgement on whether to ask someone questions or not. Then we hadn't talked about the case any more and had sat down for a nice dinner.

I picked Julia up at her place and drove both of us to the guy's house in one of the small villages not far from Amsterdam. As we sped through the relentless flatness of the polder, the early-morning sun created golden edges along the thick dark clouds and I could see as far as I wanted; nothing interrupted my view. The long, straight road followed a small canal from field to field. There were no other cars. There was just Julia and me on this road late in the morning.

When the door to the farmhouse opened, we were greeted by a woman who only came up to my shoulder. I was conscious of wanting to bend down to speak to her. Her blue trousers were clean and she wore pink slippers with pompoms at the front.

'Hi, I'm Julia Nieuwkerk. Kars called me. I arranged to see him?'

The woman stuck out her hand. 'Frida Borst,' she said.

'Detective Lotte Meerman,' I introduced myself. I wasn't sure what exactly Kars had to tell us. It could be purely personal, but I wasn't going to run the risk of being accused of subterfuge.

She showed us through to the kitchen and called her husband on his mobile. He would join us in a few minutes, she said.

We sat at the large table and were offered cups of filter coffee, which I gratefully accepted. One wall of the kitchen was adorned with photos of family holidays; they all seemed to be in winter. Smiling children and parents. Three children. I got up and looked at the pictures more closely. Dark-haired mother, blond father, two dark-haired children, one blond.

'You like winter sports?'

'It's busy on the farm in summer.'

There was silence again and I drank my coffee. 'This is a lovely house,' I said, looking around the kitchen.

She made a disapproving noise, as if I'd said something out of order. Her mouth tightened until it looked like a prune, pulled into wrinkles that hadn't been there before. 'We liked it here,' she said. She poured more coffee into her mug, but spilled it over the edge. She grabbed a dishcloth from the sink and scrubbed the coffee away with more force than was needed.

I didn't know what I'd said to upset the woman. I stopped the small talk, as it wasn't doing any good, and took a gulp of coffee.

The outside door opened and the farmer, Julia's classmate, came in: a man in his early forties, in blue overalls. He took off his wellies in the corner of the kitchen that was specific-ally used for this: multiple pairs stood underneath a row of coats. He stepped into a pair of slippers and came further into the kitchen. His wife poured him a coffee without ask-ing. I wouldn't have automatically picked him out as a farmer; like his wife, he seemed too slight a figure, a man who would depend on tractors rather than dig himself. But then what did I know about farming?

'Julia,' he said. 'It's been a while. Do you remember me?'

'Of course I do.' She introduced me and we shook hands. His hands were clean but I could feel the rough skin and calluses when he gripped mine.

'I never really talked about what happened,' he said as he pulled out a chair to join us at the table. His wife put his coffee in front of him, then sat next to him and put her hand on his thigh. 'When the story about your brother initially broke, when they identified the skeleton, the police came to school. Do you remember that?'

Julia nodded. 'I do.'

'I talked to them then. We weren't taught by Verbaan any more at that point – we'd moved to another class years before – but I told the officers some of what had happened. Then, when he killed himself, it seemed that everything was in order. It was all fine. There was no point dragging his name through the mud any further.'

'How old were you then?'

'Seventeen, the year we were all graduating.'

'Not dragging his name through the mud,' I said. 'Was that your decision?'

'It was what my parents said. I think they also wanted to protect me. They were shocked when they found out.' He looked at Frida. 'It was harder to tell them than to tell the police. I hadn't told them about it before, it all happened because we weren't getting on.'

'What do you mean?' I asked.

'Verbaan preyed on kids who were lonely. Outsiders. Like I was, like your brother was.' He nodded at Julia. 'You knew that, right?'

'I didn't at the time,' Julia said.

'You knew your brother didn't fit in.'

'I knew that. I didn't know about the abuse.'

'I was really into art,' Kars said. 'I loved drawing, painting, that kind of thing. I didn't like sports, I didn't really like school, I just liked other things and Verbaan noticed that. He knew my parents were upset that I wasn't studying harder, that I wanted to focus on what they thought was just a little hobby. He'd talked to them at parents' evening. That was when he started to single me out. Take me aside, talk to me, tell me that it was possible what I wanted to do, that I was talented, that I was special.' He stopped talking.

Frida put her hand on his arm and squeezed it softly.

'Nobody had told me that before. I wanted him to keep saying it, so I . . . I did what he wanted me to do. I didn't like it, but I liked the attention. No, let's be honest. I was desperate for attention. I was desperate for anybody to think I was worth talking to. That I deserved someone's time. I was fourteen, I had no friends, no mates in school. I had nobody to talk to . . .' His voice trailed off.

'I'm sorry,' Julia said.

'I'm not saying it to have a go at you. I'm just telling you that this was what Verbaan did. This was what he was like. First your brother, then me. Two other kids came after me. I was angry. Not because of what he did, but because it turned out I wasn't special after all. Can you imagine? I think that's why I talked to the police. They say abuse victims often only speak out to protect others but I wasn't like that. I spoke out because I was jealous. It was a messed-up time.'

'It ended when you were no longer in his class?' I asked.

'No longer in his class, no longer fourteen, no longer young enough. Any or all of those reasons. You can pick. Part of me hates him, but there's a tiny piece of me that is grateful to him, because he did say that my art was important, that painting was important and that I should pursue it. That's what disgusts me about my art sometimes: that it was an abuser who made me take it seriously. That he was grooming me.'

'It's very common,' Julia said, 'to feel conflicted about abuse. But remember, he was right to encourage you. That was his job. He was right to give you time. You were not complicit in the abuse. You were fourteen. You were a kid.'

I was impressed with Julia. She'd gone into supportive-social-worker mode to help her ex-classmate. Even though this must be tearing her apart, she still said the right thing.

'I know that,' Kars said. 'Intellectually, I know. Emotionally, it's harder. Frida and I met at art school. I'd moved out of my parents' house. We argued too much. Verbaan gave me the name of a place that could help, can you believe it? That place helped me get into art school.'

He grabbed his cup, downed the last of his coffee and pushed himself up from his seat. 'Come out to the back. You might want to wear a pair of these. What size are you?'

I tried a few pairs of the most unflattering footwear known to man, then followed Kars outside.

He showed us a field where bulbs were planted and covered by a layer of hay. The next field was empty apart from high grass and impressive weeds. 'For the subsidies,' he said. 'I get paid more to leave it empty than I get for growing food. Who'd have thought it, with food prices where they are?'

'How long has it been empty?'

'Three years now. I'm not even allowed to keep cattle on it. Good for the bees, they say. It's good for my pocket.' He laughed. 'But it seems insane: prime land and we're not even farming it. Here's my studio.' He walked up to a large shed. 'I paint; Frida does mainly pottery.' He opened the double doors and I could see a sea of canvases: wild flowers, the coast, fields with animals. I liked them. I could tell what they were.

'Do you get any government subsidies for your art?' I asked. Maybe we could hang some of them at the police station.

Chapter 25

I went to have lunch in the canteen. I had a cheese sandwich, an apple and a glass of milk and stared out over the water. It was turning out to be another nice sunny day and I watched a few tourists sitting outside on a bench with their own lunch. It was as if we were eating together.

As soon as I got back into the office, I could almost feel the crackling of tension in the air. Charlie gave me the accusing look of a dog who'd been left alone for too long. Thomas only stared. I didn't want to think about what had happened while I'd been out. I wasn't going to ask.

After Thomas left to have his lunch, Charlie checked his watch and suggested we have a coffee. To round off my meal, he said. He'd like my advice on something. I wasn't sure what he wanted to talk about. Maybe Thomas had said something that told Charlie more about the opinion he had of him.

'Shall we go to the little café around the corner?' he said.

'Sure,' I said. I knew the one he meant; they did good coffee there. I didn't know what had happened, but things must be pretty rough if he wanted to talk to me away from the police station.

I followed him across the bridge. The lights were on in the large houseboat moored in the water behind the police station. Some days you could see the couple who lived there eating their lunch together. Today I didn't see them. If the lights had been off, I would have assumed they were out, or still asleep, but now I wondered where they were.

Did they know we watched them most mornings as we came into work?

If I'd been by myself, I might have waited on the bridge until either one of them showed themselves, but now I just kept walking and entered the café with Charlie.

He ordered our cappuccinos from the guy behind the bar. I offered to pay but he refused. I was about to joke that I was impressed that he knew what coffee I liked when I noticed him nodding to a guy sitting at a table by the window. The man was handsome, with black hair and darkish skin. He wore the uniform of a traffic officer, and his thick fluorescent jacket was hanging over the back of his chair.

'One of your former colleagues?' I asked Charlie. He'd been a traffic cop before he joined us in CID.

'Yeah, let's sit with him,' Charlie said, and he carried our coffees over before I could point out that I thought he'd wanted to talk to me about something.

'What's this about, Charlie?' I said.

'He wants to ask you a favour.'

I narrowed my eyes. I could tell I was being set up for something. I pulled the chair out and sat down.

'It's about the man who beat up Peter de Waal,' Charlie's mate said.

Now why would a policeman of Turkish descent want to talk to me about Peter de Waal's assault? 'You know him?' I asked.

The man had the good grace to look sheepish. 'His father and my father are cousins.'

At least he didn't lie. I stirred my cappuccino even though it had no sugar in it and it would only mess up the foam. 'I'm sorry, what's your name.'

'Mehmet. Mehmet Yilmaz.'

'Mehmet Yilmaz.' I got my notebook out of my handbag and slowly wrote it down. 'I wonder if I should tell anybody about this little chat we're having. You want to convince me that he's innocent?'

Mehmet blushed, and shuffled on his chair. 'He said you talked to him the other day, and I didn't know what to make of that. You've got a reputation for . . .'

'For what?'

'For investigating things properly. Maybe he beat this guy up. Maybe he didn't. I don't know. But I know some other people are completely convinced he did it without looking into it.'

'And you said you didn't think he did,' Charlie said. 'That's what I told Mehmet.'

'Seriously?' I turned to face him. Maybe Thomas was right. Maybe Charlie was very stupid, or just too naïve for words. Either way, he really was rubbish at the political shenanigans.

'That *was* what you said, wasn't it?' The tone of his voice was that of a small boy disappointed in his mum. But what mattered here wasn't whether I thought Erol was guilty or not; it was that Charlie had set up this meeting away from

231

the police station. I wasn't sure whose idea that had been, but they could have come and talked to me in our office.

I held my coffee cup between both hands, leant back and had a good look at Mehmet Yilmaz. I could see the family resemblance: he was built in the same way as his cousin. Like I'd thought about Erol, I also wouldn't be surprised if Mehmet could floor a man with a single punch. Maybe that was more useful for a police officer than for someone who had been harassing his ex-wife.

Mehmet squirmed under my scrutiny. He seemed embarrassed.

Erol would have looked angry.

'Do you know your cousin well?' I asked.

'He's not my cousin. My father—'

'Whatever.' I cut short the family explanation. 'Do you know him well?'

'Not that well. I've met him a number of times, of course, but we're not friends.'

'He wasn't really forthcoming with answers,' I said.

Mehmet nodded. 'I know. He can be like that.'

'He's older than you?'

'A couple of years.'

'You know this isn't our case, don't you?'

'Yes.' Mehmet shot Charlie a glance. 'I know.'

'And it's a bit of an insult,' I folded my arms, 'to assume the team wouldn't do the right thing.'

'No, no, it's not that. It's that . . . Peter de Waal's wife, you know who she is, right?'

'She's Erol's ex-wife.'

'Exactly.' He paused for a second. 'So here's a Turkish guy

232

whose Dutch ex-wife shacked up with her high-school boyfriend. Then the new husband gets beaten up. What do you think everybody is going to think?'

'He had a restraining order. It's got nothing to do with his background.' But I understood his concern.

'You actually believe that? I know what people think. I'm just asking you to not see the Turkish guy with the restraining order.'

'Okay, instead I'll see the guy whose cousin was desperate to talk to me.' I smiled to pretend I was joking. I didn't think Erol was guilty, but I knew the pressure those TV interviews were putting on the team, and suddenly I wasn't so sure any more that this was all going to work out fine without my interference. 'Check if he's taken a photo of his hands as I told him to. If he hasn't, get him to do it straight away. With a witness if possible. And make sure he can prove which day it was taken.'

'Why?' Mehmet said. 'Are you trying to stitch him up?'

I shook my head. 'Didn't you want to talk to me because I was impartial? Then just get him to do it.'

'He should take photos of himself?' Charlie asked me.

I wasn't going to fill in the details. Let them figure it out. I stared out of the window, pretending this had nothing to do with me, and let the two guys discuss it amongst themselves. The less I said, the better. I didn't think I'd done anything here that could be seen as actively damaging Ingrid's case. If I made the new member of our team do some thinking, surely that was a good thing.

'If he'd beaten up that guy, there would have been cuts and bruises on his hands,' Charlie said.

Good boy, I wanted to say, but I kept quiet. I was pretty sure I hadn't told Charlie why I believed Erol Yilmaz was innocent.

Mehmet thanked me and headed out. He obviously understood the significance of this. Through the window, I could see him getting his phone out. I hoped he was calling his cousin to have those photos taken. They might need proof of his innocence. Or at least proof that the assault hadn't happened the way Peter de Waal stated.

I took a gulp of my coffee. 'Don't do that again,' I said to Charlie.

Because I knew that even though we hadn't really done anything we shouldn't have, it wouldn't give a good impression if anyone found out about this meeting.

Chapter 26

I went to talk to the chief inspector. As soon as I told him what we'd discovered about Andre using Theo Brand's identity, and Theo going missing right around the time that the Body in the Dunes was murdered, he insisted on calling the commissaris to join us. It didn't surprise me at all.

It was probably a sign of how seriously Commissaris Smits was taking this that he came down to the CI's office rather than making us go up to his. Or maybe he felt he hadn't been commissaris for long enough yet to summon us upstairs.

'Tell me what happened,' he said before he'd even sat down.

'I went with Julia to London, to Andre Nieuwkerk's flat, and I found a note of the people he'd been planning to see on his visit. One of the names was Robbert Brand, and that made me think that maybe Andre hadn't just changed his name but had taken someone else's identity.'

The commissaris took a pen out of the inside pocket of his jacket. 'Can I use this?' he asked the CI, pointing at a notepad that was lying on his desk. At the CI's nod, he tore a page out, folded it in four and started writing on it balanced on his knee.

It would have been easier to just use the notepad itself.

'So there really was a Theo Brand?' the commissaris said.

'Yes.'

'Please tell me he's still alive.'

I shook my head. 'His family haven't heard from him in over thirty years.'

'And Nieuwkerk was using his identity?'

'Yes. We think Theo Brand left home some time before Andre Nieuwkerk did. I'm assuming the two of them met at some point.'

'Give me some dates here. What facts have you got?'

'Theo Brand's parents last spoke to him in early May 1988. Andre Nieuwkerk went missing in February 1989. Theo Brand's passport was renewed in London in October 1991, and his family thought he had moved to the UK. I now think it was Andre who did this.'

'Any evidence for that?'

'No evidence.' But before the commissaris could ask another question, I added, 'It wasn't Theo who renewed the passport because he'd already been killed. He could have been the Body in the Dunes.'

The commissaris looked at me. 'Why do you think that?'

'Nieuwkerk met with Theo Brand's family and suggested it. Then I showed photos to Forensics – of Theo Brand and of the skull – and they said they couldn't rule it out.'

'Nieuwkerk met with Brand's family?'

'His father and his brother. Andre's neighbour in London said he had been very upset about a month ago when he found out about his mother's death. But his mother died three years ago. It was Theo's mother who died recently.'

236

'No,' the commissaris said. He tapped his pen on the piece of paper. 'This makes no sense.'

I looked at the CI as if to get some support, but he stayed quiet. 'What doesn't?' I finally said.

'Why would he be upset when a woman he'd never known died?'

'Because he felt guilty?'

The commissaris shook his head. 'I'm not buying it,' he said. He looked up at me. 'And I'm not just saying that because you wanted me to do a press conference about a guy who now might have murdered someone.'

I wondered if he was laughing at me.

Well, it was better than being shouted at.

'I'm not suggesting Nieuwkerk necessarily killed Theo Brand. His actions don't seem to imply that.'

'Because why come and see Theo's family if that was the case.' The commissaris nodded. 'I get what you're saying.'

'He could just have got the papers from somewhere,' I said. As soon as the words left my mouth, they suddenly made sense. 'Maybe he thought he'd acquired a forged passport and was shocked to find out that Theo Brand had been a real person.'

'Did they look alike?'

I thought of the two photos I'd seen. 'They had different-coloured hair and Brand was two years older, but they were alike enough for Nieuwkerk to have travelled on Brand's passport and for Forensics to have misidentified the skull.'

'That's good,' the commissaris said. 'It's good that it wasn't a glaring mistake by the police.' He made some more notes on the piece of paper that he'd taken out of the CI's notebook. 'Thanks, Detective Meerman,' he said. 'I think I can work with this.' He got up, nodded towards the CI as if that was enough of a goodbye, and left the office.

I sat there confused. 'What does he mean by that? Work with it?'

'Damage control,' the CI said. 'That man's all about damage control.' He pulled the notebook towards him and picked the edges of the page that the commissaris had used out of the spiral in the middle. 'He should have been a press officer, not a commissaris.'

I understood what the boss was saying, but on the other hand, the commissaris had pushed me to a conclusion that I liked: Nieuwkerk needn't have killed Theo Brand to have ended up with his papers. I wondered how much the going rate for a passport would have been back then, and where he'd got the money from.

Maybe he'd just stolen it. The money, or the passport.

I left the CI's office and saw Mehmet Yilmaz in the corridor. He seemed to be waiting for me. This was not a good place to talk.

'We took the photos.' His words were cautious.

I realised there must be an urgent reason for him to want to talk to me here, where my boss could see us at any moment. 'Is there a problem?'

'We got him a lawyer.'

'What did he say?'

Mehmet paused. 'He said the photos were taken too late. It would have been better if we'd done it the morning after the assault.'

'I saw his hands the morning after the assault. They didn't have a single mark on them. No cuts, no bruises.'

Mehmet gave me the same look that my cat gave me when she thought I was doing something strange but there was a possibility that my actions could lead to her getting fed. 'Are you willing to testify to that?' he said.

'I can't. Seriously, I can't.'

'Then what was the point in telling me?' he said, and walked off.

It was really annoying when people just walked away like that.

Chapter 27

I went home. Pippi seemed delighted to have me back. She weaved through my legs to show affection with the entirety of her body and purred loudly when I finally did what she wanted me to do and sat down on the sofa. She jumped up onto my lap and stared at me with total adoration in her green eyes.

I didn't have the heart to push her away, so I stayed sitting. The architect's table in my study was calling me to come and draw what I knew about this case so far, but I didn't listen. Instead I stared at the dark windows and rubbed the soft spot behind my cat's ear. It was soothing and I let my thoughts drift. I had nothing to do other than think, because the TV was off as well as the radio, and both my laptop and my phone were out of reach.

The cat dug her claws into my arm to show me how much she liked being scratched underneath her chin. I rested back against the sofa cushion and Pippi meowed at being shifted slightly, then settled in a more comfortable position on my lap, her head resting heavily on my stomach.

Before, I'd thought that Andre's decision to change name

and nationality had been a deliberate act to make a completely new life for himself away from the Netherlands.

Now, I knew that it hadn't been like that at all. He hadn't merely changed his name but had taken someone else's identity. So what was with the corkboard in his office? Did it make any sense? He had looked into his own murder. He had seen the press coverage.

It meant that he could have guessed what was going to happen as soon as he went public: this could be a huge story. He was the man who had died but who had come alive again. There would have been no hiding, no more privacy for him ever again.

That was why he'd told Daniel in person, and said that everybody was going to know soon anyway.

But that press coverage would mean that everything would be out in the open. Including the fact that he'd taken Theo Brand's identity.

I thought back to the morning I'd first met Andre, when there'd been a camera crew at the hospital. I'd turned my back towards the cameras to avoid my face being on screen. I didn't like the publicity my previous cases had brought me and I would much prefer to stay anonymous. Maybe Andre had wanted the same thing. As he'd taken Theo's identity, he wouldn't have wanted to go public with this, but he had still had an urge to tell people. His sister needed to know. The family of the man who'd been accused of his murder needed to know.

This felt like a real possibility: he had come to the Netherlands only to tell the people who needed to know, but had done his best to stay anonymous otherwise.

He had tried to tell the Brand family too. Did that make sense? I tried to think back to when I'd met him. He'd been calm and collected. Not someone running from the police or trying to hide the fact that he'd murdered someone. So why had he come up to me that morning and said that people needed to know? Why tell the police after he'd worked so hard to change nationality, to destroy the paper trail, to make it seem that Theo Brand had still been alive?

Why had he come to Amsterdam? Why would anybody do what he'd done?

I rubbed Pippi's ear in the hope that this would make me think better. She stretched out on her side, extended a paw and seemed to hug my stomach, making a soft meowing noise when my fingers dug too hard into her fur.

Once again it dawned on me that Andre had made things worse for everybody.

Everyone he had spoken to was in a worse position than they had been before he'd come to Amsterdam.

In my head, I went through the list of the people he'd visited one by one.

Julia used to have a clear view of who she was: the sister of the boy who had been murdered. She had become a social worker to make up for what her parents had done, to protect other children from what her brother had gone through. She'd felt guilty about the fact that her parents had kicked her abused brother out of the house, and had worked hard to make amends. Just when she felt she'd succeeded, Andre had come back and pulled the rug out from under her. He hadn't been murdered. He'd moved to London and never contacted his family again.

I was just glad that she didn't know about Theo Brand. I was glad she didn't know that Charlie was convinced Andre had been a murderer.

When Andre had gone to see Daniel, he'd been very specific about the childhood abuse and had even made Daniel aware that his own mother had known what had happened. She had been complicit. She had blamed the victim and gone to Andre's parents' house. She had been the one who'd got him kicked out. Andre had made matters worse for Daniel not just by telling him all this but also by then committing suicide. He hadn't done what Daniel had wanted. He hadn't cleared Paul Verbaan's name. Not only had he given Daniel knowledge that he probably didn't want, but he had also taken away Daniel's faith in his father.

Then there was the Brand family. He'd suggested that their son had died, but hadn't given them any proof, no evidence. He'd only given them more questions. Why had he talked to them? He could have told them how he'd met Theo after he'd been made homeless. He could have filled in some of Theo's movements. If he'd wanted to make amends for murdering their son, he should have told them what had happened.

In fact, he hadn't given answers to any of the people he'd been to see.

Had that been what he'd set out to do? Not apologise, but take revenge?

Had I helped him make everybody's life worse?

I moved and wriggled until Pippi decided it was better to get off my lap. I needed to start writing things down, if only to sort out the mess in my head. I went to my study to make that drawing.

Everything I'd found out about what Andre had been doing in the Netherlands seemed to confuse me. There were really two different, but potentially linked, things going on here, and I thought it would be useful to separate these. First of all, if his friend Carol was to be believed – and I could see no reason why she would have lied – Andre had decided to do some investigation into his background after he'd found out Theo Brand's mother had died. I chewed the end of my pen. Did I believe this story? It was possible, of course, that it had happened like that. Andre had been completely unaware of everything, wanted to make amends and rushed to the Netherlands to talk to his sister, the son of the guy who'd abused him and the family of a boy he thought might have been the real murder victim. He also met with his ex-partner.

I wrote the first three names on the left-hand side of my paper and Laurens Werda's name on the right. There were differences between these two groups. The left-hand people had something to do with Andre's past and his disappearance. The person on the right belonged to a much more recent past. The ones on the left had been visited because he'd wanted to apologise. All three had told me that he'd been very clear about that. He'd said sorry.

The ex-partner had just been a social call maybe. Laurens didn't know anything about the Body in the Dunes or that his partner's real name was Andre Nieuwkerk. There was something that bugged me about this. I scratched the back of my head with the pen, as if that would help me bring the thoughts to the foreground.

What kind of person wouldn't tell their partner of more than ten years what their real name was? The answer came to me: someone who had something big to hide.

Someone who had murdered a man and subsequently stolen his identity.

It was an answer I didn't like. It should make me feel better, less guilty about Andre's death, but somehow it didn't.

My doorbell rang and I reluctantly left my drawing.

It was Ingrid. I hesitated for a second, then buzzed her in. I stood by my door and waited for her to come up the three flights of stairs.

'Come in,' I said. 'Can I get you anything? Tea? Coffee?'

'I'll have a cup of tea if you're making some.'

I wasn't going to but I also didn't mind. It would only take two seconds. Ingrid plopped down on the sofa and I went into the kitchen.

'We're going to arrest Yilmaz,' she said from the front room, as if it was the distance between us that allowed her to say it. Maybe not being able to see me made it feel as anonymous as confessing to a priest.

I held the kettle under the tap. 'Ingrid, don't do this,' I said.

'Don't do what, Lotte?'

'You know Erol Yilmaz didn't beat up Peter de Waal.'

'You don't know he's innocent.'

'It will never stand up in court,' I said as I put the kettle on. 'Arresting him now will cost him his job.' I joined her again in the front room. I would be able to hear the kettle click off from there.

'And not arresting him will cost me mine.' She turned away from me angrily, maybe because she'd said more than she wanted. 'It's easy for you to do this; you don't care. You're happy staying a detective all your life. Me, I want a career. I want to get promoted. I do what the boss wants me to do.'

'This is insane. You can't do this.'

'You were there with me that morning. You saw how angry Yilmaz was. Did he look like an innocent man to you?'

'He looked like a man who was sure we wouldn't believe him. And he was right, wasn't he?'

'Don't interfere, Lotte. Just don't.'

In the kitchen, the kettle whirred and bubbled and then clicked to let me know it had finished boiling. 'Hold on just one second. I'll be right back.'

I dipped a tea bag quickly in both mugs and went back into the living room. I put the mugs on the table and sat down. 'I was there that morning, you're right. I chose to come with you instead of listening to Andre Nieuwkerk, and he ended up killing himself.' I wanted to sound factual, but thinking about the choice I'd made that morning made me feel awful. 'And you know what?' My voice sounded thick and unnatural however much I tried to control it. 'I regret that. I'll probably always regret it. I chose to help out another police officer. I chose to help out my friend.'

'You see me as your friend?' She picked up her mug, probably just to give herself something to do, and blew the steam away.

I was quiet for a few seconds, taken aback that she was questioning what to me was the least controversial thing I'd said. Would I have told her how guilty I felt if I didn't see her as my friend? I wouldn't have told any other colleague. I would never have told something like this to Thomas or Charlie. 'Don't you?'

'I'm just surprised,' Ingrid said. 'You tell me I'm your friend and then you try to persuade me not to arrest this guy. Now I know how you treat your friends.' She took a sip of her tea.

I shook my head. 'I know what the pressure's like, Ingrid. I know what working for Bauer is like. But I can't let this go. A man killed himself because I chose to help you.'

'I talked to Bauer. I talked to the commissaris. I told them what happened that morning. They still want to go ahead with this. The prosecutor has signed the arrest warrant. We all want the same thing, all apart from you.'

'I know what I saw is inconvenient . . .'

'Inconvenient? That's what you call it?' Her hands started to shake and she had to put the mug down to stop the tea from spilling. She tucked them under her legs.

'. . . but I saw what I saw.'

'And so did Peter de Waal!'

'I don't believe him.'

'I know you don't, Lotte, and I've done my best to work with you on that. I interviewed him again.'

Pippi sauntered back into the room. I stroked her and she purred. 'You asked me to go with you to talk to his colleague.'

'Because I wanted you to agree with me! Don't you see? You say you're my friend, but to me you're my mentor. I want you to believe in me. I want you to think I'm doing a good job.'

'You honestly think Yilmaz did this.' The reality had only just dawned on me.

'It's what the top people think. It's what public opinion thinks. It's best for the police force if we all act the same.'

'The same?'

'Don't step out of line. Please.'

'But I would be lying.'

'You don't have to lie. You just have to stay quiet.'

I'd seen it that morning, I'd seen how tired Ingrid was. I'd gone with her because I'd been worried that lack of sleep would cause her to make wrong decisions. Of course everything would be easier if I hadn't done that, but I had. I couldn't undo it. I couldn't unsee what I'd seen.

'I wish you'd made another choice that morning.' Her voice was bitter.

'So do I, Ingrid, so do I.' But I hadn't. I'd seen Erol Yilmaz, and I couldn't stay quiet.

'Maybe then I also shouldn't ignore what I saw that morning. I saw you refuse to talk to a man who ended up killing himself. But you haven't told anybody about that. I've been keeping quiet about it for you, but maybe I shouldn't any more.'

IV

The Victim

Chapter 28

The next morning, I was still in bed, scanning the news headlines on my phone, when the outcome of the commissaris's way of dealing with things stared me in the face.

Body in the Dunes finally identified, one headline said.

Andre Nieuwkerk stole victim's identity.

Was assumed victim really the killer?

I called Julia's phone, but there was no answer. I jumped out of bed and got dressed as quickly as I could. I didn't know when he had briefed the press, but I could read their reaction on my screen.

I rushed down the stairs. I had my car keys in my hand, ready to drive over to Julia's, but I paused at the car door. Going on my bike would be slower than getting a clear run in the car, but the chances of that were slim at this time of day. The chances were that I would be stuck in traffic. The cold of the morning was starting to bite, but I put my keys away, fished my gloves and hat out of my handbag and got on my bike.

The air felt like winter, cold and crisp, but cycling to Watergraafsmeer would warm me up in no time.

In the end, it took about twenty-five minutes, crossing

from old areas to new. I turned into the road of small houses, and if I hadn't already known where she lived, I would have been able to guess it from the crowd of people outside her door.

I hadn't expected the invading army in front of her house. I'd thought there'd be one or two reporters and that was it. On both sides of the street, net curtains twitched as neighbours tried to find out what was going on.

'What's it like to find out that your brother was a murderer?' one woman shouted loudly in the direction of her window. The curtains were pulled tightly closed and not a trace of light escaped from inside the house. 'Talk to us, Julia.'

I remembered that she had told me her flat did not have a back door. I remembered how small the place was. I could only too easily imagine her sitting at her table trying to ignore the noise outside. I pulled back a little way – I didn't want the reporters to see me – and called her again.

'You must be shocked,' a man shouted. 'Or do you still think he was innocent?'

Her voicemail picked up. 'Are you inside?' I said. 'Call me back if you want me to get you out of there.' I wasn't going to barge through a mob of journalists if Julia wasn't even at home. Plus, if I was going to ring her doorbell and she wasn't going to open up, there was no point anyway.

'Give us your side of the story.'

Maybe she was trying to ignore everybody.

When the commissaris had told me I'd given him information he could work with, what he'd meant was that he could spin it to the press. They had drawn their own conclusions. That these conclusions were not that far away from my own didn't make it any better. And that the commissaris had told the press before I'd told Julia only made it worse.

Should I have realised that this was what he was going to do?

I called her again, but she still didn't answer.

I didn't want to get unnecessarily worried. Just because her brother had killed himself, that didn't mean Julia would do the same. She hadn't seemed suicidal at all the last time I'd seen her. She'd been her own grounded self. She had probably switched off her phone.

I called her landline number, the one that Andre had had in his diary, but she didn't answer that either. It didn't even ring; just went straight to voicemail. That was the number that was in the phone directory, so I hadn't expected her to answer. Disconnecting the phone from the wall was the first thing you did when journalists tried to contact you.

On the other side of the street, I saw a car pull up. It stopped close to the swarm of journalists. The door opened and a man got out. It was Daniel Verbaan. He was wearing his baseball cap again, but this time with the peak pulled low to hide his face.

It concerned me that he was here. I monitored the journalists' faces closely, but none showed any sign of recognising him. They hardly gave him a glance; they were too focused on Julia's front door. Daniel must have seen the newspaper headlines too. What was going on in his head? Not only had his father been innocent of murder, but the man who was presumed to have been the victim had actually been the murderer?

I could only imagine how angry he must be right now. He'd punched Andre in a fit of rage.

I propped my bike against a lamppost and quickly pushed the lock shut. I shoved the key into my pocket and walked up to Daniel. To my surprise, I saw Julia's front door open. The journalists pushed in, cameras at the ready. She held a hand in front of her face. Daniel stepped up to her and put his arm around her shoulders.

I barged in and showed my badge. 'Police. Let these people through.' I recognised Monique Blom. I was surprised she was here.

'Do you have a comment for us? Anything?'

I shook my head. I did my best to guard my face with my arm to stay out of sight of the cameras and helped Daniel shepherd Julia out of the house and towards his car. She got in the back and I followed her.

She turned to me. 'Why are you here?' she said. 'This is all your fault.'

'I'm sorry,' I said. 'I had no idea this was going to happen.'

Daniel rushed around the car and opened the driver's door.

'You should have told me,' Julia said. 'If you had found out something about my brother, you should have told me, not the press.' She stared out of the window. 'You found something in his flat, didn't you?' She said the words to the world outside.

The feeling in my stomach was the weight of guilt being stacked on top of guilt.

Daniel threw me a glance in the rear-view mirror but didn't object to me being here. Instead he started the car and drove us away.

If I'd been worried last night that I'd helped Andre make everyone's life worse, here was evidence that I had definitely made things worse for all the people I'd spoken to in the last week.

Even if it wasn't my doing directly, because I hadn't personally made the calls to the press, it was clear that I'd assisted the commissaris in protecting the reputation of the police force at Julia's expense.

I told myself that nobody had done anything wrong. The commissaris was just following up with the press on the Andre Nieuwkerk case. I had done the right thing by keeping him informed. Andre could well have been a murderer. He had definitely taken Theo Brand's identity. He wasn't the innocent victim we'd thought he was. That Julia had always believed he was.

So why did I feel that I hadn't learned anything from what had happened when I'd ignored Andre to help Ingrid?

It hit me that I'd made the same choice I'd made that morning: I'd put the police force over a member of the public. I wondered why that felt like the wrong choice again.

Daniel parked the car. We crossed under the railway bridge and over the main road and walked in silence along the Amstel to the café by the river. It was located in a beautiful eighteenth-century house that was slowly getting swamped by the new-built glass towers around it. The past was once again being crowded out by the present.

The living rooms of the original house had been converted

into sitting areas with wooden tables and chairs. I chose a table where we had a bit of privacy. A bookshelf behind me seemed to indicate that at one point this had been the library. It could all be pretence, of course, but it made for a good space to have a private conversation but with all the security of being in public. It was best to be careful, even though Daniel didn't seem angry. He went to order our coffees.

I couldn't help thinking that this case was very much like the area around us, with past and present fighting for control and precedence. Because what was more important: the mistakes the police had made twenty-five years ago when they misidentified the Body in the Dunes as Andre Nieuwkerk; or the mistake I'd made last week when I'd ignored him?

If I blocked out part of the view from the window, modern times felt far away. Large barges floated over the wide water of the Amstel at a pleasantly bucolic speed, as if nothing had changed over the last two hundred years. But if I turned my head slightly, it became impossible to avoid the tall glass towers of the office park by the Amstel station. They were shouting that obviously the present took priority over the past.

Both mistakes had caused a suicide. The suicide of a child abuser and the suicide of the victim of his abuse. Even though I didn't want to, it was hard not to agree with what my surroundings were telling me: that the present mistake had been worse. I shook my head. This wasn't helping.

Daniel came back from the bar. 'The waitress will bring our coffees.' He sat down next to Julia. 'I knew I had to get you out of there. I saw the papers and I knew the press would be at your doorstep.'

It was weird to be here with Daniel and Julia. To sit here with two people who had once been friends and who had ended up hating each other. Or had they? Julia said she'd always been willing to talk to Daniel.

He'd had the same thought as I had, and the same reaction. She hadn't opened the door for me, but she'd opened it to him. You wouldn't do that for someone you hated.

'I know exactly what it's like to be accused of being the family of a murderer,' Daniel said. His voice was calm. I could tell he wasn't saying it to be confrontational; he was telling Julia that she wasn't the only one this had happened to. Again I wondered what it must have been like for him after his father was named as Andre Nieuwkerk's murderer. Had he seen the photos in the papers when the family were banned from church? The headlines screaming about the abuse? Had he struggled with reporters outside their house? Had he known they'd taken his picture at his father's funeral? I couldn't imagine he'd been able to avoid all of that. As he'd said, he'd been the son of a murderer.

'They asked me if I knew,' Julia glared at me, 'and I didn't know what they were talking about. But you knew, didn't you?'

'Knew what?'

'That Theo Brand was a real person. And that Andre took his identity.'

'Yes,' I said. 'That I knew.' And I'd made the decision not to tell her. It had been my fault that she'd woken up to that bank of journalists without knowing what was going on.

With no idea of what they were going to throw at her. 'But I didn't know it had gone out to the press. I'm really sorry you had to hear it this way.'

'Why didn't you tell me?'

Why hadn't I? Because I wanted to spare her the thought that her brother might have been a murderer. 'You had enough to deal with.'

'That's rubbish,' Julia said. 'You could have told me yesterday, when we were going to Kars's. We were in the car together for half an hour; you could have said something then.'

'He probably didn't do it,' Daniel said. 'Just believe that.'

'Like you believed your father didn't do it,' she said, and nodded to herself as if she only now realised that this was a perfectly reasonable reaction.

It felt really weird to me that the two of them could have this conversation, say these words without throwing them in each other's faces. In the circumstances, I would have thought it was going to descend into a shouting match, but in fact it just felt as though they were having a sensible conversation about how to deal with a member of your family being accused of murder.

It was a surreal experience and it made my head spin.

'I knew my dad hadn't murdered your brother,' Daniel said. 'I said so to the police at the time, but nobody listened to me. They all said I'd been too young to notice or that I'd misremembered. They ignored me.'

I hadn't found any statement from Daniel when I'd gone through the files of the previous team. He'd been twelve when Andre went missing, eighteen when the bones had been found and identified. I could understand why the police hadn't taken his testimony too seriously, but I was surprised that they hadn't even made a record of it. 'You thought your father didn't do it, or you knew?' I stressed the last word.

'He came to our door,' Daniel said. He looked over at Julia. 'He came to us, Juul.'

She smiled. 'Nobody has called me Juul in a long time.'

Daniel leaned forward and rested his arms on the table. 'Your brother came to see my father.'

The smile dropped from her face. 'When?'

'I think it was probably the night he went missing. I saw him talking to my father.'

'Did you hear what he said?' I asked.

'He said your parents had kicked him out.' He spoke directly to Julia, as if I wasn't there. 'He asked my father for money. I was surprised when Dad gave him some, because I didn't know why he would do that, I didn't know about what had happened between them. He gave Andre money and then he wrote something down. An address to go to, I'm pretty sure of that.'

'Do you know where?'

'No, he wrote it down. I couldn't see it.'

'Why didn't you tell me this at the time?' Julia said. 'You knew I'd reported him missing. If you'd told me then, I could have tried to find him and none of this would have happened.'

'My mother told me not to. She said your parents knew where your brother had gone; that they didn't want to talk to him and I shouldn't stir things up.'

The waitress came over with our coffees. Julia gripped the saucer as soon as the woman put it down, dragged it across the table until it stood in front of her and lifted the cup to hide her mouth.

I didn't think it was the need for caffeine that made her do that.

Eventually she put the cup down and wiped her mouth. She rubbed her hands over her face, then sat back on her chair. 'My parents knew where he was? Your mother said that my parents knew? That can't be right. They can't have known.'

I took a sip of my cappuccino, enjoying the bitterness. I looked out of the window at a barge floating on the Amstel. The past moved slowly compared to the present, but it couldn't be avoided.

'I don't know,' Daniel said. 'Maybe she lied about that, I know she wanted to keep me silent about Andre.'

I could tell he'd said it to make Julia feel better, not because it was what he actually thought.

'I didn't know about the abuse until all those years later,' he continued, 'but I knew that your brother was still alive when he left our house that evening. My father didn't threaten him, he didn't hit him, he didn't follow him.' He looked my way. 'The police weren't interested. Especially not after my father had killed himself. They had their story, they were done. Instead the papers printed that photo of me at the funeral. The son of a murderer. The son of an abuser. That was who I was, so who was going to listen to me, a kid with an inconvenient truth to tell?'

An inconvenient truth. I knew our circumstances couldn't

be more different, but Daniel's words reminded me of the situation I was in with Erol Yilmaz. I had seen him the morning after, and nobody wanted to hear it. Daniel had seen Andre visit his father – and walk away alive – and nobody had wanted to hear him either.

Julia's mobile rang. She checked the display to see who was calling. 'It's Kars Borst,' she said. She looked at Daniel. 'Remember? He was in our class.' She answered the call and listened for a few seconds, then said, 'Kars, I'm going to put you on speaker.'

'Julia, I saw the papers this morning and I wanted to tell you something. Because maybe you're feeling guilty over Verbaan's death. Well don't. I'm not. Your brother did a good thing. He took revenge for all of us. Verbaan was an abuser. He would never have been convicted. Nobody would ever have talked, I mean. God knows how many boys had gone before Andre.'

I looked at Daniel. He was so pale, it was as if he was going to be sick.

'Even if a kid had gone to his parents,' Kars continued, 'and if the parents had gone to the school, it would all have been brushed under the carpet, you know that. If your brother hadn't pretended to be dead, if he had come forward immediately, Verbaan would still be alive. He might have gone on to teach for another twenty years.'

Daniel put a hand in front of his face. Julia reached out and patted him on the arm, as you would do with a crying child. As she had probably done often enough with people in her job. She was comforting him, but she was probably the one who needed the support most

'Don't feel bad,' Kars continued. 'Just remember that once Andre kept quiet, he couldn't come back. I don't think he did it because he hated you. He didn't do it to cut you out.'

I looked at Julia. Tears were streaming down her face. I could see that she was shaking.

'Don't feel bad,' Kars repeated. 'I know it was tough for you and your family, but I think Andre felt he had to do it. Verbaan died. That was a good outcome. I know it's been hard on Verbaan's son – you two were friends, weren't you?'

'Yeah,' Julia said, looking at Daniel. 'We were friends.'

'But don't forget that the guy was a child abuser and would have ruined many more lives.'

Something Daniel had told us earlier jogged my memory. 'Kars,' I said, 'this is Detective Lotte Meerman. Sorry to interrupt. When we came to see you the other day, didn't you say that Verbaan gave you the name of a place to go? After you had problems with your parents.'

'Yes, he did, and they were great. They really helped me.'

'Can you remember what they were called?'

'Side Step.'

I looked at Daniel, but he shrugged. I needed to know if maybe one of the other runaways had gone there. Someone like Theo Brand.

Julia thanked Kars and disconnected the call. 'It reminds me of this area,' she said. 'Did you know they had to build the apartment blocks around this house because it was so old? The past,' she said. 'It always shapes the present, doesn't it?'

Chapter 29

I'd thought Theo's father might have information on where
his son had gone, and I'd taken Charlie with me to talk to
him. Robbert Brand gave us a tired smile when we arrived
on his doorstep.

'I knew you'd come to talk to me again,' he said. 'Is it all
certain now? Is Theo dead?'

The last time I'd spoken to him, he'd seemed an energetic
man. This morning he looked old, as if the hope that his son
was still alive was what had kept him charged all this time,
and the news of his death had sucked the life from him. With
journalists chasing him and speculation about his son's death
in all the papers, he'd aged a decade. A pile of newspapers
lay by the side of his chair. The front page of the local paper
showed an old picture of his son side by side with one of
Andre as a teenager. Luckily it wasn't one of the photos that
Robbert had given me the other day. I would have hated it
if the commissaris had passed one of those on to the press.

I'd only thought of the information I wanted when I was
on the way over, but now I was hit by the father's grief. If
I'd thought it was bad that Julia had found out through the
papers that her brother had used Theo's identity, Theo's

father finding out that his son was most likely dead was a hundred times worse.

I should have briefed him. Someone should have told him. 'We still don't know for certain,' I said, 'but it seems likely.' I should have rushed over to this house instead of Julia's this morning. My bad decisions only kept multiplying.

'Is this true?' He gestured at the paper. 'Did the guy who came here the other day murder him?'

'We know that he used your son's identity. His name and his passport. We don't know if he killed him.'

'Why didn't you tell me this last time?' The old man's voice was soft and small, as if he didn't even have the strength to be angry any more.

It didn't make me feel any less guilty. 'We don't have evidence for any of it,' I said. 'We don't know where he got your son's passport from.' Charlie and I were sitting side by side on the sofa as if we were in this together, even though I was mainly to blame for how upset the old man was.

'You said the ashes had been scattered.'

'That's right.'

'Do you know where?'

I knew what he was thinking: that those had been his son's ashes. 'I'll ask for you. I'll ask Julia, Andre Nieuwkerk's sister. She'll know.'

Robbert rubbed his eyes. 'Yes. My son was cremated by the family of the guy who the papers say was his murderer. Why did he come here? If he was going to tell people he'd murdered him, he should have just said. Why didn't he tell us? If he was going to kill himself anyway, why not tell us what he'd done. What he'd done to Theo.' He looked at me as if I had all the answers, but unfortunately, I had none. I'd come here only with questions.

'Can I ask you some things about your son?'

The old man didn't answer me, but got his iPad out. 'Here are some photos of my wife's funeral,' he said. 'Barbara's funeral. There were a lot of people. Everybody loved Barbara. Everybody knew her; she talked to people, made time for them. When we went for walks, we'd always bump into someone who wanted a chat, asked her for advice.'

There used to be a time when old-age pensioners weren't up to date with the latest technology, but Robbert seemed to like his gadgets even though he still read the newspaper in old-fashioned print.

'We should have had something like that for Theo,' he said sadly.

'Why did he leave home?' I asked.

'He was old enough to do that.' Robbert showed me a photo of a group of people talking, looking solemn, dressed in black, at the edge of a cemetery.

'You said you spoke to him for the first month or so. Did you know where he was?'

'He stayed with one of his mates at first, slept on his sofa. Look, this is my cousin Frank,' Robbert said. 'I hadn't seen him in years, but he still came.' I could see the tears in his eyes. 'He's called me a couple of times since. He knows I'm not lonely because Harry lives close, but I think he likes to keep in touch with me. It's nice of him.' He swiped and showed the next image. 'It's nice of him,' he said again.

'He stayed with one of his mates first. Do you know where he went after that? Was he at a place called Side Step?'

'Side Step? No, that doesn't ring a bell. He went to London.' He paused for a second. 'No, you now think he didn't go to London, don't you? I read about that. That it was Andre Nieuwkerk who went to London on Theo's passport.'

The article had been very in-depth.

'So I don't know.' He swiped a few more times. He held the iPad away from him when he looked at the next group photo, and narrowed his eyes to get the picture in focus.

'Do you remember the names of any of his mates?' Charlie asked. 'The one he stayed with maybe?'

'It's all such a long time ago. Harry might know. He tried to find him a few times. Went looking for him when he first moved out, but if someone doesn't want to be found . . .' Robbert turned back to the photos. 'Ah look, here's Katja. It was nice that she came.' He planted a finger in the middle of his iPad. 'She's a good girl.' He enlarged the image for me, so that I could see her more clearly.

It also enlarged the image of the man she was talking to. A man I recognised straight away. I took the iPad from Robbert's hands and angled it so that Charlie could also see the picture clearly.

I heard him take a sharp intake of breath.

'Katja?' My voice was tight with the effort it took to keep calm.

'Harry's ex-wife.'

Of course. It came back to me. I'd spoken to Katja when I'd called the number in Andre's diary. She'd told me she didn't know a Harry; that I'd dialled the wrong number.

And now here she was, at Theo Brand's mother's funeral, chatting to Andre Nieuwkerk.

I called Katja and spoke to her for the second time in a week. At least this time she didn't say I must have the wrong number. I'd confirmed that the address Andre had written down in his diary was actually the right one, and Charlie and I drove out to her house.

'I can't believe it.' Charlie kept his eyes on the road in front of him while he talked. 'Andre Nieuwkerk came to Theo's mother's funeral. Why would he have done that?'

'To be honest, I've got no idea. Let's wait to talk to Katja.'

'Can I lead the questioning?'

'Of course you can.' This latest turn of events made me think I'd been asking all the wrong questions anyway. Charlie couldn't make more of a mess of things than I had. 'What do you think we should find out?'

'What she talked to Andre about at the funeral.'

'And what else?' I asked. We were coming up to a large roundabout and Charlie stopped to let a stream of cyclists pass. I thought of Andre cycling in London and getting into an accident that ultimately caused him to lose his job, giving him time to google himself and find out about Theo Brand's mother. The accident had also got him hooked on prescription painkillers. In Amsterdam, cyclists and cars were kept separated as much as possible precisely to stop these kinds of accidents. When they did happen, they were often racing bikes, deciding to cycle on the main road instead of staying in the designated lanes full of cyclists in no particular rush.

When I'd gone to London with Julia, traffic had seemed confusing enough already without trying to get through it on a bike.

'Is there anything else?' Charlie asked.

'He came to her house last week,' I said. 'Harry told me that she said there'd been another nutter.'

'I didn't know that,' Charlie said.

I became aware that I probably hadn't kept him informed as much as I should have done. 'He told us that when Thomas and I interviewed him and his father the first time.'

'Last Saturday.'

'That's right. He didn't mention that his ex-wife had talked to the man a month before that.'

'Maybe he didn't know.'

'Worth a question,' I said.

Charlie nodded, his eyes on the road. 'Lotte, I spoke to Mehmet. Did you know that Erol has been arrested?'

I'd expected that question. If anything, I was surprised that he'd waited this long to bring it up. 'Ingrid told me it was going to happen.'

'What are you going to do?'

'Do? Nothing.'

'Don't you think you should?' He looked at me. 'You don't believe he did it.'

'I'm not going to mess with Ingrid's case any more than I already have.'

'Don't you think you have a duty?'

'I have a duty to a fellow police officer.'

Charlie was shaking his head. 'You also have a duty to the truth.'

The truth. I'd talked to Ingrid last night and she was convinced that Yilmaz was guilty. It was also the truth that I'd talked to Andre Nieuwkerk. Did that make me guilty of his death? Did it make me culpable, and did I want Ingrid to tell other people about that?

I didn't want to think that this was the reason why I wasn't more willing to help Erol Yilmaz. Surely I could trust Ingrid? She wouldn't have arrested someone unless they had some evidence.

We pulled in to Katja's street. The house looked like a typical family home, with a pair of garden gnomes in the front guarding two recycling bins, and a patch of pebbled ground only a little bigger than a car. It was that time of year when gardens looked their worst, and Katja's was no exception. I was glad I didn't have a garden at my place. I couldn't even keep potted plants alive.

Katja opened the door and let us in. She was a little younger than Julia and had her hair cut short in stark straight lines that did nothing to soften her angular features. She wore bright blue eyeshadow; the kind we wore as teenagers because we were told it brought out the colour of our eyes. She hadn't moved on from that look, which hadn't even been flattering on young girls. The house was filled to the brim with plants, large bunches of flowers stood on every surface, and the air was so full of unseasonal pollen that it made me sneeze. She mainly seemed to favour large lilies that reminded me of nothing so much as a funeral home.

She led us through to an open kitchen, the only place where there were no flowers.

'You met Andre Nieuwkerk at your mother-in-law's funeral?' Charlie said.

It was good that he wanted to lead the questioning, because Katja gave him her undivided attention. 'He was looking for Theo,' she said. 'Was he at the funeral, was he going to come, when had we spoken to him last, those kinds of things.'

'What did you think?'

'I tried to get rid of him. I thought he was just trying to get information from me. We'd had some other people pretending to be Theo in the past.'

Harry had told me about people like that.

'I was quite short with him, told him we hadn't seen Theo in years. That I had never met him. When Harry and I started going out, Theo was already out of touch with the family.'

'You saw him again last week?'

'Yes, he came to my front door, told me he had something to tell me about Theo. I knew it was just rubbish, so I didn't stop to talk to him.'

'Why do you say that?'

'A month before, he was asking me if I'd seen Theo, and now he was saying that he had information for us? Of course I didn't believe him. I told him to leave. Then you called,' she nodded at me, 'so I was short with you as well.'

'Did he say anything else?' Charlie asked. 'When he came to your place?'

'Like what?'

'Like what information he was going to give you?'

'No, I didn't wait to hear what he had to say.'

I swallowed down the saliva that had rushed into my mouth. That was what I had done. Did it matter if Ingrid was going to tell everybody about it? It had happened. I'd refused to listen to him. I had made that mistake.

'What did he seem like,' I asked, 'when you met him at the funeral?'

'What do you mean?'

'How did he react when you told him you hadn't seen Theo in a while? Was he surprised, upset, angry?'

Katja paused. 'I'm not sure.' She widened her baby-blue eyes as far as they could go. 'He was sad, maybe? But then it was a funeral, it was normal to be upset. I was upset.'

'Did he tell you why he'd come?'

'I got the impression,' Katja said, 'that it was because he hoped Theo would be there. So maybe he was disappointed? Yes, that's it. Disappointed.'

I could feel Charlie's eyes on me. 'I know what that feels like,' he said. 'To be disappointed.'

Chapter 30

Charlie and I drove back to the police station in silence. This seemed to be his method of showing disappointment. I filed it away for future reference. Thomas would normally demonstrate annoyance with sarcastic comments. Silence was much preferable, and I tried to convince myself it was good because it allowed me to do some thinking. It disturbed me that Andre had expected Theo to be alive. That he had come to Theo's mother's funeral expecting to meet the man whose papers he'd used. It made me think of what his neighbour had told me, about Andre being different after he'd found out about Theo's mother's death.

As soon as I was back at my desk, I put a call in to Carol Reynolds, Andre's London neighbour.

'I was going to call you,' she said. 'I wasn't going to tell you about this, but I've been really disturbed by all the press interest in Theo. Andre, I mean,' she corrected herself.

As she was talking, I googled *Andre Nieuwkerk London* and was immediately presented with a set of pictures taken outside his place in Putney. I really didn't want to hear someone else complaining about reporters camping outside their house. I could only imagine what her quiet street was now like. Still, I had a duty to listen to her. After all, this mess was partially my fault. It was largely my fault if I wanted to be honest about it.

'I'm a psychiatrist,' she said. 'And even though I wasn't his psychiatrist per se, he did tell me a lot of things. He felt he could share things with me and that I would understand. Or at least not judge him.'

'What did you want to tell me?'

'He tried to commit suicide before, about six months ago, and I found him just in time.'

'How did you know?'

'He called me and told me what he'd done: taken an overdose of his painkillers. I called 999 and then I went upstairs. I knew where he kept the key – he'd had one hidden downstairs. It was a cry for help.'

'Was there a reason for it? Did he tell you?'

'He'd gone through a really rough time. He'd had the accident, it had taken him a long time to recover, then there was the dependency on the painkillers. But most of all, I think he suddenly had a lot of time on his hands to think. He always used to be busy at his job, but when he couldn't go to work for two months, they laid him off. That's what tipped the scales, I think.'

'Were they allowed to do that? Is it legal?'

'British labour laws aren't that strict. He got a big payout; he said he didn't mind. But sitting at home all day, I don't think it was good for him at all.'

'That's why you told him not to go.'

'Yes, I was very concerned. I told him that if things got too much, he should call me. He should come back.'

'His sister didn't believe him; Verbaan's son hit him. Was that what made him do it?'

'I wonder. Surely he would have expected Verbaan's son to be angry at him. That's why I thought something had happened with the Brand family.'

'Did he tell you something about them?'

'I think they were important to him. That those were the people he obsessed about, that's all. I just wished he'd called me. After his previous attempt, we'd agreed that he would.'

'Did he tell you anything about Theo Brand, or about what he was planning to do?'

'No, he didn't. He never even told me that Theo wasn't his real name.'

'Did he tell you anything about his early days in London?'

'Not really. He did tell me about the childhood abuse. Not in detail – I never knew it had been his teacher – but he told me about being young and being taken advantage of. That seemed to be the big thing for him: thinking that someone loved him and then realising he'd just been used. He said it was a pattern. He'd got it into his head that he had to go to Amsterdam to break this pattern.'

'A pattern? A pattern implies more than once.'

'Yes,' Carol said. 'Yes it does, doesn't it?'

I thought about the photos in his study. The photos that seemed like a gallery of people he'd hated. His teacher. His father. 'You think he'd been abused before Verbaan.'

'Before, after, who knows? Who knows what happened between him and Theo Brand?'

That pulled me up, because it wasn't the direction my

mind had been going in at all. 'Theo Brand? Did he say anything about him?'

'No, but I think I knew my upstairs neighbour well enough to know that he wasn't a murderer. If the two boys were together and one of them ended up dead . . . Well, I just think that something must have happened.'

This was completely different from what Katja had been thinking. She thought that Andre had come looking for Theo. Carol thought Andre might have had something to do with his death. 'Why do you think the two of them had been together?'

'He'd been researching his family tree. Only it wasn't his family tree, of course, but the real Theo Brand's. He'd spent hours going over Theo's family.'

I remembered what Harry Brand had told me about putting messages on all the family research websites, looking for Theo. If Andre had been researching Theo's family tree, he would have found those. 'When was this?' I asked. 'Was it before or after he was shocked about his mother's death?'

'Before,' Carol said. 'I think that was how he found out about it.'

He would have found out that Theo's family were still looking for him. He'd gone to the mother's funeral. In Katja's opinion, he'd hoped that Theo would show up. Was it possible that what he'd been shocked about wasn't the mother's death but the fact that Theo was still missing?

'Her death must have been a real wake-up call for him,' Carol continued. 'For years he would have seen himself purely as a victim, dealing with the effects of the childhood abuse, accepting that what he'd done had been necessary to survive. If he'd had something to do with Theo's death, seeing the family must have brought with it a huge amount of guilt.'

She sounded as if she was giving her professional opinion, and I wrote as much of it down as I could. 'Guilt that he wouldn't have felt before, you mean?'

'Yes. I think he would have gone to Amsterdam to make amends and I don't think it went as he'd hoped. It wouldn't have taken much for him to tip. To kill himself. It could have been something that the Brand family said to him, for example.'

'Thank you,' I said. 'This has been incredibly useful.'

She told me that if I had any further questions, I could call her at any time. What she'd said had made so much sense. I could imagine that shift between seeing himself as a victim and seeing himself as someone responsible for a man's death. Had those photos in his flat been to remind himself what he'd gone through? What Carol had said about the Brand family possibly being the trigger to Andre's suicide was possible. I thought we should talk to Harry and Robbert again. But before I could go to them, I got a call from the commissaris saying that he wanted to talk to me. I needed to keep my anger hidden just as carefully as he disguised every single emotion. I kept my hands stuffed in the pockets of my coat. That way he wouldn't be able to see that they were balled into fists.

The walk up to the floor where the commissaris's office was located was long enough to make me even more angry. I pictured Robbert Brand's face as he'd sat in his chair this morning, and I knocked on the door with more force than was necessary.

'This wasn't what we agreed,' I said.

The commissaris looked up. 'We agreed something?'

'I briefed you but I didn't know you were going to leak this to the press.'

'What did you want to do instead, Detective Meerman?' My job title sounded like an insult. 'I think I'm right in saying that you're getting nowhere with this case. There will never be any forensic evidence. You've got nothing on Andre Nieuwkerk's death or Theo Brand's potential murder. What we need are witnesses who might have seen something thirty years ago. We need press coverage.'

'I promised the family—'

'You were in no position to promise them anything,' he interrupted me pleasantly. 'What we do is solve crimes with whatever methods are at our disposal. Sure, we are sympathetic towards the families of the victims wherever possible. Here it was no longer possible.'

'I understand your position,' I said. The way I understood it and what I was going to say were not the same thing, however. 'Informing the press about Andre Nieuwkerk's death is entirely the right thing to do. However, I think it's callous to have made it known that Theo Brand was potentially the Body in the Dunes. That's the part I have trouble with.'

He raised an eyebrow. 'And I'm the person who told them? Are you sure about that?'

Frustration narrowed my throat so that the only way I

could get the words out was by talking too loudly. 'Who else? Who else but you?'

'I confirmed to the press that we'd misidentified the Body in the Dunes thirty years ago. I told them that Andre Nieuwkerk had committed suicide last week and that he had been using Theo Brand's identification papers. That's it. Maybe you should check your facts before storming in here and making these accusations.'

The photos on the wall looked at me and judged me. The eyes of one particular criminal who was posing with a politician next to a racehorse told me that I was angry with myself more than with the commissaris. I knew I could have told Robbert Brand all this in person when Thomas and I visited him after I'd got back from London, but that we'd decided not to. I could have told Julia as well. I should have briefed both of them as soon as I'd briefed the commissaris. I'd been too preoccupied with other matters to do the decent thing. 'There was a mob of journalists outside Julia Nieuwkerk's flat,' I said.

'I know. I got my secretary to write her a letter of apology.'

'An apology?'

'I shouldn't have apologised? Is that how you deal with things in Amsterdam? I'll make a note of that for next time.' He actually wrote something down on his pad. I had no idea it was possible to pick up a pen in a sarcastic way.

It had taken three meetings with the commissaris before I'd finally come to realise that this was what he did. This was how he dealt with tricky questions: he attacked any part of them he possibly could. Keep it short, Lotte, I told myself.

278

One topic in every sentence. Don't give him the slightest gap to squirm out of. 'Why didn't you tell me beforehand?'

'I really don't see what the problem is here.'

'If you're going to do something that affects my operation, at least tell me. Don't keep me in the dark. I felt as ambushed as the victim's family did.'

'You weren't ambushed.'

I relaxed my fists in my pockets. 'Next time tell me so I know when to expect stories in the press. Give me an hour's notice or so.'

'I will.' He looked me in the eye, to make himself seem more sincere. Or to check my reaction. 'At least we got Yilmaz. Did you hear?'

My reaction was the only sensible one: I said 'Yes, I heard,' and walked out of his office. This had been pointless. He would do exactly the same thing next time. My boots made pleasing stomping noises in the carpeted corridor.

I left the police station to get some fresh air. I walked along the canal behind the building and didn't go back in even when it started to rain. I had forgotten my umbrella, but I kept walking. I stood at the back of the police station and looked at the statue of the woman with the sword, seemingly ready to take on the world in the name of justice. The rain in my face forced me to think. It dared me to consider my options. Wasn't I supposed to uphold justice? Wasn't that at least part of my job?

I could no longer do anything about what my superiors had leaked to the press. I couldn't undo any of the mistakes I'd made, the one that might have cost someone his life. The only thing I could do now was to make sure that an innocent man didn't end up in prison because of the pressure of public opinion.

This wasn't revenge on the commissaris; I didn't want to ruin his victory in being able to go on TV and tell everybody we had the perpetrator of those violent muggings. No, this was about what I'd seen. This was about telling people about my 'inconvenient truth', and if that meant Ingrid was going to tell everybody how I'd ignored Andre Nieuwkerk that morning, then so be it.

I raised my face to the rain. It had helped me to make up my mind and I was grateful to it, even as it came down harder and harder.

Chapter 31

The police station was solid and immovable in the driving rain. The statues depicting the various tasks that the police had to perform were as dark as the sky. 'Protect the public' was one of them. As if I needed reminding of that.

Just because I knew I was doing the right thing didn't mean I had to feel good about it.

I swiped my card through the reader and watched the entry light flash up green. The traffic police were three floors up, and I took the stairs two at a time. Water dripped from the hem of my raincoat onto the bottom of my trousers and my shoes. My shoes squished in complaint at every step I took. They told me I was going to betray a friend in order to rescue someone I didn't like. They seemed to question my choices with a wet squishing sound.

I didn't need their reminder.

I hoped that Mehmet wouldn't be at his desk, but he was. I paused in the doorway to the traffic police's office and gestured at him to follow me. I could see two of his colleagues looking at each other with raised eyebrows, but I didn't care. He didn't ask what I wanted but walked behind me through the corridor and back down the stairs to

Interrogation Room One. I sat at the seat where the suspect would normally sit, facing the mirror.

'Go and switch it on,' I said.

'Switch what on?'

'Don't you want to record this?'

'What . . .' he started, but then left the room again. The red light came on on the camera in the corner. The microphone in the centre of the table was ready to record my every word.

Mehmet came back in. He sat down on what would normally be my chair.

I saw myself in the one-way mirror, my wet raincoat, my hair glued to my face by the rain. I felt ancient. I looked ancient. The first morning I'd met Erol Yilmaz, I'd thought he'd looked like someone who was guilty. Today, I looked like someone who was going to step into an abyss with a gritty determination. This was what it must feel like to go bungee jumping.

'What do you want me to ask you?' Mehmet said. He shook his head as if he wasn't sure what was going on. As if he thought I was playing games with him, leading him towards a trap that he didn't see coming. 'What are you going to say?'

I sat back on my chair and undid my raincoat. 'Why don't you just assume,' I said, 'that I'm going to tell you the truth.'

'Should I get Erol's lawyer here?'

'You're a police officer.' I gestured towards the camera in the corner. 'You're recording this.' I peeled my raincoat off and dropped it on the floor. There was something about sitting here, about to be questioned, that clearly brought out the worst in me. 'You can do this.'

I probably should have asked him to switch on the recording equipment after we'd had this chat, then I could have pretended that he'd called me in. Though nobody would have believed that anyway.

'You saw Erol on the morning of the assault,' Mehmet said.

Not the right place to start, but I wasn't going to correct him. 'That's right.' The same part of me that dropped my wet coat on the floor was now not going to volunteer any information.

'Did you notice anything weird about him?'

I raised my eyebrows and tipped my head sideways. 'Weird?'

Mehmet shook his head as if he needed to clear his brain. 'Sorry,' he said. 'Can we start again?' He sat up straight on his chair and made eye contact. 'You saw Peter de Waal after he'd been assaulted.'

'That's right.'

'You interviewed him in hospital.'

'Yes.'

'He stated he'd recognise his assailant.'

'Yes.'

'He told you how the assault happened.'

'Yes.'

'Did you think the attack happened the way he said?'

'I knew it didn't.'

'Why are you saying that?'

283

'He said he'd been hit once, but his face and body clearly showed marks of more than one blow.'

'More than one person?'

'Possibly. Not necessarily.'

'Did that rule out that the assailant was the man he mentioned?'

'No, of course it didn't. He could have been unconscious after the first punch and that was all he remembered.'

'Did he get a good look at the man?'

'He said the man called his name; he turned around, saw him and was immediately punched.'

'What time was this?'

'Between three and three thirty a.m.'

'It was dark?'

'Yes.'

'Was it near a streetlight?'

'No.'

'It would have happened quickly.'

'Correct.'

'The man was sober?'

'No, one of his colleagues told us he'd been drinking heavily.'

'But you followed up on the victim's witness statement.'

'That's right. Detective Ingrid Ries and I went to visit Erol Yilmaz.'

'How soon after the assault was this?'

'We saw him around ten a.m., so at most seven hours after the assault.'

'You didn't immediately arrest him.'

'True.'

'Why was that?'

'There was no physical evidence on him to suggest he'd hit someone.'

'Please explain that.'

'There should have been marks on his hands, bruising or cuts, if he had been the one to cause the damage I'd seen on Peter de Waal's face and torso.'

'What conclusion did you draw?'

'That Erol Yilmaz was not the person who'd assaulted Peter de Waal. Or at least not in the way that de Waal described.'

'So either de Waal's statement was incorrect about the method the attacker used, or Yilmaz wasn't the man who assaulted him.'

I nodded. 'That's exactly it.'

'That makes the witness statement groundless.'

'Given that de Waal was drunk when it happened, that it was dark, that the attack happened very quickly, I would find it difficult to arrest Yilmaz based on the witness statement alone.'

'Just to make sure: you checked Yilmaz's hands.'

'It was one of the first things I looked at.'

'Seven hours after he was supposed to have hit de Waal, there was no physical evidence whatsoever to corroborate the victim's story.'

'Correct.'

'So why would the team still try to pursue him for it?'

I didn't answer; just shook my head with a tiny gesture and threw a glance at the camera. Mehmet got the hint. I wasn't going to go there. I was willing to go on record with what I'd seen that morning, but I wasn't willing to say anything else.

He got up, left the room again and switched the equipment off.

'Make a copy,' I said when he came back. 'Because I might not do that again.' I picked up my wet raincoat from the floor.

'Thanks, Lotte,' Mehmet said.

I didn't respond. It wasn't that I disliked him for having put me in this position – it wasn't his fault – but I didn't feel particularly good about myself for having torpedoed Ingrid's case.

I could only hope she wouldn't put her threat into action.

Chapter 32

Even though Robbert Brand hadn't known anything about where Theo had gone after he stopped sleeping on his friend's sofa, I couldn't help thinking that the missing information might give us important clues about his murder. Theo had left home in February 1988 and his father had last talked to him in May of that year. Andre had been kicked out of his parents' house in February 1989. If the two had met, which seemed likely, where had Theo been in the ten months between May and February? I called Harry to ask him if he knew anything. He said he didn't, but that I was welcome to go through Theo's stuff. It had been kept exactly as it had been. Also, his father had been doing research into Theo's movements and there might be something there that would help. I said I'd come over and look through the papers.

His father was at a weekly meeting with some friends and Harry let me into the house. The low daylight crept through the net curtains. 'It's in the attic,' he said. 'Right under the eaves. It used to be Theo's bedroom.'

I followed him up the stairs. 'How long did they keep it like that?'

'They didn't move his things until years after I left,' Harry said. 'They redecorated the whole house. Got rid of my bedroom and turned it into a spare room, and made Theo's into a study. About ten years after he'd gone missing.'

'Did they think he wouldn't come back?'

'No, Dad always thought he would. That's why they never moved. This house is clearly too big for him, but he always hoped that Theo would come home one day.' He paused on the landing and opened a door to a bedroom on the left. 'This is the spare room. Half the things in here are still mine.'

A bed with a bedspread with blue stripes; a large table. I could see the bare bones of a teenage boy's room there.

'Did you mind?' I said. 'Your parents' long search for Theo, I mean.'

'Mind?' He turned away and went up the second flight of stairs. 'What was there to mind? I wanted my brother back just as much as my parents wanted their son back. If anything, I felt sorry for them. My father never moved on. His life was stuck at the point that Theo went missing. He's spent the last thirty years looking for him. I don't know what he would have done in his retirement otherwise.'

He opened the door to the attic room and displayed what thirty years of research had gained Robbert Brand.

'I don't mind this.' He indicated the walls lined with ring binders. 'I minded all the people who were trying to take advantage of my father. People like that man who said he was my brother. People like the psychics who told him where Theo was. Only clearly he wasn't there.'

'And you thought Andre was one of those people?' I picked up a sheet of paper from the desk but didn't look at it. I looked at Harry's face instead.

'Poor Andre. Yes, I did think he was one of those people at first, but then I realised he wasn't. He didn't ask for money. I've ended up wondering,' he said, 'if he wasn't worse than the others. He hinted that he had answers but he never gave them to us. Did he do that on purpose?'

'You didn't meet with him after that first time, did you?'

'No, I tried to reach him but I couldn't. Because he'd already died.'

Yes. He'd already died.

He took off his small black-framed glasses and rubbed the lenses.

'Did your father ever say that he suspected someone of having murdered your brother? Was Theo seeing anybody at the time he went missing?'

'I don't know,' Harry said. 'I really don't. I don't even know if he ever had a girlfriend. It just wasn't something we talked about. He was seventeen, he was a good-looking kid, he used to hang out with a group of his classmates.'

'Was there a boyfriend?'

'I don't think so. He and his mates would go to pubs together, they'd go clubbing together. I can't imagine that he never met anybody he liked, if you know what I mean, but I have no idea how serious any of it was. I always thought he liked girls. If he was gay, he never told me.'

'Perhaps that was what the argument with your parents was about.'

'I don't think my parents would have made a big deal out of that. I'm sure they couldn't have cared less.'

'Then what? What happened?'

The light was low in this space that had been Theo's

bedroom. I felt closer to the boy who'd disappeared thirty years ago than I had before. I hoped it was the same for Harry. That he would tell me why Theo had left home. That he had knowledge of what had happened, like Julia had had about her brother.

But he stayed silent.

I knew I was trying to force the reality into a version of events that would make sense to me, but I couldn't stop myself from trying to find a link between Andre and Theo. I could picture the two of them together. The key thing was to find out how they'd met. 'Are there any photos of Theo and his friends?'

Harry got up and took a photo album down from the shelves. 'This was in the eighties, when everybody still took photos.' He handed it to me.

I sat down at the desk and opened the album. Four photos had been glued down on each page. The first one showed a group of six boys, smiling broadly, waving at the camera. They were getting ready to board a bus.

Andre had been a quiet boy, his sister had said. Kars had been one of those boys who'd had no friends. Theo was different. Confidence blasted from his eyes and out of every centimetre of his body. Looking at these photos, he wasn't anything like Andre. If you'd put the photos of the two boys side by side, you'd think their identities could never be confused. Still, Andre had been able to pass for Theo because on the small passport snap you probably couldn't see what I could see in those photos. It wasn't about the way they looked; it was about their attitude.

The thought entered my mind that – unlike Andre and

Kars – here was a kid who probably wouldn't have kept quiet.

'This was Theo's first trip abroad. They were going to Spain.' Harry tapped one of the faces. 'That's him,' he said. 'That's my brother.'

I'd already recognised him from the other photos I'd seen, but he seemed so alive here, with an exuberance that bounced off the page. It was in the light in his eyes and the wide smile. A joy, a pleasure in life spoke from every part of him. 'How long before he left home was this photo taken?'

'Three months. This was the first and last foreign holiday he ever took. I remember my parents were really against him going, but I'm glad he did, otherwise he would never have got to do this.'

'Did you go too?'

'God, no, I didn't have any money and my parents wouldn't pay for foreign holidays.'

'Theo had money?'

'He always did little jobs here and there. He was good at making cash. Unlike me.' Harry smiled ruefully.

I scanned the faces of the other boys in the photo. I'd hoped to recognise Andre, but he wasn't one of them. I should have known he wouldn't be. Theo's parents would have known if one of his friends had gone missing or been killed. Nobody in the photos looked familiar. Snaps of beaches, of girls joining the group of boys on their holiday, all with deeply tanned faces and slightly red noses. Had any of them been girlfriends? Who could tell? More photos of the friends with their arms around each other's waists. I felt like turning the pages more quickly. Other people's holiday photos were never very interesting. I made myself slow down. I made sure I looked at every face, every pose, every person who joined them or was in the background. I didn't see anybody I recognised.

'How many of these albums are there?' I asked Harry.

'A lot,' he said. 'He liked photos. Can I help? What are you looking for?'

'I'm looking for a photo with anybody else in it. A girl-friend, a friend, anybody who could have seen something or who could have killed your brother.'

Harry looked at me as if he thought I was crazy but it was best to just humour the police detective. He thought right. Of course it crossed my mind that if he'd been involved in his brother's disappearance or Andre's death, he might skip certain photos, but there would be photos with him in anyway so that didn't tell me much. I didn't think there was a lot of mileage in it for him to not help me out. I sat down on the floor next to him, and for a few minutes all I could hear was the sound of Harry turning pages, every so often pulling back sticky paper and putting photos on a pile.

I was going through another album myself: it seemed to be the one of Theo's high-school days. There was a photo of the entire class of seventeen-year-olds. I examined each of the twenty-odd faces, but nobody looked familiar. At Harry's side, the pile of photos grew steadily.

'I don't know who half these people are,' he said.

'Would you have known at the time?'

'It just makes me realise how little I knew about my brother. It's a bit upsetting.'

'Or maybe how much you've forgotten? It has been thirty years.'

He handed me the pile of photos he'd selected. 'These are all the ones that have other people in, even if they were just walking past.'

'Good,' I said. 'That's good.'

Harry went downstairs and I kept going through the pile. I was at it for more than an hour and must have looked at about two hundred photos. There was nobody of interest in any of them.

I got up from the floor with aching knees. I had pins and needles in my right leg and gave it a good rub, then sat down on the chair. The desk had two drawers on either side. I pulled open the top left-hand one and revealed a fascinating collection of pens and pencils. The one beneath it mainly held computer stuff, printer cartridges and so on. The top one on the right had bits of paper in it. It was a mess, like Andre's flat in miniature. I took the stack out and went through them. Old receipts, a menu for a Chinese restaurant.

I was reminded of being in Andre's office, moving the keyboard and finding that vital slip of paper. I opened the top left-hand drawer again, the one that contained the pens and pencils, and lifted the velour-covered insert.

Beneath it was a leaflet. It looked as if it could have been here for thirty years, kept out of sight by the green insert.

On the front was printed: *If things are getting too much, come and talk to us. We can help you.*

Underneath were the words: *Side Step.*

Chapter 33

The offices of Side Step were behind Centraal station, in an area that was now up and coming. I'd called Charlie to meet me behind the station and we had taken the little shuttle ferry across the IJ. It was as if we were on a mini cruise, the two-minute highlight reel of the Amsterdam water tour.

We were met by Servaas Laan, the head of Side Step.

'Our location is convenient,' he said. 'A lot of runaways end up at Centraal station at some point, so we're close, but the water forms a firm separation from the other possibilities these boys have. Drugs, crime; we like to say we're the ones who can ferry them away from that.' He laughed. 'It's a bad pun, I know.'

'We met with one of the kids you helped. He spoke very highly of the organisation.'

A broad smile broke out on Laan's face. 'That's great to hear. We know it doesn't work out for everybody, but we try to keep the kids in school, if at all possible, provide them with a roof over their heads, do all the paperwork.'

'What about the parents?' Charlie asked.

'It's not always the right thing to get those kids to go back home,' Laan said. 'If they want to, great, if they can be reunited with their parents, great, but only if that's what they want. We've got a team of people who help mediate between the kids and their parents. Sometimes that works, sometimes it doesn't.'

'And you purely help boys.'

'Yes, boys between thirteen and eighteen are welcome here.'

'We're looking for information about two boys who might have come through here in the late eighties. We know this might be tricky.'

'No, we've kept records of everything from 1985 onwards.'

'Why is that?' Charlie said.

'There were problems before. We had some people working here in the early eighties who were preying on those kids. As soon as we found out, we kept records.'

'You . . . kept records?' My voice was more sarcastic than I'd meant it to be. 'You didn't try to do anything about the abuse?'

'Oh don't get me wrong,' Laan said. 'We keep a very close eye on all the people who work here. Also on all the boys who turn up. Sometimes it's hard to tell whether a kid is really seventeen or maybe a few years older. But in case something does go wrong, at least we've got all the details. At least we'll be able to help the police bring the culprit to justice. Isn't that much better than what a lot of other charities do? Stick their heads in the sand, assume that all their staff are good people and try to keep matters quiet at all costs because it might harm their reputation? We try to be open, transparent, but we also understand that even the best safeguards might not always work. What is it they say? Drunks like to work in bars.'

And people who were sexually attracted to children tried to work with them. Like Verbaan. I nodded. I completely understood Laan's attitude and found that I agreed with him.

'You might have information for us then,' I said. 'We're looking for Andre Nieuwkerk.'

'The Body in the Dunes guy? I've been following that story, of course. You think he came through here?'

'We don't know for sure, but we know that his abuser gave the name of your organisation to another kid.'

Servaas Laan grimaced. 'You don't think we had anything to do with the abuse, do you?'

'The other kid is the one who spoke highly of you, so there's no suggestion that he was passed on to another abuser.'

'I didn't know this. Well, let's go down to the archives in the basement. Someone suggested the other day that we should clear it out – we could house another six boys if we do – but I really don't want to get rid of any of the paper.'

'You could computerise it,' Charlie said.

'And then have someone wipe it? I don't think so.'

The basement was a large room with pillars at regular intervals. It smelled of old paper and a hint of damp. Row upon row of pink folders lined the walls.

'What year are we looking at?'

'Andre left home in February of 1989.'

We followed Laan along the shelves.

'Here we are, 1989. It's all in alphabetical order.' He trailed

296

a finger over the dusty spines. 'No, I'm afraid not. He isn't here.'

'What about Theo Brand?' I asked. 'Have you got him?'

'Let me check.' Laan studied the files again. He didn't point out that it would have been easier if I'd given him both names at the same time. 'No, nothing in 1989,' he said.

This was going to be a pointless visit.

'Maybe 1988?' Charlie said. He was an eternal optimist.

I took a step back and watched Laan check the spines of a whole new row of files.

'Here he is!' The man's voice was triumphant. He took out a thin folder and opened it up. 'Okay, he arrived in February 1988 and left in May.' He looked at me. 'He wasn't here long.'

I should have come here as soon as Kars Borst gave us the name of the charity, rather than going to the Brands' house. It would have saved us half a day.

'Can you give me all the details you have? Where he went to school, where he went from here.'

'Oh, wait. There's this,' Laan said. He studied a piece of paper. 'He accused a member of staff of touching him up. Those were his words.'

I pulled my hair away from my face and held it together at the back of my neck for a second. So much for perfect safeguards. I'd thought it when I'd seen his photos: here was a kid who wouldn't keep quiet. 'What happened?'

'He withdrew the accusation a day later. Said he'd just been pissed off with the man. Again, his words. He left a couple of months later. This place clearly wasn't working for him.'

Much more likely that he never left; that he was killed in May 1988 and his body buried in the dunes nearby. I took my notebook out. 'What's the name of the member of staff he accused?'

'I'm . . .' Servaas Laan hesitated. 'I probably shouldn't tell you that.'

I raised my eyebrows. 'Didn't you say you kept records so that you could help the police?'

'The man was cleared.'

'The kid was murdered, Servaas.' I used his first name on purpose. 'He was murdered and he accused one of your staff of sexual abuse.'

'Of touching him.'

I held out my hand. 'Give me the file. Or do you want me to come back with a warrant? The result will be the same, only an hour later.' Or two hours, depending on how busy the prosecutor was.

Laan rubbed a hand over his face. He looked down at the sheet he was holding. 'Werda,' he said. 'Laurens Werda.'

Charlie made a loud noise next to me, an involuntary gasp of surprise.

I just felt sick, but I needed to get all the facts so I knew I had to keep my emotions under control. 'Laurens Werda? What exactly happened between him and Theo?'

'I'll get Werda's file too. Hold on a second.' He scuttled along the shelves and pulled out a green folder. He opened it. 'They had a tribunal.'

I was intrigued by how 'we' had suddenly become 'they'.

'Werda said nothing happened. He was closely monitored

for the rest of his time here, but there were no more complaints. Not from Theo Brand or any other kid.'

'You didn't fire him?' Charlie said.

'Well, no, not after the kid withdrew his statement. You have to understand: the people who work here have rights too. Some of these boys are really troubled.'

He'd withdrawn his statement, like Kars had done against Verbaan all those years ago.

'Oh, here,' Laan said. 'Theo had been expelled from his previous school for falsely accusing a teacher of touching him up. A female teacher.'

'Okay. Fine,' I said. There was no point in arguing with a guy who must have joined the organisation long after all this had happened. 'Give me those two files. Don't worry, I'll return them to you.' I wouldn't want to mess up his perfect paperwork; paperwork that clearly hadn't kept these kids safe.

Laurens Werda had worked at Side Step from October 1987 until February 1989. He'd been there for four months before Theo Brand arrived, and resigned from his job two days after Andre Nieuwkerk had been kicked out of his house and Paul Verbaan had given him the address of a place to go.

On the walk back to the ferry, the files seemed to burn in my bag and my fingers twitched with a desire to read through everything. The ferry arrived and we boarded. I got one of the files out of my handbag, but the wind kept pulling at the papers, trying to tear them from my hand and throw them into the water of the IJ. I put it away until I got back to my desk.

At the police station, Charlie and I sat side by side and read through the files. I gave him Theo Brand's file and took the one covering the tribunal myself.

'He said he left home because he was scared his parents would find out about the teacher, and that he'd been expelled from school,' Charlie said.

There was no denying that Side Step had been thorough in their investigation of Theo's claim against Laurens Werda. They'd interviewed Theo's previous teacher. I scanned through her statement. 'She said he demanded money from her; if she didn't cough up, he'd claim she'd been touching him.' I flipped a few pages. 'Laurens said something similar.' I read from the piece of paper. '"Theo approached me for an advance on his allowance, and when I refused, he threatened to report me for abuse."'

Charlie looked at me. 'You think he was telling the truth?'

I shrugged. 'Who knows? Either that, or he had had access to Theo's file and knew what to say to sound innocent.' I went back to the teacher's statement. She'd said she'd given Theo 400 guilders, but that he kept wanting more. She finally stopped paying and he went through with his threat and reported her. The school sided with the teacher and expelled the kid.

Her statement sounded credible, but I couldn't help but think of Paul Verbaan abusing those boys and getting away with it for so long. I remembered what schools were like in the eighties. They would have sided with the teachers by default. Even in my school there'd been a teacher who'd had a reputation, so that the girls would not want to go to his classroom after lessons had finished.

300

On the other hand, I remembered the photos of Theo going off on his first foreign holiday. Of Harry telling me he'd been jealous of his brother's ability to earn money.

'There's nothing much else here,' Charlie said. 'He didn't enrol in another school. Nobody seemed to have been worried when he left Side Step in May 1988.'

Chapter 34

The interrogation room was brightly lit to indicate that we wanted to get answers to everything and look into every corner. Laurens Werda sat opposite me. His lawyer was by his side. As soon as we'd called him in for questioning, he'd said he wanted his lawyer. This was his right, of course. I'd filled Thomas in on the way to the interrogation room on what Charlie and I had found out. I knew I needed someone experienced by my side. Charlie had been disappointed, but getting this right was more important than his feelings.

'You worked for the Side Step charity,' I began.

'That's right,' Laurens replied. 'Between 1987 and 1989. It was my first job.' He grimaced. 'I don't think I quite knew what I was getting into.'

'Tell me about Theo Brand,' I said.

Laurens looked down at his hands.

'The real Theo Brand,' I added. 'The one you met at Side Step.'

He sighed but met my eyes. 'He was a really troubled kid. I'd only been at Side Step a few months when I met him. He said he wanted to confide in me about his past, and I didn't have the experience to deal with him. I remember that five minutes into our chat, he grinned at me and said: I've got you now.'

'He said you touched him up.'

'I never touched him.'

'Were you angry with him?'

'At first. Then he withdrew his statement.'

'Did you pay him?'

'No.'

'Then what? You killed him?'

'He left one day and we were all relieved. I wasn't the only one.'

'He didn't really leave, though, did he? You killed him, took his possessions, buried his body and then ran away with Andre, who was using Theo's passport and name.'

Laurens shook his head. 'No. Theo left some of his things behind and I gave them to Andre.' He looked at his lawyer and she nodded. They must have agreed beforehand what he was going to admit to. 'Andre came to Side Step but didn't want to stay. He told me about his teacher, his parents. I only wanted to help. I went to the storage area and gave him the stuff that Theo had left behind.'

'You took him to London.'

'No, I gave him some money and Theo's passport.'

'Because he looked like Theo? Because you fancied him too?'

'He was a kid. He was upset. I helped him.'

'You helped him leave the country.'

'I didn't know he was going to do that.'

'That wasn't helping,' Thomas said. 'You were covering for killing Theo.'

'I didn't kill him. But I did realise I couldn't work at Side Step any more. Too many kids with bad stories. I resigned the next day.'

'I don't know why you've asked my client to come here,' the lawyer said. 'You're looking into a suicide and an out-dated case.' She gave me a stern glance over her reading glasses.

'We're trying to get Theo's family answers about what happened to their son. You can understand that, can't you?' But I knew the lawyer had a point. There was no crime we could arrest Laurens Werda for. No reason to keep him. His version of events could so easily be true.

'Okay,' I said. 'You're free to go. For now.'

Laurens stood up. He threw a glance at his lawyer. He looked relieved.

Thomas escorted the duo out. I stayed behind in the interview room. I realised he thought we had called him in for something else.

Thomas came back in. 'Did you see how he looked at his lawyer?' he said. 'We've missed something, haven't we?'

Talking through the facts to fix the timeline and come up with a probable chain of events was the first thing to do. That might help us understand where we had to poke. Where we had to look to get proof.

'We've got nothing,' I said. 'But look at this list I found in Andre's flat. At first I thought Laurens was separate from the others, but in fact these were four people he wanted to talk to who all had something to do with the Body in the Dunes.'

304

Thomas shook his head. 'So what? Are you saying that Laurens killed Theo and then ran off to London with Andre?'

'I don't know,' I said. 'It's possible that he told us the truth: that he simply gave Andre the passport. But maybe he suggested Andre should go to London to get Theo Brand officially out of the country. To hide his death. After all, when Andre renewed the passport in 1991, everybody assumed Theo was still alive. Giving Andre that passport was a master stroke if Laurens had murdered Theo.'

'Would Andre have known that at the time?' Charlie said.

I had to think about that. I'd wondered from the start why Andre had decided to come back to Amsterdam. Now I realised that this might have been the catalyst. It could have been exactly what made him come here. 'I think he had no idea until a couple of months ago,' I said. 'I don't think he knew that Theo was dead. Laurens probably told him that the guy had done a runner and left his passport behind. Then Andre did a bit of research and realised that Theo had been missing all those years.'

'He'd been looking him up online,' Thomas said.

'Right. He could have found the family tree, or one of the notices that Harry had put up for his brother when his mother was seriously ill. His neighbour told me that Andre had been really shaken up when he found out about his mother's death. I now think he was shocked because he found out that Theo had been missing for thirty years. He'd realised that Laurens had given him a dead kid's passport.'

When Laurens moved to London, maybe he had looked Andre up. Found out where he lived, arranged to meet. The runaway kid and the guy who'd helped him all those years ago. It was easy to picture it. Laurens was also the only person who knew Andre's real name. His real identity. The one person who knew his past and understood him. Maybe his hero. I could only imagine how intoxicating that must have been. Then Andre had found out that Laurens had had his own reason for helping him.

'He must have come here to find out what happened,' Charlie said.

'He must have come here to talk to Laurens about it,' Thomas said.

'Laurens told us Andre was his ex. That they'd been living together in London.'

'And that must have really thrown the poor guy off balance. Enough to make him kill himself in disgust at having been played all that time.'

I was suddenly reminded that Carol had mentioned Andre talking about a chain of abuse. His relationship with Laurens must have felt like that in hindsight. Thinking about Carol also made me remember her saying that she'd had a pact with Andre about suicide; that he had promised he would call her if things got too much.

I wondered if he'd ever made an agreement like that with someone else.

Someone he'd called really early in the morning. Someone he'd hoped would stop him.

Someone who'd had a reason not to come when he called.

Then another thought popped into my head. What if it was someone who *had* come?

We needed to go back to the hotel. Maybe someone had seen Laurens Werda that day.

The Hotel Mondrian was quiet this afternoon. A couple in thick winter coats, a little too thick for the weather, were sitting in the lounge area. I guessed they were waiting for others to join them, to go out sightseeing. A young man in a suit was staring intently at his laptop screen at a table in the corner. On the opposite side, a woman pushed a trolley piled high with cleaning products. It was that time of day. She turned a corner and went into the ladies'.

'Wait for me here,' I said to Charlie, and followed the cleaner. Because I'd recognised her. She wasn't wearing a pale green scarf this time, but one with a gold and orange swirled pattern. She was a block of colour in the otherwise stark surroundings of the hotel.

I pushed the door to the ladies' open. The cleaner was an unpleasant reminder to me of that morning. Of how I'd felt when I'd seen Andre Nieuwkerk. Only a week ago, I had doubted his identity. How far we'd come since then, and how little had we achieved.

I could tell from the way she looked at me that she recognised me too. She made eye contact, then dropped the hand holding the cleaning cloth to rest it on the basin in front of her. 'I saw,' she said.

I met her eyes in the mirror. 'What did you see?'

'I saw on TV. That man, he was famous?'

Famous? He was now, I guessed. Famous for having died twice. No, for having been declared dead twice. There was nothing like a mystery combined with police failings to capture the imagination of the press.

That morning, the cleaner had made sure not to look into the room. She had looked at the floor in front of her.

Almost as if she knew what was inside.

That didn't mean anything. This was a hotel. Guests died in their rooms; maybe not frequently, but it wasn't as if it had never happened before.

After all, there had been two police detectives in the hallway.

No, she couldn't have known that. Charlie and I hadn't been in uniform; we could have been normal guests, accompanied by the manager. We could have just forgotten our key.

I rested my hip against the basin. 'What did you see?' I said again. 'When did you see him?'

She grabbed a bottle of detergent and sprayed the glass, blurring my face.

'Did you see his body? Did you find him?'

She rubbed the mirror as if it was her enemy. That first morning, it had been the street cleaner who had called an ambulance.

'Why didn't you call the police?' I said.

'He did.'

'Who did?'

'Manager. He called you.'

'He called us after you'd opened the door. After you'd seen the dead body.'

She went back to rubbing her cloth over the glass.

'You were the one who found him?'

She shook her head but didn't stop cleaning. 'The manager did.'

'Did you take anything? Was there anything in his room?'

'He was dead. We called you.'

'Did you take anything?' I asked again. 'Did you find a note?'

'No. We didn't take anything. There was no note.' She said it softly.

'If only the CCTV hadn't broken.'

The cleaner scoffed. 'Wasn't broken. It's a fake. They're all fake. To keep down cost. He has installed real ones now.'

'Just in that corridor?'

'No, all. All was easier, he said.' She stopped cleaning and looked at me via the mirror. 'Don't tell him I said so. I'll lose my job.'

'I won't.'

'I was sad,' she said, 'because he was a nice man.'

'A nice man? How did you know that?'

'I talked to him on Saturday. I let him in; he'd lost his key.' She rubbed her forehead. 'I let him back into his room because I recognised him. He left me a big tip. Then I found him dead.'

'He'd lost his key? Did you have to make him a new one?'

'No, the second one was in his room. Guests always have two keys.'

'And you said this was Saturday?'

'Yes, Saturday morning. Maybe eight o'clock? Half past eight?'

'Thank you,' I said. 'Thank you for telling me.'

She went back to wiping the mirrors.

On my way out of the ladies', I bumped into the hotel manager. 'How's your CCTV now?' I said. 'All fixed?'

'Yes.' He smiled his super-professional smile. 'It's working perfectly again now.'

It was on the tip of my tongue to tell him that I knew they'd been fakes previously. It would have been satisfying to wipe the smile off his face. The only reason I didn't was because the cleaner reminded me of the street cleaner that first morning, the man who had called the police when everybody else had ignored the slumped body of Peter de Waal. However my decisions that morning had worked out, that man had done a brave thing in the face of his fear. Just like the hotel cleaner had been brave to tell me. She needn't have done. She could have kept quiet.

Keeping quiet was so often the easy solution. Keeping quiet about someone having been beaten up; keeping quiet about your boss being the first person to open the door to a hotel room and find a dead man; keeping quiet about interviewing a suspect and noticing his hands.

I knew only too well how difficult it was to speak out. I knew how it could make your life so much harder. I could only imagine what would happen to the cleaner if I didn't control my tongue right now. If I did anything other than smile.

I shouldn't make life unnecessarily difficult for the people with the guts to speak out.

'I'm glad to hear that,' I said to the manager. 'Having working CCTV is really important.'

I walked away so that I didn't need to hear his response, found Charlie and tapped him on the arm. 'Let's go,' I said.

'Didn't you want to talk to the manager?'

'Nope,' I said. 'Don't need to talk to him any more.'

'What happened?'

'Let's go,' I repeated, 'and I'll fill you in.'

Once outside, I told Charlie about the CCTV.

'Leave it with me,' he said.

I liked the determined look on his face as he scanned the other buildings on the street.

My phone rang. It was Ingrid. I hesitated before picking up, but there was no point in avoiding her.

'What the fuck?' she screamed. 'We had to let him go because of you.'

'I'm sorry,' I said. Having just done the same with Laurens, I understood only too well how upset she must be.

'You know he most likely did this, don't you?'

'You know he didn't.'

'He was there, Lotte. He was in the vicinity of the Lange Niezel on the night of the assault.'

'What do you mean?'

'His mobile phone. He was there.'

I pulled my hair away from my face. 'Why didn't you tell me that last night?'

'Why didn't you just trust me?'

I started to say again that I was sorry, but she'd disconnected the call.

Chapter 35

I went straight to the traffic department when I got back to the police station. Mehmet was at his desk and gave me a huge smile. 'Thanks, Lotte,' he said. 'They let Erol out.'

'We need to talk to him,' I said. 'Right now.'

'Why?'

'Did you know that he was actually there that night? You're coming with me. Let's clear up this mess.'

'He was there?' Mehmet said. 'Shit.'

'Call him,' I said. 'Tell him we're coming to his place right now.'

To be fair, Mehmet didn't argue. He made the call.

When we got to Erol's flat, he didn't seem pleased to see me, but at least he didn't look as if he wanted to beat me up. It was interesting that I'd tried so hard to get justice for someone I didn't particularly like.

'Thanks,' he said with seeming reluctance. 'My lawyer said your testimony made all the difference.'

'You should have taken photos of your hands as soon as we'd been to see you. As soon as I told you to.'

Erol smiled. It changed his face. 'I'll know for next time. Instead I had a detective testify for me. That was a first.'

'If you're so grateful,' I said, 'you can tell us what happened that night. You were there.'

He folded his arms. The shutters came down again. 'I had nothing to do with the assault.'

'They've got your phone at the location.'

'I didn't beat him up.' Erol sighed. 'I don't want anything bad to happen to them. I never went to their house. I didn't harass them. I didn't do most of the things they said I did.'

'But they got a restraining order.' I was puzzled.

'Based on no evidence whatsoever. I didn't send Peter de Waal anonymous emails. I never said I was going to kill him.'

'You sure?' Mehmet leaned forward. 'You never sent threatening emails?'

'Never.'

'Did you make any threats towards them at all?' he asked.

Erol pulled both hands through his hair. 'I really don't think I should tell you any of this.'

'All these things are on record,' I said. 'According to your file, you've done them all already anyway. Tell me what you did do.'

Erol frowned. 'Okay. The only time I said I was going to kill him was when I signed the divorce papers. He was there with Caroline, being all smug, and just got on my nerves.' He rubbed the back of his neck. 'To be honest,' he said to Mehmet, 'if you hadn't held me back, I probably would have punched him.'

Mehmet had neglected to tell me about that. So forgetful, that man. He must be closer to his cousin than he had implied.

'But I didn't do any of the other things. I didn't send any

anonymous emails. I didn't stuff dog shit through their letter box either. I didn't break their windows.' He looked me in the eye. 'And I didn't beat the living daylights out of him. Peter came to pay me a visit. All friendly like. We had a chat. I thought it cleared the air but then they started claiming I'd been harassing them.' He sighed. 'I've kept my distance and he still got me anyway, didn't he?'

'Your phone,' I repeated. 'They've got you at the scene of the assault.'

Erol scratched the back of his head and pulled a face.

Mehmet pointed to me with a thumb. 'You can trust her. She testified for you.'

'Trust? She's still a police officer. It's in her best interests to turn me in as soon as she gets a chance.'

'Believe me,' I said, 'I really don't want to see you arrested again. But help me out here.'

'Okay, yeah, I was there.'

My jaw tightened as my teeth locked together. I had to force myself to relax. 'You were there?' I knew I sounded incredulous. I threw an angry look at Mehmet, even though it wasn't really his fault.

'I didn't beat him up,' Erol said quickly. 'I came around the corner and I saw a group of guys kicking a man on the floor. They took his stuff and ran.'

'You saw it?'

'There were four of them.' He fell silent.

'Then what?'

'Then ... I realised that the victim was Peter and I walked away.'

'For fuck's sake, Erol.' Mehmet's sharp voice took me by surprise. 'You walked away?'

'I know, I should have called an ambulance, but . . . I knew he'd try to lay it on me. I never harassed them, and I didn't want to get involved.'

I kept my temper under control. I didn't say that he'd been a coward, unlike the street cleaner. There was no point in going on about what was morally right and wrong. Instead I focused on what was useful. 'You saw them?' I said. 'The guys who did this, you actually saw them?'

Erol nodded.

'Any chance you recognised them?'

'I took their number plate.'

'You fucking idiot,' Mehmet said. 'Why didn't you tell us any of this before?'

Erol shrugged. 'Nobody would have believed me.' He didn't even sound angry about it.

Mehmet and I were back in the little café where we'd first talked, the one just behind the police station. The only difference was that Ingrid was here instead of Charlie. I'd asked her to join us for a coffee. This strategy had worked well enough for Charlie last time. Part of me was surprised when she agreed to talk to me, and she definitely looked pissed off with me when she walked through the door. It didn't get any better when she spotted Mehmet.

'What the hell is this?' she asked. 'Some kind of weird ambush?'

'If we can get you evidence to arrest the real people who are carrying out those assaults, would you like it?'

'What do you mean?'

'There's evidence. Someone saw the number plate of the car.'

'You found a witness?'

'Yeah,' I said. 'There's a witness.'

'And the problem is . . .'

I didn't say anything.

'I know you too well, Lotte,' Ingrid continued. 'You wouldn't be here with this guy if there wasn't a problem.'

'You're not going to like my witness.'

She narrowed her eyes. 'You're talking about Erol Yilmaz. I knew he'd been there around that time.'

'What do you want to do, Ingrid?'

'Are you saying Yilmaz was there when de Waal was assaulted? He knew the guys who did it?'

'He saw them. He took down their number plate.'

Ingrid shook her head. 'What the hell, Lotte, you can't believe he was there by accident?'

'I did a trace of the number plate; the car belongs to someone with a lot of previous. These guys would fit for all the assaults. All we need to do is talk to Peter de Waal. If he confirms what Erol said, we can get the guys who really did this.'

'What if it *was* Yilmaz?'

'He said he never sent those emails. That he never harassed the de Waals.'

Ingrid swore under her breath and then took a sip of her coffee. She looked out of the window, as if the answer to how to deal with a stubborn colleague could be found in the water of the canal.

'Fine,' she said finally. 'I'll double-check the emails. Give me some time. If there's anything out of the ordinary, we'll go talk to Peter de Waal again. Is that good enough?'

'Yes,' I said. 'Yes, that's great.'

Chapter 36

I hadn't been to Peter de Waal's house before. The only time I'd talked to him was when he was still in the hospital. It was an average house in this row, which meant it probably belonged to the ten per cent most valuable pieces of property in Amsterdam. It had that solid square shape that screamed of money. It was larger than Mark's place.

'Thanks for not saying anything to anybody about that morning,' I said as we arrived at the front door. 'About Andre Nieuwkerk.'

'We've all messed up sometimes,' Ingrid said. 'I wasn't going to rat you out.' She threw me a glance. 'I'm still annoyed with you for testifying for Yilmaz.'

'I know.'

'But I also know that that morning you chose to help me.' She rang the doorbell. 'Even if Peter retracts his statement, we can't arrest anybody on Yilmaz's say-so. Not after what's been in the papers.'

'Once you know who they are, you can trail them. Wait until they mug someone else.'

'Do you think we've got all the time in the world?'

'Not all the time in the world.' I grinned. 'But I think you've got time to do that.'

Before Ingrid had time to reply, Peter de Waal opened the door. Last time I'd seen him, his face had been badly bruised, but it had gone back to a normal patrician shape and colour. He'd probably been very attractive a decade ago, but now the skin was slack around his jaw and there was weakness in the bags under his eyes.

'Caroline isn't here,' he said.

'That's fine,' Ingrid responded. 'We wanted to see you anyway. Get some things clear.'

'Sure, we can go over everything again.' He pulled the door open and invited us to follow him. He pointed towards a sofa in the middle of the light, airy room.

'This time,' Ingrid said after she'd unzipped her coat, 'when we go over things, can you not lie? That would be really helpful.'

Peter looked as if he'd been punched in the face again. His features mainly reflected total shock.

'We checked those emails that you printed out, the ones you claimed Erol sent you,' she said, 'and they actually came from an IP address in your wife's office. So either the two of you have sent them to yourselves, or your wife really hates you.'

'We ...' Peter's eyes shifted from mine to Ingrid's and back, like those of a dog following a tennis match. 'We didn't lie. She forwarded them from her work email address to my private one. That's what you must have seen.'

'Don't,' Ingrid said. 'Just don't. Stop lying. I've checked it all.'

'Why are you doing this?' he said. 'Is it because we talked to the press? Because we made you look bad?'

'Your wife is at work,' I said. 'If there's anything you want to tell us without her here, now's a good time to do it. We want to stop those assaults. Get the people who are really doing it.'

'I don't know what you want me to say.' Peter folded his arms.

'Be honest about the night you were assaulted,' Ingrid said.

'I'm not going to change—'

'Tell us the truth,' I interrupted him, 'and we'll forget that you sent those emails yourself and pretended that Erol Yilmaz harassed you.'

'I don't really remember,' Peter said.

'Your colleague told us you were drunk that night, that you refused to go home, that you were aggressive. We've kept all of that quiet and will continue to do so.'

'But I'd be changing my testimony.'

I stopped myself from smiling, but I knew we had him. Just a bit more pressure was needed.

'We need to get those people,' Ingrid said. 'And we can't do that if you still maintain that it was Erol.'

'Why?'

'We've got a witness from that night,' I said. 'But your testimony contradicts what he says, which makes it hard for us.' Which meant that Ingrid didn't believe me. None of this needed to stand up in court; all I needed to do was convince my colleague that Erol had told the truth.

'But if I say something else now . . .' His voice trailed off.

'We won't do you for wasting police time, if that's what

you're concerned about.' I would love to pursue him for what he'd done to Erol, but then Erol hadn't called an ambulance for Peter either, so in my head the two men were pretty much square. Sometimes policing was all about what you could prove in court plus getting the best solution for all concerned.

'I really thought it was Erol,' Peter said. 'At first. I thought I'd seen him.' He paused. Then he made up his mind to talk and the words flooded out. 'The next day I remembered that there had been more than one attacker. That it hadn't been him. I wanted to tell you but I couldn't.'

'Why?'

'By then it was in all the papers and Caroline kept telling everybody who was willing to listen that it been Erol, and I couldn't go back on what I'd said. I wanted to come clean, but she hates him.' He seemed relieved to get the story off his chest.

'She hates Erol?'

'Yeah. Because he left her.'

I narrowed my eyes to see Peter more clearly. 'I thought she left him.'

'That's what she told everybody, but in reality he'd had enough of her. He never understood her and she hated him for that. She wanted to stitch him up, so even when I told her that it probably hadn't been him – this was when I was still in hospital – she said: let's destroy him now. You have to understand her,' he added. 'Nobody likes to be left behind. I know I shouldn't say this, but I think she could have killed him when he first said he wanted a divorce. It came as a real shock to her.'

'What about the restraining order?'

'Caroline did all of that. She really went off the deep end. Made up a story, made Yilmaz's life hell. I thought she'd moved on, and then this happened. It's all my fault.'

Ingrid and I exchanged a glance. 'You said there was more than one guy?' she asked.

'Yes,' Peter said. 'I think there were four of them. They shouted something. I turned round and saw them.'

Ingrid showed the mugshot of the guy who owned the car.

'Yeah,' Peter said sheepishly. 'That could have been him.'

Ingrid was still shaking her head when we left the house. An hour later, my mobile rang. It was Charlie.

'I got it,' he said. 'I've got it.'

Chapter 37

'What is it?' Thomas said. He'd also come to the office.

'Just wait.' Charlie grinned. He was like a schoolboy saying: not telling you. He inserted a memory card in the PC
and played the footage.

It was granular. It wasn't high-definition by any stretch of
the imagination. It showed a pavement, cars going past, a
tram rattling by.

'Where is this?' Thomas asked.

'The luxury watch shop,' Charlie said. 'The one next door
to the hotel.'

The camera must be installed somewhere inside the shop
window. If anybody was going to smash the window to grab
the watches on display, at least there'd be footage of that.
That didn't mean we'd ever be able to identify who was on
the screen, but it made shops feel better.

'Look, here he comes,' Charlie said.

The man walking into the picture hurried along.

'Well done,' Thomas said, and Charlie smiled as if he'd just
been given the biggest compliment on earth.

I would have liked to think the man on the screen had
been in a rush because he'd been desperate to save someone's

life, but instead I was pretty certain he was hurrying to make sure that someone died.

'What time is this?' I asked.

Charlie pointed at the screen. The clock was in the bottom corner and seconds were ticking away. He rewound the footage a bit: at the moment that Laurens Werda walked past the watch shop, the clock said 08:32.

Nearly two hours after Andre had called him.

Charlie wound the footage forward. 'Here's when he leaves. He stayed for half an hour or so.'

It was 08:58 when Laurens came past the watch shop again. The grainy footage meant that I couldn't see the look on his face.

I looked back through the notes I'd made the day we'd found Andre dead. We thought he'd come back to his room at 8.37, because that was when his key had been used. But that hadn't been him. That couldn't have been him.

It had to have been Werda. Did he have a key to Andre's hotel room?

The cleaner told me that she'd let Andre into his room on Saturday morning because he'd lost his key.

The morning after he'd had dinner with Werda.

This all made so much sense.

I got up and scribbled on the whiteboard.

'Andre called Laurens at 6.43 a.m. We know from Carol that he had tried to commit suicide before and that he'd called her and she'd saved him. How long would it have taken Laurens to get to the hotel?'

'Half an hour at most,' Thomas said.

So he'd waited for more than an hour to set off. That bastard.

'Do you think he murdered him?' Charlie said.

'Not that. But I wonder if the reason he came to the hotel wasn't to stop Andre from committing suicide, but to check that he had successfully done it.'

'You're saying Andre didn't die after Werda came to the hotel but before?'

'Yes. And Werda had a key; the cleaner had to let Andre into his room the morning after he'd spent the night at Werda's place.'

'So he came to the hotel, let himself in with the key, made sure that Andre was dead, and then left?'

'Yes,' I said. 'That's exactly what I think happened.'

Thomas rubbed his chin. 'He called him at 6.43 to say he was going to kill himself, hoping that Werda would stop him, as the arrangement had been with Carol, only Werda had no intention of stopping him. Not with what Andre knew. He waited over an hour and then went to the hotel. Now how the hell are we going to prove any of that?'

That was a good question.

'Andre's death was very convenient for him, don't you think?' Thomas said. 'If you hadn't called his sister, we would never have found out that he really was Andre Nieuwkerk.'

It hadn't been because I'd called his sister. It had been because I'd talked to him that morning, but nobody knew about that.

'If you hadn't spoken to her,' Thomas continued, 'none of this would have come out, not about the Body in the Dunes, not about Theo having been murdered, not that Verbaan didn't kill Andre. It would all have been buried. You did well.'

I shook my head. I hadn't done well at all. 'You're right about one thing,' I said. 'Andre's death was very convenient for Werda. There was no way he was going to stop his suicide.'

'Is that even a crime?' Charlie asked.

'Let's go pick him up again,' I said. 'We'll see what we can get him to admit to.'

Laurens' sanctimonious smile made me want to throw up. Of course we'd had to wait for his lawyer again. At least we knew who she was, so she was only a quick phone call away.

'You don't feel bad for what you've done?' I asked.

'What did I do?'

'Andre Nieuwkerk called you that morning to tell you he was going to kill himself, and you didn't stop him.'

'You're wrong. I went to his hotel, but by the time I got there, he had already died. I was so upset that I sat by his side for half an hour. He was the man I'd loved. I was torn apart.'

'You didn't think to call an ambulance?'

'He was dead. I checked his breathing. Yes, he called me and I didn't stop him in time. I didn't call the police after he contacted me. If that was what he wanted, then why would I interfere? Yes, I was very sad, but to stop him would have been selfish. My wish, not his. When you love somebody, or even when you loved somebody years ago, you should do what's best for them, not for yourself. Don't you think?'

'How did you get into his hotel room?'

'He stayed at my house on Friday night, after we'd had dinner, and he left his key behind. I thought he'd done it on purpose. He said he still loved me.'

I shook my head. That dinner had been about something completely different.

'He wanted me to visit him, spend more time with him,' Laurens continued. 'But it would have been a mistake to rekindle our relationship.'

By this point Andre must have known that Laurens had killed Theo. That must have been why he'd come to Amsterdam: to talk to his ex-partner about it, the man who'd given him Theo's papers and got him to go to London.

Either way, what were we going to be able to prove? That Laurens had gone to Andre's hotel room. That Andre had died either just before, or while Laurens had been there. His visit was right in the window of the time of death the pathologist had given us. Not interfering with a suicide attempt was not a crime. Working at a charity for runaways was not a crime. All I had was a whole bunch of circumstantial stuff and no evidence whatsoever.

Andre had told Daniel that soon everybody was going to know what had happened.

I could imagine him calling Laurens. Giving him one last chance to prove that he'd loved him. No, giving him one last chance to prove that he was a decent human being.

A chance that he hadn't taken.

'Was he still alive?' I asked. 'Was he still alive when you got to his room?'

'What do you think?' Laurens said. 'Surely you don't think

I killed him. You think I sat with him and watched him die? I told you, he was already dead. He committed suicide.'

'What happened with Theo?' I asked. 'Did he want more money? Did he threaten you? Blackmail you again?'

Laurens stayed silent.

'You murdered him; that's why you had his belongings. You gave his passport to Andre and made Theo come alive again. Did it feel good?' I asked. 'Did it feel good to meet Andre in London, to be with the man you'd lied to? Did it feel good to know you'd got away with murder?'

His lawyer made a movement. 'The statute of limitation on Theo Brand's murder has long passed. Can we stop talking about this?'

I knew I had no grounds for arrest. 'Sure, let's move on to Andre Nieuwkerk if you prefer. You killed him too,' I said. 'You killed him and I'm not going to stop until I can prove it.' I didn't care that I was talking to their backs. 'I'm not going to stop.'

But we still had nothing at the end of the twenty-four hours that we could keep him locked up for. The prosecutor refused to extend the arrest period. He pointed out to me that we had one case where the statute of limitation had passed and another that looked like a suicide.

Chapter 38

The next evening, the doorbell rang. I wasn't expecting anybody and pressed the button on the intercom with resigned annoyance. It would probably be someone wanting to convert me, or to sell me something.

'It's Laurens Werda,' the disembodied voice said. 'I'm here with my lawyer. Can we talk for a moment?'

Why the hell were they here? 'I'll come down and we can go to the police station instead,' I said. 'Let's talk there.'

'I don't think you'll want to,' a female voice said. The lawyer.

Without her there, I wouldn't have let Laurens in. Even though I had my gun in my flat, I wouldn't choose to be alone with a man who, I was pretty sure, had murdered someone, even if it was thirty years ago.

I pressed the buzzer that unlocked the communal door downstairs. 'I'm all the way at the top,' I said. 'Third floor.'

I waited by my front door until I saw them coming up. Laurens' face was flushed red from the exertion of climbing the steps. The florid hue clashed with the pink of his shirt. I stepped aside to let him and his lawyer in. The woman must be in better physical shape than Laurens, because she hadn't even broken sweat.

I went ahead of them, led them to the dining table and sat down. It was the closest to a formal interrogation area I could offer in my flat. There was no way I was going to sit on the sofa with them.

I indicated seats at the other side of the table, one of them the place where my mother used to sit when we played cards. The place from where it was easiest to cheat.

'We thought we'd talk to you,' the lawyer said, 'so that you can drop the investigation.'

'Right,' I said, 'and why would I do that?'

'We've got evidence that Andre Nieuwkerk's death was suicide.'

'Evidence that you're willing to share with me?'

The lawyer opened her bag and took out a large sheet of paper in a plastic cover. Laurens looked at me with an expression on his face that could only be described as smug. 'It's how I knew you'd talked to Andre,' he said. 'He mentions you in his suicide note. He wrote that he spoke to you but that you didn't believe him. I thought I'd give it to you. If you take it, you'll know it's suicide but nobody else needs to learn about your part in it.'

I held out my hand. 'Give me that.'

'He was already dead,' Laurens said. 'I got there too late.'

The lawyer kept the sheet of paper in front of her.

'What about Theo Brand?' I said. 'What about the boy you murdered?'

'It was twenty-five years ago,' the lawyer said. 'The statute of limitation has passed.'

'Then tell me,' I said. 'Just tell me if you killed him.'

'My client won't answer that question,' the lawyer said.

'Tell me something else then, for the family. Were those remains Theo Brand? At least tell me that.'

The lawyer gave a single nod. Confirmation of everything I had guessed but was unable to prove.

Laurens Werda didn't say anything. He just pushed the suicide note in its plastic cover across the table. 'The paper will have my fingerprints on it,' he said, 'but it's definitely Andre's handwriting.'

'Why didn't you call the police?' I said. 'When you found him.'

'I assumed the hotel staff would find him later that morning. I didn't know it would be another full day.'

'There's no legal obligation to report a dead body,' the lawyer said. 'My client didn't commit a crime by not calling the police.'

I knew that. I knew it wasn't a crime. 'Wasn't there a moral obligation, though? Towards someone who'd been your life partner for two decades?'

'One decade,' Laurens said. His grin told me that he knew I'd been trying to catch him out.

The lawyer stood up. 'You've got the note. I hope that clears up any suspicions you might have had about Laurens killing Andre Nieuwkerk. I'd suggest you keep it to yourself. It makes it clear that you're far more to blame for his death than my client is.'

I avoided reading the note. All I saw was that it had been written in blue pen.

On the way out, Laurens stepped close to me and whispered, 'He was still breathing. I sat with him until he stopped. Until I knew for sure that he was dead.'

He closed the door behind him.

I heard his footsteps go down the steps, following his lawyer.

My eyes were drawn to the note. I couldn't stop myself.

To the hotel staff, it began. *I apologise that you'll find me dead. Please pass this note on to Detective Lotte Meerman. I talked to her this morning. She didn't believe me then but hopefully she'll believe me now.*

Chapter 39

The whole day I pondered on what to do whilst pretending to work, and by the time Mark came to my flat for our Sinterklaas celebrations, I was emotionally drained. As tradition demanded, we waited for dark to fall before we started swapping presents.

I handed Mark one of his, wrapped in colourful paper. He shook it.

'When I was a kid,' I said, 'my mum used to add poems to the presents. Did yours do that?' That was one of the Sinterklaas traditions, along with putting straw for Sinterklaas's horse in a shoe in front of the chimney – or in our case the central heating boiler – and then finding it miraculously swapped in the morning for a present.

'She did. It always freaked me out how much Sinterklaas knew about me. Especially all the things I'd done wrong during the year.'

'Me too!' I said. 'My mum loved to point out what I could do better. She thought I was much more likely to listen to Sinterklaas than to her. I hope you didn't add any poems to my presents.'

'No,' he said, 'I didn't. I thought that if there were things we needed to talk about, we could do it as grown-ups. Not in a poem.' He handed me a present.

It was the same size and shape as the one I'd given him. I followed his example and gave it a gentle shake. It sounded like something bumping against cardboard. I grinned. I knew what it was.

He tore the wrapping paper off his present to reveal a letter M made out of chocolate. Milk chocolate with nuts.

Mine was an L in white chocolate. I liked white chocolate.

It was a good thing we'd had that discussion.

'Do you feel you can talk to me?' he said.

'Yes,' I said. 'We talk. Don't we talk?'

'But I know you try not to talk about your work.'

'It's not good to always talk about death and violence. I want to have conversations about other things too.' I put my chocolate L on the table with more care than I needed to. Worry suddenly sat at the base of my throat, thick and troublesome. I picked up my glass of wine and took a big gulp to try to wash it away.

'I understand,' he said, 'but don't shut me out.'

'I tell you more than I tell anybody else.'

'Like what?'

Like how I talked to Andre Nieuwkerk that morning, I wanted to say, but that would lead me to telling him that Laurens Werda and his lawyer now knew about that as well, and he wouldn't be happy that I'd let them into my flat. 'You were the first one I told about the guy that morning. The one who said he was the Body in the Dunes.' That wasn't even a lie.

'That became really big, didn't it?'

'Yes. Big and problematic. Like the assault case the same day.'

'What happened with that?'

I just wanted to open another present. I didn't want to talk about work. 'It turned into a mess because the victim lied.' A mess we'd hopefully sorted out.

'You can tell me about things like that. You don't have to carry them around with you all by yourself.'

'Sometimes I don't want to talk about them, though. Sometimes I want to sit here and pretend that what I do is normal, drink wine and chat about ordinary things like the weather and politics.'

Mark paused. He handed me a small present. It was a diary.

'If you don't want to tell me, you can write things down. It's good to write about your problems.'

I looked at the diary. Just the fact that it would record my thoughts terrified me. 'Thanks. I'll do that,' I lied.

'I'm serious,' he said. 'Tell me. Tell me what's going on.'

Instead of responding immediately, I handed him an envelope containing the paperwork for the course I'd enrolled him in. I waited until he finished reading the details of where and when to go. I didn't want to talk about what had happened that morning and what had happened since, but I also realised that our relationship was pretty much doomed if I continued to stay silent. I remembered my mum telling me not to mess this one up; maybe for once I needed to heed her advice.

Once I'd put it in those terms in my head, it was no longer a difficult choice.

I told him.

I told him that I felt responsible for a man's death, and how I was planning to fix it.

Mark held out his hand. 'You're doing the right thing,' he said. Even though he'd seemed happy enough with his knife-skills course, his broad smile said that me talking to him about what had been going on had been the bigger present.

Chapter 40

I could hear the rain pattering on my roof, telling me in Morse code that it might be best to stay in bed. My cat sleeping peacefully nestled against my feet, my duvet lovingly embracing me and Mark's arm heavy around my waist with his hand warm on my stomach all reinforced the message. So what if Ingrid was waiting for me in the red-light district, telling me that I had half an hour to come over if I wanted to do this?

I had thirty minutes. Only thirty minutes. I'd better get going. I slid out of the bed, scaring Pippi into an annoyed meow that turned into a catty yawn and stretch, and grabbed some clothes. What would be the right thing to wear? It didn't matter, I decided, because listening to the weather, I would look like a drowned rat before I even got there.

'Good luck,' Mark muttered. It sounded as if he was talking in his sleep.

Jeans, jumper, waterproof coat. I did go as far as putting on a little bit of make-up.

I grabbed my large umbrella, and slung my bag with my papers over my shoulder.

Downstairs, I got on my bike and set off with my

umbrella aloft to keep the worst of the rain off my head, but more crucially to keep my bag and its important contents dry. It was still dark, and it felt as if the whole of Amsterdam was asleep. Only here and there were lights on behind windows.

Ingrid stood on the same corner where we'd been that first morning. 'What kept you?' she said. The awning of a shop provided shelter from the rain. I folded up my umbrella, locked my bike and joined her.

'Have you been here all night?'

'Pretty much. But we got them.'

'How careless of them to go for the same place,' I said.

'We had to follow them for two days before they finally made a move.'

'Bauer must be delighted.'

'He is. Catching villains in the act is his favourite thing.' Ingrid didn't sound pleased, though; she just sounded exhausted.

I could make more chitchat, ask her how Tim was, or if she had any plans for the weekend – other than sleep – now that they'd finally caught these guys, but I let her stand in silence, gave her some peace and quiet.

We waited, with the rain falling down on the awning and forming a small waterfall at its edge. I looked at my watch. 'I thought you said half an hour.'

'That's what Bauer told me.' She threw me a look. 'I couldn't ask for more details. I had to pretend not to be interested.'

'Sure,' I said. 'I appreciate it.'

'And now we're even, right?'

I was about to say that we were only even if her information was good, but just at that moment, the cars pulled in.

'Yes,' I said. 'Now we're even.'

The camera crew got out using a forest of umbrellas. In
a country where it rained on average ten hours a day, they
were used to shooting under these circumstances.

The next car was the one I'd been waiting for. Commissaris Smits climbed out.

Now that it was about to happen, I didn't feel too good
about this. The first morning, I had turned my back towards
the cameras to avoid having my face on screen again. When
I'd liberated Julia from the throng of journalists with Daniel's
help, I'd guarded my face with my arm. This felt like a desperate attempt even to myself. A desperate attempt that
nobody was going to appreciate.

The commissaris was in position, Monique Blom opposite him, both holding see-through umbrellas. The cameras,
sheltered by plastic, were aimed at them like searchlights.

They were thirty metres away from us.

I just had to wait for the right moment. I opened my
handbag.

Monique Blom congratulated the commissaris on the
police's success in capturing this gang.

'Gang,' Ingrid muttered. 'It was just four guys.'

'It's making you sound good,' I said. 'Don't knock it.'

'Maybe I'll get a pay rise.'

'Don't hold your breath.'

Even though I was talking to Ingrid, I was paying close
attention to the interview. The commissaris had just finished

answering a question about the problems with open borders and gangs from Schengen countries coming over.

It felt as if the boring part was going to start.

I made my move, stepping out from under the awning.

The rain hit my face, woke me up and dared me to think about what I was doing.

If it thought it could make me change my mind, it was wrong.

The commissaris saw me coming. He narrowed his eyes and subtly shook his head, probably hoping against hope that he could stop me.

I reached into my handbag. Monique Blom turned to check what the commissaris was looking at.

'Detective Meerman,' she said.

For once, it was really useful that the press recognised me.

I took out the photo of Theo Brand and held it up towards the camera. 'This is the man who was the Body in the Dunes,' I said.

The commissaris made a grab towards the photo and got hold of the top left-hand corner. I fought him for control and managed to keep a grip of the lower corner. It was perfect. I knew the image would look as if we were holding it out together.

'I know you've been interested in this story,' I said, 'and I think your viewers would be too. Let me read out Andre's suicide note. Do you mind?'

'No,' Monique said. 'That would be really interesting.'

I took the sheet of paper in its plastic cover out of my handbag. I didn't want to read it out, but it would cement everything. I cleared my throat.

'*I met Laurens Werda in February 1989, when I came to Side Step. I was in a bad place: my parents had thrown me out of the house and the man who I'd thought loved me did nothing but give me money and the address of a charity that would put me up for a short while. Laurens gave me Theo Brand's passport and some clothes that other boys had left behind, and bought me a bus and boat ticket to London.*'

I lowered the paper for a second and lifted my head to the rain. Laurens had given him a passport and put him on the boat. Purely to cover his own tracks. He'd seen the similarities between Andre and Theo and realised this was his chance to make a dead boy come alive again.

I continued reading.

'*He told me that Theo had gone to France on a false passport.*

'*I believed him.*

'*I wanted to believe him.*

'*The police identified the Body in the Dunes as me and I kept quiet. I know I should have spoken out, but I was afraid of what would happen. Then Paul Verbaan killed himself and I had a man's death on my conscience. He had died because I'd been afraid. But part of me felt good about that. This was justice for the man who had abused his students for years.*

'*Laurens Werda and I met again and I thought he loved me.*

'*When I found out a month ago that Theo Brand hadn't gone to France but had gone missing, I decided I couldn't be afraid any more. I had to tell people what had happened.*

'*I tried to get Laurens to tell me the truth, but he laughed at me and told me that nobody would believe me.*

'*He was right.*

341

'*My sister wouldn't believe me, the family of Theo Brand didn't believe me, the son of my abuser only believed what he wanted to believe.*

'*This morning I tried to tell the truth to Detective Lotte Meerman and she didn't believe me either.*

'*My supposed death brought some justice. Hopefully my real death will bring justice too. Now the police will have to reopen the investigation into the Body in the Dunes case.*

'*I know in my heart of hearts that the dead boy was Theo Brand. That Laurens Werda had his passport and other belongings because he'd been the one who murdered him.*

'*I trust that the police will be able to find proof where I have failed.*'

After I'd stopped reading, I had to fight hard to control my tears.

'This case is more than twenty-five years old,' Monique Blom said, 'so the statute of limitation has expired.'

'That is correct,' the commissaris said. 'With these cold cases, the real importance is to get answers for the family of the victim, and I'm sure you understand that this has been a tough time for both Andre Nieuwkerk and Theo Brand's families.'

'But you still don't know who really killed Theo Brand.'

I held up a photo of Laurens Werda. I hoped the camera would zoom in on it. 'Knowing and proving are two different things,' I said.

'I understand,' Monique Blom said.

Someone in the background gave her a signal. It seemed that her live broadcast slot was up. The cameras stopped rolling.

The commissaris grabbed my arm and dragged me away to stop me from saying anything else to the reporter.

When we were out of earshot, he let go.

'Perfect,' he muttered, and walked back to his car.

Chapter 41

Julia was sitting at the front of the room, next to the commissaris. He was in uniform. She was wearing another one of her embroidered jumpers, this one dark green with stitching in pale blue around the neckline. She looked like a woodland creature, slight, elfin, ready to run away as soon as she was startled. I knew she was tougher than that. She would deal with this just fine.

The journalists in the audience were chatting to each other, not paying too much attention to the two people at the front. I sat in the back row. Nobody was paying any attention to me. Only Julia looked my way as she adjusted the papers in front of her. The commissaris leaned towards her and, hand over the microphone, whispered something. She checked her watch and nodded. They were going to start.

'Thanks for joining us this afternoon,' the commissaris said. His voice boomed through the small auditorium. 'I want to brief you about the grave error the police made twenty-five years ago when we mistakenly identified the Body in the Dunes.'

There was a small murmur as well as the sound of fingers tapping on keyboards.

'This recently came to light because Andre Nieuwkerk was still alive.'

There it was: the sentence I'd needed to hear.

I would always feel guilty about not talking to Andre that morning. But I felt good for having done what he had wanted: now the world knew that he'd still been alive.

I got up from my seat, trying to make as little noise as possible, but the people in front of me were riveted by the story the commissaris was telling them, and fascinated by Julia's explanation that she hadn't recognised her brother and had found it hard to believe until DNA confirmed it. I was out of the room before the questions started. I had achieved what I wanted.

The next day, we stood together at the river's edge. The rain had abated, as if it accepted that this occasion was sad enough without the weather making it worse.

Julia held the urn containing the ashes. She threw the first handful up in the air. The wind carried them, dispersed them, until they landed in the gently flowing water.

She held the urn out to Robbert Brand. 'This is the same place,' she said. 'This is where we scattered Theo's ashes too.'

The old man held Andre's ashes as carefully as if they were his son's, before finally letting go.

Acknowledgements

I would like to thank everybody who helped me with this book, especially all my friends who had to listen to me complain how hard this one was to write, and all those who helped me get it over the finishing line.

I'm fortunate to work with a great team of people. In Allan Guthrie from the North Literary Agency, I have a fantastic writer as my agent. My editor Krystyna Green, editorial manager Amanda Keats, copyeditor Jane Selley and all at Constable and Little, Brown have worked hard to make this book the best it could possibly be.

Finally, I would like to thank all the readers who got in touch to say how much they enjoy my books. Especially when you write a series, it's great to hear that people like the characters and are eagerly waiting for more. On the tough days, it's what keeps me going.